THE TRIALS OF NAHDA SINCLAIR V-LOG PA884/R

Published by Merita King
Eastleigh
Hampshire
United Kingdom

Cover art by JL Stratton

The Trials of Nahda – Sinclair V-Log PA884/R

OTHER WORKS BY MERITA KING

The Lilean Chronicles: Book One ~ Redemption
The Lilean Chronicles: Book Two ~ The Sleeping
The Lilean Chronicles: Book Three ~ Changing Faces
The Lilean Chronicles: Book Four ~ Avalanche Effect

Floxham Island ~ Sinclair V-Log AZ267/M
Bygora Vandos ~ Sinclair V-Log LB734/A

Acts of Life
Delectus Morbidium
A.W.O.L

ABOUT THE AUTHOR

Merita King has loved the science fiction and fantasy genre in both books and movies since she was a young child. She has been greatly inspired by years of watching movies and reading books and has wanted to make a contribution to this genre for many years. Her stories all contain a spiritual thread as she believes that spirituality is universal and crosses all boundaries. She believes that the creative process is largely intuitive and can be very effectively blocked by too much pre-planning. "Plot lines, characters and events all come to me intuitively," she says, "and this makes the act of writing a constant pleasure." She lives alone, with her vivid imagination, in Hampshire, UK.

DEDICATION

For Sammy.
Your vain streak and irreverent sense of humour are a constant inspiration.

CHAPTER ONE

This is Sinclair V-Log PA884/R, data log reference point 1957365/7984. Sam Sinclair, Tag Code Sinclair 27593-4/167AZP commencing report.

Hi there, it's me again, and this time, what I have to say represents an unusual experience for me. It made me question everything I believe in to a far greater degree than I would ever feel comfortable doing. I consider myself a grounded sort of person. Magic, fairies or any other sort of weirdness requiring the suspension of my natural scepticism have never been within my capacity for belief. My job involves witnessing all sorts of very real horrors, and after a while, people's capacity for evil would destroy anyone's belief in magic. The job I am going to relate to you today though, made me rethink everything and for a time, when we were down in the thick of it, I was on the brink of believing that maybe there is such a thing as magic after all.

My boss at the Inter-Galactic Law Enforcement Agency back home on Sigma Prime, called me up and offered me the job because I was the nearest law enforcer to the vicinity of the crime. If I had been anywhere else in the galaxy at that moment, I would have missed a life changing experience. I know this makes it sound like the job was something amazing, and I suppose it was on a personal level. When it was all over, I felt like I had never known myself at all until then, as if I had met a stranger for the first time. This stranger is a nice person and I like him better than I like the old Samelan Sinclair.

I was taking a few day's holiday on Kalima 2 to visit with some friends after finishing a job that had taken the wind out of me, when Tinnias called me and changed my life. The way I was feeling at the time, I almost turned him down flat. Looking back now, I am glad I accepted the job.

"Hi Sam. How are you?"

"Hi Boss. I'm okay thank you. How's the family?"

"They're great. Grellina says hi and Ambella sends a hug."

I grinned at the thought of his wife and daughter, who are both like family to me, my own parents havi7ng died years ago. "Tell them both I said hello and kiss them for me."

"I will. Now I have a job to offer you if you're feeling up to it. You can say no if you're not ready to get back to work just yet, so don't feel coerced.

The Trials of Nahda

You always say it's through your work that you find your equilibrium best, so I thought I'd offer it to you first."

I was not sure I was ready for another job yet. "Well I err, I don't know. What's the job?"

"Some guy from a museum on Nahda 4 has absconded with a valuable artefact. A priceless artefact actually, and the Nahdan security force has so far failed to apprehend him and retrieve their little piece of history. They know he hasn't left the Nahdan system, so he must be still down there."

"How do they know he hasn't made a run for it?"

"The whole of the Nahdan system is surrounded by a very fancy piece of technology. It's a network of inter-communicating lasers that protect the system. Nothing can enter or leave without permission. As soon as anyone tries to enter or leave the system without the security forces say so, they're fried. It's wrapped around the system like a bubble and is impossible to cross safely or unnoticed."

"Wow. They must be paranoid folks down there."

"They are, but with good reason. They are one of the galaxy's few sources of Esplonite TX5, so security is a major priority for them."

"What the heck is Esplonite TX5?" I groaned inwardly as I realised I had laid myself open to a scientific lecture I would not be able to understand. "And remember I'm no scientist Boss, so keep it simple huh?"

I heard Tinnias laugh. "Okay. I don't know much about it myself either. It's some kind of metal with weird magnetic properties. It doubles the energy production of fusion reactors. Apparently, if you use the stuff in your fusion reactor, you get twice as much energy output, for the same input of raw material. A hundred percent profit."

"So it's bound to be of interest on the black market."

"Correct. So they are naturally cautious about who they let in and out. When this museum guy ran off with the artefact, the net prevented him from leaving the system and it's been on ever since. That's how we know he's still down there somewhere. It has all the hallmarks of a simple job so I thought I would offer it to you as a way of getting your balance back without too much obvious danger to give you additional worry."

"Thanks. I'm okay really. It just took it out of me when all those people got killed when I was so close to catching that psycho."

"I know Sam, and you take all the time you need. I'll find someone else for this, don't worry."

The Trials of Nahda

"No. I'll take the job."

"Are you sure? There are other freelancers I can call."

"Yeah, I'm sure. My friends here have helped me a lot, but now I have to find myself again, and the best way to do that, is by doing what I do. So tell me, what is the artefact he stole?"

"It's an ancient sword, made by the Nahdan ancestors. It's called The Singing Sword. They discovered it seven years ago. This guy, Zaavi Dhilam, has been working on it since it was first discovered. He and his assistant, Cristik Noya, have been trying to translate the inscription that covers it. Apparently, Dhilam was excited about some new bit of the inscription he had translated, and disappeared with the sword a few days later."

This was something I had not come across before. "The singing sword?"

Tinnias laughed at my incredulity. "Yeah. Noya says there's some legend about it singing when in the hands of the right person."

"Wow, well I hope it has a better voice than the woman who won Galacti-Talent last year."

"Hey now, I bought some of her music."

I could not believe this of my boss. "You bought her stuff? Are you shitting me Boss?"

"No, I'm not shitting you and when you next get home and come to dinner, I'll make you sit and listen to her, so be nice to me okay."

"Hey, whatever you say. Anything but that."

"I'll send you through all the information we have, and I'll consult with the Nahdan Security Force so they know you're on your way. Give me a day and I'll get back to you."

And so it was that I set off once again, after a fabulous last meal with my friends, during which I thanked them for helping me when I needed them, and found myself heading off into the cold of the cosmos. It felt good to be back at work and the familiar surroundings of my ship were a great comfort to me. I plotted my journey to Nahda and flipped her into auto flight mode, before heading down to the cargo hold to work out. Working out every day was something I took up after my ex-partner Ren taught me his people's martial art, and after he died, I promised his memory I would continue everything he taught me. I am in better shape now than ever, and I was not happy to let my discipline slip. Travelling between systems takes a long time, even with the

3

most powerful spaceships, and the long hours alone can get boring. Working out gives me a way to use up some time and stay healthy. Having recently had my ship's engines overhauled, she was now capable of half-light speed, but the journey to the Nahdan system was still a long one.

Tinnias was true to his word and got back to me the next day with the information he had on the case, which was not much, and also a bit of history about the Nahdan people.

"Wow, they're weird looking people Boss. What is he? Seven feet tall?"

"Seven three. That's at the shorter end of the scale for these people Sam, the average is seven feet ten inches."

"Jeez. And look at the haircut; I hope that doesn't become fashionable on Sigma." I heard Tinnias laugh and I joined him. Zaavi Dhilam's white hair went from mid-forehead to the nape of his neck, in a two-inch wide strip, and stuck right up from his scalp. It reminded me of those cartoons I used to watch with Tinnias' daughter Ambella, where the bad guy was struck with electricity and all his hair stood on end. The hair on either side of Zaavi Dhilam's head was no more than a few millimetres long, which accentuated the long strip running down the middle.

Tinnias educated me about Nahdan hair. "All Nahdan men wear their hair like that, so don't offend them about it. It's some kind of male sexual prime thing. Boys are bald until they reach puberty, when their hair grows like that. The women are all bald."

"Are they? Wow, that's umm," I struggled before giving up. "Those eyes are weird too." I looked at Zaavi's bright orange eyes and vertical pupils. This was one of the few occasions I would call someone an alien. This word is something of an insult, as everyone is an alien to someone, but from time to time, my job brings me into contact with people who are very different indeed. This was one such occasion.

"Yeah, I know."

I scanned the information on his file. "He seems like an ordinary sort of guy to me. Apart from his physical appearance I mean. He's not been in trouble before, had a good job, is respected in his field, and has a girlfriend who loved him. Why the sudden leap into crime?"

"That's one thing you will need to find out. Although, as you're well aware, it's not necessary to know why he did what he did, just that he did it. But I know you don't like loose ends so feel free to answer that question if you can."

The Trials of Nahda

"Am I getting predictable?"

"Sam, it's my job to understand my freelancers. That's one of the reasons I'm the Boss."

"Sure thing. I'm glad you do; you've been good to me over the years and I appreciate it."

"You take care, and call me regularly okay?"

"I will."

Between working out, eating my unpalatable nutri-vend meals, sleeping, and checking the ship, I read and re-read the files on Zaavi Dhilam, his assistant Cristik Noya, and the girlfriend Shyola Mastak. They were your average clever nice people and the reason for Zaavi's sudden change of heart nagged me. I knew I must find the answer or I would go nuts with frustration. Doing this job as long as I have makes you good at reading people, understanding them and anticipating their next move. I pride myself on being something of an expert at reading people, and Zaavi's sudden detour into crime was out of character. This made him unpredictable, which means I would not be able to do my job effectively, and that annoyed me.

Zaavi Dhilam was an only child, was well educated and showed an early interest in the history of Nahda and its people. When he finished his education, he went straight to work at The Museum of Nahdan History in Lanis, a large city on the bigger of Nahda's two landmasses. There was no record of him ever being in trouble with the Inter-Galactic Law Enforcement Agency and there was no mention of him having problems with the Nahdan Security forces either. He had a girlfriend and they planned to marry during the traditional Nahdan wedding month. At the time of his disappearance, he was thirty-five years old.

Cristik Noya, Zaavi's assistant, looked very similar. The same white hair, the same orange eyes and vertical pupils, but he was much taller at seven feet eight inches. Twenty-six years old and unattached, he worked with Zaavi for four years and helped him translate inscriptions and ancient texts on the various artefacts that found their way to the museum. He worked on translating the inscription on the sword with Zaavi for the whole four years of his employment. Like Zaavi, there was no record of him ever being in trouble or committing even the most minor of offences. He noticed the sword was missing when he arrived at work and found Zaavi, and it, missing. He called the museum security guards and reported it.

The Trials of Nahda

Zaavi's girlfriend, Shyola Mastak, was twenty-nine years old and, as Tinnias told me, bald. Her head appeared to be covered in an intricate design of curvy lines and symbols. Coupled with her large orange eyes, she was striking. Being seven feet five inches tall meant she looked down on Zaavi. The file said she went to his home to share lunch with him, as was their usual arrangement, but he never showed up and never returned home. The next morning, she called him at work, to be told he had not arrived. She was worried and called the security forces.

I sat back and groaned. The files told me precious little, and knowing how paranoid the Nahdans are as a people, I got the distinct impression that there was more to this than the files told me. More than anything else, I hate when people lie to me, and although I understood it was not personal and maybe was not a deliberate cover up, I was annoyed. It made me determined to find out what I knew was missing from those files. Those details I knew from experience should be there were all the more obvious by their absence, and I knew that once I found them, everything would be much clearer. No one has a spotless record for thirty-five years. Everyone gets into trouble at some time in their life. Kids are told off by teachers, grounded by angry parents and protest at having to do chores. Neighbours have disputes, lovers fall out, men get drunk and beat each other up in dark alleyways. Workers piss off their bosses and hate their co-workers, it's all a natural part of an average life, but none of that stuff was in those files. They were too clean for my liking, and as I approached the Nahdan system and waited to be hailed, I knew my first objective was to find out about the real Zaavi Dhilam before I could track him down.

"Unidentified vessel. You are approaching the Nahda Defence Network. Identify yourself immediately and halt your course or be destroyed."

"This is Samelan Sinclair of the Inter-Galactic Law Enforcement Agency and this is my vessel SC257. I am here to investigate the theft of an ancient artefact, to track down Zaavi Dhilam and bring him to justice for that theft. My superior officer assured me you would be expecting me. Sending you my identification signal now." I sat back and waited for a response. Their disagreeable greeting made me uneasy, and although Tinnias warned me they were a little paranoid, I expected a little more warmth since I was there to do a job they had failed to do.

The Trials of Nahda

"Mr Sinclair, we have your signal and confirm we are expecting you. The defence network is now safe to pass. I'm sending you landing co-ordinates and will have a team of officers there to meet you."

"Thank you, I have the signal. On my way." I gunned the engines and hoped this job was not going to take too long. I still felt uneasy, although I did not know why and I wanted to be away from there with as much haste as possible.

I touched down in a military base and prepared to disembark. A group of five soldiers waited for me when I lowered the hatch, and all towered over me. Having to gaze up at them made me feel more than a little intimidated, which must have showed as they all grinned and one sniggered.

"Welcome to Nahda 4 Mr Sinclair. We apologise for the brusqueness of your first communication from us, but we have good reason to be cautious of visitors."

"My boss told me." I craned my neck up to meet his eyes. He gazed down at me and several seconds of silence passed between us as we both sized each other up. It would be a terrible idea to get on the wrong side of these people; if they decided to get violent with me, I would be screwed. It was a few seconds before I realised I was staring, which I knew was rude and blushed.

"I'm sorry, forgive me for staring. I've never met anyone like you before, and I've been around. Man, you're huge."

"I am Laklo Sherrin and I'm the Markian around here, the Captain if you wish to use a more familiar term. I'm eight feet one inch by the way, which is not unusual here. If it makes you feel any better, we don't often get to meet little runts like you that often."

I laughed aloud. I am six feet two and never had occasion to be called a runt before. I knew right away I was going to like him, he was honest and open, which is something I do not get too often in my line of work.

"Sam Sinclair, glad to meet you." We shook hands and he enveloped my hand and wrist. For a moment, I hoped he was not going to squeeze too hard and I was relieved when he let my hand go.

"If you'd like to follow me, I'll introduce you to our Alderon, the civilian base commander. It was he who communicated with your agency and arranged for you to investigate this matter, and he is the one with all the details."

"Sure, I'll just get a few essentials. Will my being armed be a problem for you?"

"Not at all. Our exhaustive investigation satisfied us with your record and work history. We have been told to give you every assistance you might require to bring this unfortunate matter to a swift end."

"You investigated me?" I was shocked to know someone was nosing around in my business without asking.

"Of course. You surely didn't expect us to welcome anybody here without doing some background checks, did you? You know how paranoid we are."

I could not decide whether to be annoyed that his people bugged my communications with Tinnias, or impressed at their thoroughness. "You listened in on my calls with my boss?"

He saw my cheeks flush with anger. "Now Mr Sinclair don't be angry. We had to be sure that the person who came here to investigate this matter is someone we can trust. We are a cautious people, as you already know, but we do have good reason. We feel confident that you are trustworthy and I assure you that we are no longer spying on your calls."

"Well yeah, I guess I understand that." I picked up my already packed backpack, holstered my two laser pistols and sedative dart gun, slung my laser rifle over one shoulder and tucked the Damiklonian War Dagger given to me by my ex-partner Ren, into the waistband of my pants.

"You're after one man Mr Sinclair. A man who has never, to our knowledge, owned or fired a gun of any kind."

"Experience tells me it's best to be prepared for every eventuality. Better to take something I don't need, than to get killed because I didn't."

He nodded. "I get your point. Was that a Damiklonian War Dagger by the way?"

"Yes. You recognised it, how come?"

"I spent a few years on Damiklon Prime, training soldiers. I was presented with one as a gift."

"Then they must've thought very highly of you. My ex-partner was Damiklonian and he gave me one of his daggers when he began teaching me their martial art."

Laklo stopped in his tracks and regarded me, his huge orange eyes with those strange vertical pupils, showing his shock. "You were taught the martial art? By a Damiklonian? On a one to one basis? Really?"

"Yeah. He was my best friend as well as my work partner."

"Was?"

"He died." Memories of Ren flooded through my mind. "On a job. He was murdered."

"I'm sorry for your pain."

"Thank you."

We walked across the base and the air was cool but not uncomfortable. I took a deep breath and looked at my surroundings. The city in the distance appeared modern and clean and the faint purr of hover vehicles floated across the base. They built everything for the size of the inhabitants, which was a little too big for me. The steps we climbed into the base headquarters were a little too high; the doors too tall, the reception counter was level with my neck and the chair the civilian base commander offered me left my legs swinging. I felt like a child and it showed, as he called for a lower one immediately. I sat in relative comfort facing a middle-aged man whose size, combined with his rank, intimidated me.

"Welcome Mr Sinclair. I'm Teesho Pretik, the Alderon of this base. Forgive me for forgetting to have a more suitable chair waiting for you."

I nodded in response. "Of course." I knew this was an attempt to further intimidate me, to make a subtle gesture of dominance. His reference to the difference in our heights made it clear to me that this was something they viewed as a mark of superiority over shorter races. The way he made my lack of height into an inconvenience for which he needed to make a special effort, was typical of the usual jockeying for position I tend to expect with military types. Tinnias calls such behaviours, pissing contests.

"Now let me fill you in on everything we know about this matter, and you can decide how you wish to proceed."

I was not surprised to learn that he knew precious little more than I read in the files Tinnias sent me. If he did know more, he was not about to tell me. Zaavi Dhilam disappeared thirteen days before, with the artefact, The Singing Sword of Nahda. There was no apparent warning that he was going to commit such an act and everyone was very surprised when he did. As Pretik went on about Zaavi's excellent education, his profound knowledge of the ancient Nahdan people and their culture, my gut told me they were still holding out on me. I decided on the spur of the moment not to question him about it; I could use my time to better effect questioning those in closer contact with Zaavi who knew him well.

9

The Trials of Nahda

"So that's all we know Mr Sinclair. Now, what do you need from us?"

"My immediate needs are a room to make my base, and permission to question his work colleagues, family and friends."

"Not a problem. Here are the names and addresses of those who work with him, his female mate, and his mother. His father died some years ago. They should be able to tell you of any friends he has, I don't have such information. The museum has arranged a room for you on site, and I'll get one of our men to drive you over there. Staff who live on site have access to a staff restaurant, and there are facilities for you to take care of laundry etc. They will give you details of that when you arrive. Your first contact there is Harsh Briel, the museum curator."

I took the details from him and stood. "Thank you. I hope I am able to bring this situation to a satisfactory close quickly." I offered my hand, which he shook with a smile that did not reach his eyes. His lips drew back into something more reminiscent of a grimace, showing his icy white teeth with a little too much force, and I knew it was fake. I offered one of my own, equally as fake but crafted by an expert.

The grimace remained, and it seemed from his reply that he knew me far too well. "If anyone can, you can. If you need anything that the museum staff cannot provide, call me. Oh, and please keep me informed of any further developments." He tried to make it sound unimportant that I keep him in the loop, and I got the distinct impression that I would not need to keep him informed. He would ensure he knew what I was finding out without me having to tell him.

"I will, and thank you." He led me out of the office, and I allowed him to show me out to a waiting military hover car.

The journey into the city was more pleasant than I would have anticipated. It was warm on Nahda 4, and the cool breeze flowing in through my open window was enough without being intrusive. The driver was quiet and I was grateful. It allowed me time to think about the case and the irritating lack of information about my target, Zaavi Dhilam. I knew I would find it hard to proceed unless someone opened up to me about him, and there might come a time when I would need to have a showdown with someone about it. My mind filled with images of an angry exchange of words at some time in the future, and I hoped with every fibre of my being that I found out what it was they were all hiding from me without such an interaction. The city was indeed very modern and clean, and I could not see a single building of any great age.

10

The Trials of Nahda

It was as if they built everything a few weeks ago, like a brand new city without roots to an ancient past.

I broke the silence between the driver and myself. "Everything is so new here. Is this a new city?"

"Everywhere on Nahda 4 is new." By the way he looked me up and down; I was one of the few non-natives he had ever seen.

"What do you mean?"

"We came to this world just three hundred years ago."

"Really? So you're not native to this planet?"

"No. You didn't know that?"

"No."

"We originally lived on the neighbouring planet, Nahda 3. We had to emigrate here three hundred years ago as the planet's atmosphere was destroyed."

This was a surprise to me. "Wow. So that's why it's all so new."

"Yes. You will find nothing of Nahda's history here. For that you must journey to our neighbour, the Old World as we call it."

"What was it that destroyed the atmosphere over there?"

"It was us. We polluted and poisoned the Old World until it could sustain us no longer. Our corporate greed fuelled by our precious natural resource, Esplonite TX5, sealed our fate, and that of Nahda 3."

"So you came here."

"Yes. Our government decided to send settlers here to build new communities so that we could emigrate. Once we did, new laws were put in place controlling the reach and power of corporations."

"What sort of laws?"

"They made all sorts of new laws governing how Esplonite was to be used and who could benefit financially from it. Immigration was closed off so that foreign companies and their power hungry directors couldn't take us back to where we had been before. We have no more places to emigrate here in our home system; we have to get it right this time."

Although I am not into politics, this was interesting. "That's incredible. It takes a brave government to bring in such strict controls when everyone is used to making their own wealth and working their way up the ladder of power."

"Brave maybe, or perhaps it just takes a people on the brink of extinction to make everyone realise how their priorities need to change."

The Trials of Nahda

We pulled up at the main gate of the museum and I said goodbye to the driver, who nodded and drove away, swishing into the light flow of traffic. After announcing myself to the security guard, who looked me up and down and checked my weapons and licences, he called the curator, Harsh Briel. I groaned inwardly and knew I would have to get used to them staring at me. I was the real alien here in this world of giants. The smile he offered me as he shook my hand was no more genuine than Teesho Pretik's had been, but he was a better actor. After thanking the security guard, he showed me to the staff accommodation block. I was delighted to find the room refitted to suit someone of my reduced stature, all except the bathroom, but at least I was able to pee standing up without having to stand on a box.

He handed me the key. "Would you like some time to relax before getting to work?"

I shook my head. I wanted to get this job done and get away to somewhere else, anywhere where I would not feel like the weirdo in the neighbourhood. I dumped my backpack on the bed and shook my head. "No thanks. I'd prefer to get straight on with it if that's okay. The more time I waste, the less likelihood there is of me finding him. He's already got thirteen days start on me."

"Of course. Right, then let me show you to his department and introduce you to his staff."

The museum building was huge and although I am not into history, some of the artefacts I saw on display were impressive and I could not help but ask him about them. He gave me a brief description, happy at my genuine interest in his culture. We climbed more sets of far too high stairs and my legs ached when we reached the fourth floor and home to the Research Department. As we climbed, he talked about Zaavi Dhilam and I asked him to tell me more about him. I hoped I was going to get the lowdown on the man at last, but he gave me the same sterile crap I already knew.

"He was extremely knowledgeable about our history, especially the ancient languages of Nahda. We were lucky to have him work with us here, he researched many of the artefacts, and much of what we know about the ancient Nahdans, came from his diligence and profound understanding. He spent hours studying texts and deciphering the inscriptions and scratches on the various items brought here. He really brought the ancient Nahdans to life for us."

12

The Trials of Nahda

"So why do you think he would suddenly steal the sword and run off? You knew him well, what made him do it?"

"Surely that is what you are here to find out?" He gave me a sideways glance that I knew meant our conversation would go no further. "Ahh, here we are. This is Cristik Noya, Zaavi's assistant." I looked at the young man and saw his mouth flicker into a genuine smile. "This is Sam Sinclair from the Law Enforcement Agency. He is here to investigate Zaavi's disappearance and bring us back the sword. I was just explaining how lucky we are to have someone as knowledgeable and passionate about our history as Zaavi is, and how surprised we all are that he would steal it and disappear like that."

Cristik nodded, and I noticed a nervousness about his manner that told me he did not like Briel being around. "Yes Sir. Very lucky indeed."

Briel turned to me and looked down his nose and into my eyes. "Well I will leave you in the capable hands of Cristik here. Let me know if I can be of any further help." I watched him leave and noticed the expression on Cristik's face as he too, watched Briel leave the department. The silent deep breath and subsequent sigh of relief, the quick glance up to the ceiling, all told me he was relieved when Briel left. This small gesture on the part of Cristik made my day. I smiled at the man in front of me and knew he was someone I might be able to rely on to tell me the truth. It was not until the door shut with a click that he relaxed and turned to me.

"I'm glad to meet you Mr Sinclair." He held out his hand, which I shook. As I said, I am good at reading people and despite these Nahdans being very alien in appearance; I knew this person was an ally, so I opened up to him.

"Call me Sam, please. So tell me Cristik, just what is it that everyone is refusing to tell me?"

The Trials of Nahda

CHAPTER TWO

Cristik gave a little smirk and motioned for me to sit, before admitting there was much about Zaavi Dhilam that would never reach his official record, at least none that would ever be in the public domain. I gave myself a mental pat on the back, glad I had not yet lost my people reading skills.

He nodded. "I will tell you everything I know, if you meet me after I finish work tonight. We're horrifically busy today and I'm already hours behind thanks to Zaavi not being here to help. We have a new display going out into the museum tomorrow and everything needs to be ready. I live on site, room 83. Come for me at six and I'll take you out to dinner so we can talk privately."

I was happy to wait a few more hours to find out what I needed to know. Now that I had the promise of information, I relaxed and decided to go back to my room for a shower, then go out to interview Zaavi's girlfriend and mother.

I braved the stares of the Nahdan public, and went out to hail a hover cab into the city, towards the homes of Zaavi's mother and girlfriend. The cab driver was friendly and not native to Nahda. To my delight, he was shorter than I was, which did wonders for my rapidly diminishing sense of masculinity, but he was as glad as I was to see someone more of his own stature. I paid him extra to give me a quick tour of the city so I could find my way around alone if necessary, and I was glad to notice the Nahdans built everything on a very logical grid system. He showed me where to get the best local Nahdan food, the quietest bars, and everywhere a tourist might like to visit. Most of it was not of interest to me but I registered everything in my mind, in case any of it turned out to be relevant to the case. If it should come out that Zaavi confided his plan to a friend who works at the biggest Vidicom theatre in the city, I would be very happy to know I could find my way there in a hurry if need be. Glass and metal glinted in the mid-day sun as I craned my neck up at the modern tower block that soared into the sky like a spear. This place looked like one of the top end apartment towers back home on Sigma Prime, only available to the very richest citizens, and I was impressed. After thanking the cab driver, I accepted a card with his Unicom number on, and headed towards the entrance.

Aveyla Zaavi lived on the ninety-second floor and I was grateful to find the elevator in working order. If I had to climb all those far too big stairs, I would never recover, despite my workout regimen. As the elevator swished upward in silence, I remembered something I read in the files Tinnias gave me. Nahdan boys take their mother's surname as their first name, whilst the girls take their father's surname. This seemed ridiculous and complicated to me, but I did not want to offend anyone, so I made sure I remembered. The elevator stopped and I walked the corridor and found the apartment at the end. I rang the bell and guessed there must be a fantastic view of the city from up there.

The door opened, and I saw a woman whose appearance astounded me. She was over seven feet tall and middle aged; the lines at the corners of her eyes taking nothing from either her beauty or elegance. Her bald head was covered in intricate designs and those orange eyes with black vertical pupils gazed down at me. She was beautiful and I was standing there with my mouth open.

I blushed. "Forgive me. My name is Sam Sinclair and I'm here on behalf of the Inter-Galactic Law Enforcement Agency. I'm investigating your son's disappearance. Is it convenient to speak with you?"

"Ahh yes, I was told you would probably be visiting me. Do come in Mr Sinclair."

I was right about the view, it was incredible from up there, and the floor to ceiling windows gave a jaw dropping, stomach churning view of the whole city and beyond to a range of mountains in the far distance. Aveyla Zaavi made me a drink of herbs mixed with fruit and although a little bitter for my taste, it was refreshing and I enjoyed it. I hauled myself into a chair made for someone well over seven feet tall, and retrieved my data log to record the interview. She started by giving me the same censored shit I had received from everyone else and after an hour, I lost my patience and stuck the knife in, a little.

"Forgive me but everyone I've met since my arrival on Nahda, has told me exactly the same thing about your son. He's well educated, clever and knowledgeable about his chosen subject, and what he doesn't know about ancient Nahdan history really isn't worth knowing. I'm sorry but I need to know everything, even the stuff you don't want on his record. No living person in the galaxy of his age can rightfully claim to live such a clean and sterile life as your son allegedly does. I just don't buy it." She looked down at the floor and for a moment, I thought I had offended her. A split second later however, she returned my gaze and I knew I had unsettled her into giving away her lies. I pushed harder.

"I give you my word, as an experienced and well respected member of the Inter-Galactic Law Enforcement Agency that nothing you say to me in confidence, will go any further. You have to tell me; otherwise I might be unable to find your son."

She locked eyes with me. "Mr Sinclair." Her jaw clenched a tiny bit, and I noticed the muscles at the top of her neck move as her lips narrowed. She was not yet willing to open up any further. "You must understand that I love my son more than anything else in life. He is my only child and although he has given me cause to worry at times, I couldn't do anything to bring harm to him."

I tried a gentler poke. "How did he give you cause to worry?"

"Our world, our life, was brought back from the edge of annihilation. We were given a second chance at life when we came here to Nahda 4. It was our chance to not make the same mistakes our forebears made. Making that change has involved a measure of choice being taken away from us as individuals, so that the whole of our race can thrive. Sometimes those choices we are forbidden to make are the ones we want most of all, and we must find a way to reconcile ourselves with that. It is for the common good."

"I understand." It was obvious that Zaavi did not like having to obey the law when those laws controlled which choices he could make for himself and his life. What I did not know, was how far his anti-establishment feelings went. I needed to know though, so I pushed further.

"So was he able to reconcile himself to those constraints?"

"We all have a little difficulty with that at times." She held my gaze with her hypnotic orange eyes and I knew I would get nothing more from her. Our interview was effectively over.

I hopped down from my chair. "Indeed we do. Thank you for your time, and here's my Unicom number if you wish to talk to me about anything, in total confidence of course."

She smiled as she showed me out. "Good day Mr Sinclair."

Shyola Mastak lived in another, equally awe-inspiring tower three streets away, so I decided to walk. It gave me time to clear my head after my frustration at Aveyla Zaavi's evasion. I did understand though, and although it did hamper me in my efforts to close the case, I could not help but wonder how hard it would be to live in a society where my personal choices were not mine to make. I know myself well enough to be able to say with complete authority, that it would bother me beyond my capability to endure. My life is good; I have a job I enjoy, respect from my colleagues, but most of all I have a lot of personal freedom of choice. I can live where I want, do what I want, with whom I want, and so long as I continue to do my job to a satisfactory standard, I am left alone. To have any of that freedom curtailed would not be acceptable to me.

Shyola Mastak opened the door to her twenty-seventh floor apartment and smiled when I introduced myself. She was even more beautiful than Zaavi's mother was, and her physical strangeness did nothing to diminish the attraction I felt come to life within.

"Come in Mr Sinclair, would you like a drink?"

"Thank you, yes I would indeed." She offered me a seat by the window that afforded me another wonderful view across the city, and I hauled myself up into it. That vantage point gave the vista a calmness and serenity that I found attractive. Perhaps I should sell my own apartment back home on Sigma Prime and buy something in a similar situation to this.

Shyola re-entered the room carrying two glasses of something blue. "I was told you might be visiting me." I thanked her and took a tentative sip, to find it tasted fruity but bland.

"I'm sorry to burden you with questions. I know you must be worried sick, but I need as much information about Zaavi as you can give me. If I can understand why he did what he did, it will help me calculate his likely course of action and hopefully, enable me to intercept him quickly and return him to you."

"Of course." Her face creased with worry and I knew that I could get her to open up by playing on her emotions. Call me callous if you want, but information is the building material from which my job is constructed, and the one place I can get it, is from people. Sometimes they do not want to give it to me, and I have to encourage them to open up. In truth, I do not enjoy upsetting beautiful women, but if it helps me bring my target to justice, I have no problem with it.

"Tell me about Zaavi. About him as a man, apart from the crime he has committed I mean. What is he like? What makes him happy? What annoys him? That sort of thing."

The Trials of Nahda

"Why do you need to know that sort of thing? Surely you need details of his disappearance?"

"I have those details, but in order for me to find him, I need to get to know him. If I can understand the man, I can anticipate what he might do or where he might go. Often these little details help me in my work. Believe me; I have been doing this job for twenty years."

"Okay. Well he's very clever; as I'm sure you've already been told. He is an intellectual man, a thinker. He likes to theorise and debate and that's what first attracted me to him. Sometimes he comes across as lacking social skills but he lives inside his mind you see. I always think of him as being from the future."

I frowned. "From the future? What do you mean by that?"

"His ideas, his theories, they are very different. It's almost as if he comes from the future with ideas that the rest of us haven't thought of yet."

"Right, I understand. Carry on, please."

"He enjoys good food, fine wine, and the company of a few friends who he believes to be on an intellectual level with himself. He has an interest in politics and makes sure to attend all the public meetings. He likes to keep abreast of what is happening within our government. I tease him sometimes and say he should be a politician rather than a scientist."

"You're due to marry soon, aren't you?"

"Yes, during our traditional wedding month of Vansway."

"Was he excited about it?"

She bristled and glared at me. "Of course. Why wouldn't he be?"

"Well he's disappeared. After stealing a valuable artefact. He might be trying to finance an alternative life to the one he was leading. This sort of thing happens more than you know."

"Not here it doesn't. Besides, I know our marriage will go ahead because he left me a note telling me that he would be back for me."

"Oh?" I saw her bite her lip and look at the floor. "I'd like to see that note if I may." She left the room, returning a minute later with a small folded piece of paper.

"My darling Shyola. Fear not by my absence my love, for I will return and we shall live our lives together, as I promised you that night on the midnight shore of Rillias Noth, when you gave me your love."

"Do the Nahdan Security Forces know about this letter?"

"No. I know I should've given it to them, but it's so personal. I couldn't bear to part with it."

"I understand. Would you allow me to take a scan of it for my own records? I give you my word I won't tell the Security Forces unless it becomes absolutely necessary." She gave a reluctant nod and I got out my digital scanner. "Thank you."

"Will I get into trouble?"

I shook my head. "Not if I can help it. Now tell me more about Zaavi. What annoyed him for instance?"

"Well." She was hedging, hesitating for a moment too long and I knew she was holding back.

"I need to know everything. I give you my word I won't divulge where I got the information from."

"He wanted more responsibility in his work. He wished to attain a position that would enable him to have more control. He found the laws governing the pursuit of wealth and position, frustrating. That's why he followed our government's dealings so closely. He wanted the ability to change the laws."

"I see." Now the fog was clearing a little. The man was an insurrectionist at heart. No wonder the authorities chose not to tell me, it would be an embarrassment for them. I hoped Cristik Noya would be able to elaborate further on this when I met him later for dinner.

"Your laws do control the pursuit of wealth and power very strictly, don't they? After what happened on Nahda 3, I can understand why they would wish to avoid a similar tragedy. People naturally want to better themselves though, and they will rail against such controls from time to time."

"Yes. Most of us accept things. We know why the laws are in place and we live by them without complaining too much. Zaavi just couldn't accept it though and he would get angry sometimes during debates about these matters. I begged him to keep his feelings to himself but he couldn't always comply with my wishes."

"Why do you think he stole the sword?"

"I have no idea." She held my gaze and I knew she was telling the truth. "Maybe he was hoping to force a change in the law by keeping its location secret. It is a very valuable artefact and its worth goes beyond money. It is one of the few items we have from our earliest ancestors, and what it tells us about them, their way of life and their beliefs, is something we cannot replace.

Maybe he hoped that by using it as leverage, our government would relax the laws that angered him so."

"That is certainly a viable theory. Do you have any idea as to where he might go, to hide out?"

"No. I wish I did. I would go there myself and try to persuade him to come back if I did."

I handed her my Unicom number. "If you think of anything else, call me. In confidence of course."

She nodded. "Please find him Mr Sinclair. Find him and bring him home to me."

"I will try, I promise. That is why I'm here. Thank you for your time."

I found a cafe not far from Shyola's apartment tower and went in for some lunch. Being stared at no longer bothered me, and I found that most people were friendly once the initial shock of my appearance passed. It felt weird being the strange one in town, the alien, and I resolved to be more aware of the plight of others in such situations in the future. I may come across as the hard man, and my job requires that sometimes, but I do care about people. I am a nice person; believe me. I got talking to a few men, and they had a good sense of humour. By the time I left to hail a cab back to my museum accommodation, I had not laughed so much in weeks. I knocked on Cristik's door at six on the dot, and he ushered me inside.

"How was your day Sam?"

"Interesting, thank you. Did you get everything done for your display?"

"After working through lunch, yes. I hope you're ready for a meal, I'm starving."

"Absolutely. I might have to ask you to translate the menu for me though. I had a rather fun experience in a cafe at lunchtime."

He grinned. "Really? What did you end up ordering?"

"Umm I can't honestly remember the name of it, but thankfully I didn't find out until I'd finished eating it, that it was made from the excrement of some sea creature."

He laughed aloud. "Calimas Mot."

"That's the one."

"Did you enjoy it?"

I nodded. "It was delicious actually."

"I give you my word I won't lead you into such territory tonight."

"Thank you, I appreciate that. Where are we going?"

"There's a great place about a mile across the city. The food is second to none and the place is quiet so we can talk without being overheard."

"Okay, that sounds great."

"Shall I call a cab, or would you rather walk?"

"I'm happy to walk but by all means call a cab if you wish."

He shook his head. "I'd prefer to walk. I sit all day long in the museum and I like to exercise."

We walked through the early evening city and Cristik told me about himself, his life and work, and the more he talked the more I liked him. He was not a strict intellectual like Zaavi, but although he was clever; he liked to enjoy himself in ways that were familiar to me. We discussed sport, cars and sex like most guys do and I was happy to discover that what we had in common, far outweighed the differences between our races. I was shocked to learn that Nahdan people enjoy sex with both genders freely, and that their marriages are often not monogamous. Thoughts of Shyola filled my mind and I could not help but wonder what sex with her would be like.

The restaurant nestled at the end of a side street, its doorway lit by a single small sign. We entered and a wonderful smell assailed my nostrils. A man smiled as he approached us and shook hands with Cristik, and I guessed my new companion was known here. Cristik spoke to him in Nahdan, after which the man nodded and bade us follow him to a secluded table in a corner. I allowed him to order drinks for us and listened as he translated the menu. After assuring me that what I chose was made from something safe, he laughed.

Cristik leaned over and whispered into my ear with a snigger. "The waiter thinks you and I are umm, you know."

"What? You're shitting me."

"I needed to ensure we got the most private table, so I had to improvise."

"I hope this never gets back to my Boss. I'll never be allowed to forget it if it does."

The smile fell from Cristik's face. "Are our ways disgusting to you?"

"What? No of course not. They're just different."

"So you've never umm, with another male? Only women?"

I nodded. "Yeah."

The Trials of Nahda

"Well you must be aware that things are different here, and you may find yourself on the receiving end of a proposition or two. They will be quite direct about it too; you will be left in no doubt as to what is on offer."

"Really?"

"Yes. I thought I'd better mention it so you're prepared if it happens. If you're not interested, just say no thanks."

"Wow, okay." I have never been propositioned by a man before, and I will admit that the thought scared me. After doing this job for so long, I've become very broad minded and have known many people who prefer sex with their own gender rather than the opposite one, but in all that time, I've never had a man come on to me.

"Foreigners are something of a rarity here, so they're seen as more attractive because of that rarity."

"Does that belief apply to the women here too?"

"Yes, it does."

"Then I might enjoy my time here more than I thought I would,"

The meal was delicious and I allowed Cristik time to sate his hunger before I fired questions at him. He was able to elaborate on Zaavi's personal politics and by the time the meal was over, I felt happy that I now knew everything about the man.

"He has quite dangerous beliefs."

This was more like it. "In what way dangerous?"

"Our government has strict laws about how much power any one person or corporation can wield."

"Yeah I know. Because of what happened on Nahda 3 and the value of Esplonite TX5."

"Correct. Well Zaavi hated those laws. He wanted power and wealth, or more directly, the choice to pursue them."

I thought back to my interview with Shyola Mastak. "His girlfriend admitted as much to me earlier."

"He tried to form a political group to discuss the matter, but no one wanted any part of it. I'm pretty sure that many secretly agreed with him, but no one I know would dare be so open as to challenge our government's decisions. Word got back to Harsh Briel and Zaavi almost lost his job over it."

"That's interesting."

"He was obsessed with the way things were done years ago, back on Nahda 3 when everyone could follow their own dreams and gain whatever power and wealth they were able to achieve. He used to talk about wanting to go and live on Nahda 3 and just be on his own, or maybe to run his own kingdom in his own way. He was sure more would follow if he was brave enough to pave the way."

"And would they?"

He shrugged as he considered my question. "A few might. I'd be tempted myself actually, but not because I yearn for power, although some more wealth would be nice. Just because it would be something new, fun, y'know?"

"Yeah." Why do you think he stole the sword?"

"We'd been working on translating the inscriptions for ages, and progress was very slow. We had precious little to use as a comparison you see. It is one of only seven artefacts from that far back in our history, and none of the seven displayed as much of the ancient language as the sword does. We were able to decipher enough to realise it talks about power of some kind, and it seems to indicate that the sword is, in some way, directly connected with gaining that power."

"Oh, so it's a sort of symbolic thing. Like a badge of office."

"That's what we believed, yes. There is some kind of religious connection too though, as some of the pictographs translate as temple or place of worship."

"Why is it called The Singing Sword?"

"Now that is the most interesting thing, and the bit we know least about I'm afraid. From what we were able to decipher, it indicated that the sword would sing, or to translate more correctly, make sound."

"How?"

He shrugged. "We don't know. All we know is that the inscription on the sword talks of power, a temple, and making sound. Zaavi firmly believed that the three are connected and that if we could find that connection, we would understand what it says, and a lot more about those ancient ancestors' way of life and culture."

"So where do you think he would go to hide out?"

"I've been thinking about that ever since he disappeared, and the only thing I can come up with is a conversation I had with him the last night I saw him. He kept on about this temple and said he believed it might still be standing, somewhere on Nahda 3. He kept saying how fantastic it would be to find it."

"Had he ever been to Nahda 3?"

"Yes, several times, we both have. It's where all our artefacts are found. We have teams over there all the time, searching for anything of interest. I went on several excursions there with him. I'm sure that's where he's gone. I haven't told anyone else about this though, you're the first one to know this."

The more I thought about it, the more I believed he was right. With his obsession with all things connected with their ancestors and their way of life, and his anger at the present government's way of managing things, there was a distinct possibility that he would make for Nahda 3. There was one more thing I needed to know, and once Cristik had translated the dessert menu, I asked him.

"Do you think Zaavi was a secretive sort of man?"

"Are you kidding Sam? He hates the way our government controls our financial freedom, he steals our most valuable artefact because it talks about power, and he runs off with it without a word to anyone. Yes, I would regard him as secretive, wouldn't you?"

"I didn't actually mean in that way. I meant do you think he kept stuff from you on a day to day basis. He obviously talked to you about his ideas and beliefs. He obviously trusted you, but do you believe there was stuff that he wouldn't reveal, even to you?"

"Oh I see. Yes, I do believe that. It would make sense after what he's done wouldn't it? Besides, he obviously did keep secrets from me, because I've no idea where he went. Unless of course you feel I'm lying to you about that."

I did not want to put Cristik off, so I shook my head and frowned. "No, I know you're not lying. I think there's a lot that Zaavi hid from everyone, and I mean to find out what that is. I think I need to check out his home."

"You'd have to get permission from the Security Forces for that."

Knowing more about my target at last was a huge relief, and I was able to eat my dessert without the frustration of this case spoiling my enjoyment. "Okay, that's not a problem. I know just the man to get it for me." I tucked into something so sweet it made my teeth tingle, but delicious. "Now what do you folks do for nightlife around here?"

"There's a decent bar around the corner. You fancy a few drinks before heading home?"

The Trials of Nahda

"Why not. Since it's my first day here and I've had a busy day being kept in the dark about everything, I think I deserve an hour or two relaxation."

We left the restaurant and walked around the corner. The night was cool but pleasant as we followed the sound of music drifting on the breeze and found ourselves at a very busy club. Cristik introduced me to a couple of men he met there from time to time, and I learned the name of the local spirit, which he assured me would not cause a hangover in the morning. We listened to a band so loud that we had to shout in order to communicate. By the time we left to catch a cab back to the museum, three men had propositioned me. I turned each one down politely. It felt good to be so desirable, and I hoped that the local women would be as keen as their menfolk were. I said goodnight to Cristik and fell into bed, exhausted, my ears still ringing from the band at the bar. I slept soundly and dreamed of my ex-partner Ren, who died in my arms after making me promise to remember him in a healthy way, and not to lock his memory away inside for fear of the pain it might cause. I awoke with tears in my eyes and smiled at his memory, before getting up to shower, dress and find breakfast.

CHAPTER THREE

Teesho Pretik answered my call on the first ring. He sounded stressed and I hoped he would receive my official request without a fuss.

"Hi, it's Sam Sinclair here."

"Oh hello Mr Sinclair. How was your first day on the case? Have you discovered anything of interest?"

"It was interesting, thank you." I was not going to reveal the details of what I had discovered yet, as I still had that uneasy feeling that if I did, the local security force might leap in and fuck things up for me.

"So how can I help you?"

"I need official permission to enter and search Zaavi Dhilam's home. Is that something you can arrange or do I need to ask someone else?"

"That's no problem; I can arrange that for you. Get yourself a cab over here and I'll have the papers for you by the time you arrive. I just have to make a couple of calls to set it up."

"Thanks, I'm on my way."

Two hours later, I was on my way to Zaavi's home. Pretik had tried to push me for information on what I had discovered the day before, but I managed to side step his questions without too much trouble. He knew I was keeping it from him, and I wanted him to know that. After being kept in the dark by everyone, I felt I was justified in keeping things to myself. I remembered my promise to Shyola Mastak, and did not want to get her into trouble if I could avoid it.

Zaavi lived in several large rooms above a store selling baked goods that smelled wonderful. A gate between it, and the store selling fruit and vegetables next door, led onto a small courtyard in which sat a small table and two chairs. A hover bike sat to one side, the paintwork scratched and various dents adorning the bodywork. This must be his daily transport to work every day. It was cheaper to run than a hover car and cheaper than daily hover cabs, so I guessed Zaavi was careful with his money. The lack of pride in the machine's outward appearance smacked of someone who was either very hard up for money, which I knew Zaavi was not, or someone who was mean. I plumped for the latter and was happy that I was not wrong. The lack of plants and decoration of any kind in this stark little courtyard, that reminded me of prison exercise yards, backed up my theory.

Retrieving the key from my pocket, I struggled with the door. At first, I thought Teesho Pretik had given me the wrong key, as the door was stuck closed, but a swift knee to the side had it swinging open and I entered. A flight of too-large stairs greeted me, and I groaned as I climbed. I found several large rooms that could make a fabulous apartment if taken care of. Again, the place displayed a certain lack of care that further proved Zaavi did not care for trifles such as decorating or fine furnishings. It was clear to me that he did not care for spending money on such things. The place was clean enough, but needed decorating and refurnishing. Mismatched seating, cracks in the kitchen counter tops and badly hung doors, all spoke volumes about Zaavi's priorities. This was at odds with Shyola's description of Zaavi being something of a connoisseur of the finer things in life during our interview the day before. As I searched the apartment, it was obvious that his liking for fine wines and elegance was more of an affectation than a natural part of his character. I tried not to sigh with frustration as I draped my jacket over a chair and set about the laborious task of searching the place.

Three hours later, I sat back in Zaavi's home office and switched on his computer console. One by one, I fed the data chips I had found hidden in a paper bag at the back of his food-cooling unit, into the slot and read his notes. They were, of course, in the Nahdan language, but a few taps on the keyboard and a translation flashed across the screen from right to left. There is no need to bore you with a word-for-word transcription, and when I say boring, I mean it. The data chips consisted of two things. First, they were a political rant, and the majority of the chips contained nothing but his anti-establishment leanings. His views on the present method of governing the Nahdan people and how they could improve things for everyone if they did things his way, comprised most of the political stuff and I admit to you now, I was bored rigid within a few minutes. I scanned through the stuff without concentrating too hard. As each one finished, I copied them to my own data recorder, so I could read them later, or send them direct to Tinnias and let him do it.

The contents of the final chip made me sit bolt upright and pay attention. Copies of ancient documents flashed up on the screen, together with his translations, all connected with the ancient Nahdan's way of governing, which was much freer than the present one. A drawing of a long sword flashed up and I guessed this was the Singing Sword. It was impressive, almost five feet from end to end, and covered with inscriptions and pictographs. Drawings of each of the pictographs followed, together with his translation of their meaning and I understood what Cristik had said when he told me how the sword mentioned a connection between power, religion and the sword making sounds. When the data stream stopped, I was about to switch it off when something caught my eye. It sounded like white noise, the screen covered in flickering snow, but I was sure there was a video of someone talking behind it. I peered right up to the screen, my nose almost touching the display, but the snow of white noise was not what it appeared to be. Viewed up close, I recognised the pattern of an encryption programme. Grinning at Zaavi's bad attempt at secrecy, I retrieved my data scanner and fished for the universal docking plug I always carry. Once I connected it to Zaavi's console, I set my scanner to search for a suitable decryption programme. The Law Enforcement Agency has the largest database of encryption and decryption programmes, all gleaned from the various criminals we come into contact with. Within two minutes, a beep told me my scanner had found a suitable programme, and I sat back and waited.

Zaavi's face leapt into perfect clarity before me, the large orange eyes with their vertical black pupils, filled with excitement as he spoke, in Nahdan.

I cursed aloud. "Shit." Once again, I tapped until an audio translation reached my ears. This short homemade film, no more than twenty minutes long, explained everything to me and was the break I needed. Zaavi talked about new translations he had made of the sword, translations he had not shared with Cristik or Briel, and which he said explained much more about the sword and its power. He showed photographs of ten or more of the swords pictographs, which he said explained why the sword was so valuable. From Zaavi's secret translations, it intimated that the sword was a source of power, real tangible power and not simply symbolic. In order to gain the power of the sword, one must make it sing, and to do that, one must earn the sword's trust. Once you have achieved that, the sword will make sound, or sing, and the bearer finds himself with powers he did not have before. There was nothing much about what those powers might be, but everything pointed to what Zaavi called, the true power of the universe. All of this must occur within a place called The Temple of Power.

Next, Zaavi announced with wide eyes, that he thought he had found the location of this temple of power, and showed a photograph of another of the sword's pictographs. Three circles, at the points of a triangle, joined by three straight lines that emanated from a central spot in the middle of the three circles. This whole thing was itself, enclosed within a circle. Zaavi laughed long and loud as he held up the photograph, commented on the irony and berated himself for not realising sooner. At this point I got annoyed; I had managed to follow his thread, but now he was losing me. Irony? What irony? Come on man; explain for pity's sake.

Zaavi refused to elaborate further, other than holding up the photograph, pointing to it and exclaiming how this was the temple. He laughed and kept jabbing a finger at a particular spot. "This is the temple. Of course, it has to be. It's the temple of power." More laughter ensued. "How perfect and how funny that it should be hiding in plain sight all this time." The data stream ended and I cursed aloud.

"Fuck you Zaavi Dhilam." My shout echoed within the empty room and I banged my fist on the desk, sending a pot of pens rolling in all directions. I did not bother to pick them up, but grabbed the last data chip, switched off my scanner and left the building.

By the time I got back to my room at the museum, I was calm and able to think with a bit more clarity about the problem that now faced me. I had to assume that Zaavi had found the location of this temple, or at least he thought he had, and I surmised he had gone there with the sword to claim its alleged powers. My problem was that I had no idea where the temple was; all I had was a cryptic symbol left by Zaavi, which could mean any one of a thousand things. I decided to call Tinnias and ask for help. Knowing they bugged our earlier conversations, I used my secure encrypted channel and waited for him to answer.

"Hi Sam, how are you? Why the encrypted channel, is there a problem?"

"Hi Boss. Our previous conversations were bugged, and I'd rather not share what I have to tell you, at least not yet."

"Bugged? How do you know?"

"They told me when I first arrived. They also checked up on my background and snooped into my history."

"Yes I know they looked at your record. I allowed them to check you out. I knew they would find nothing bad. Sorry, I should've told you. I didn't know they were listening in though. Damned cheek."

The Trials of Nahda

"That's okay, no problem, but yes it would've been nice to know they were snooping."

"Sorry Sam."

"No problem. I also felt that they were holding out on me, right from the start. Everything they told me about this guy Zaavi Dhilam was nothing more than what was in the file. It was just too sterile y'know?"

"I know what you mean."

"Anyway, it wasn't until I met with his assistant Cristik Noya that I finally found out the truth about the guy. He's got form as a bit of a political insurrectionist."

Tinnias was as surprised as I had been. "Really? Wow, that makes it more interesting."

"Yeah. Anyway, I interviewed his mother and got nothing from her. I knew she was hiding something from me, but she made it clear she wasn't about to be persuaded to open up. I got more from the girlfriend though. She hinted that he was unhappy with the government here and the control they put on the people's ability to gain wealth and power."

"So is this a political crime do you think?"

"Well I thought so at first, but now I'm not so sure."

"Oh?"

"You see, Cristik Noya told me that Zaavi got into trouble several times for making noises about his anti-government feelings, and he almost lost his job once because he tried to get some others to form some kind of pressure group."

"But that still makes it feel like he acted out of political anger."

"Yeah but Boss, listen to this. I turned over his apartment and found some data chips hidden away at the back of his food cooler unit, and one of them was a heavily encrypted video he made about the sword. He's been doing secret translations of the inscriptions on it, without involving Cristik, and he kept his findings secret from everyone. From his translations, it seems he believes that the sword gives the bearer what he calls, the true power of the universe, when you go to a place called The Temple of Power. You have to do something with the sword, which sings, or makes a sound of some kind. Then you get these special powers. So his translations say anyway."

"That sounds crazy Sam."

"I know it does, but he believes it and that's the important thing. He also said he reckoned he'd found where this alleged Temple of Power is, but he

31

didn't say exactly where. He just showed a photo of a symbol and said that was the temple. I'm sending you the photo now and I'm hoping you can find out what it means."

"Okay I have the file coming through now. Let me have a look. Oh, I see what you mean, how annoyingly cryptic of him."

"Exactly."

"Right, give me a couple of hours. I'll get some guys onto the database and see what we can come up with. I'll get back to you soon. Go have some lunch or something and wait for my call."

"Thanks Boss, I appreciate it."

"No problem, take care Sam."

By the time I had taken a shower and sampled the museum's staff restaurant for a late lunch, which was delicious, I headed back to my room to wait for Tinnias' call. I was drifting off to sleep when he called.

"Hey Boss, what do you have for me?"

"It's interesting Sam. That symbol is what the Nahdans use on their maps to identify the location of their fusion reactors."

"Oh, power."

"Yeah, I knew you'd get that. Now, we scoured the global web for anything about the Nahdan fusion reactors and we almost despaired. I was just dialling to call you to say we'd found nothing, when one of the guys yelled at me that he'd found it."

"Found what?"

"We assumed that Zaavi would run somewhere on Nahda 4. We restricted our search to there, and when the guys suggested we search Nahda 3, I almost said no, that it would take too much time. Since we hadn't found anything on Nahda 4 I relented and I'm glad I did."

"Come on Boss, you're killing me here. Out with it."

"Sorry Sam, it's fun making the moment last. There is a disused fusion reactor on Nahda 3 called Temple Circle."

"Wow. That's umm, got to be it, hasn't it?"

"It's tenuous I know, but it's the only connection we can find. I suggest you go there and check it out. You won't have any problems getting there; your entry papers give you permission to enter both planets unhindered."

"Okay." I thumped a fist into the air. At last, I had a direction in which to chase him.

The Trials of Nahda

"Keep in touch okay?"

"I will, and thanks, I owe you one. I was at my wits end with this and thought I had no choice but to involve the local security forces. I don't want to let them in on anything yet, I just don't trust them."

"I trust your instincts Sam, but remember you're under their jurisdiction while you're on their planets, so don't piss them off too much. Do your job to the limit of your rights, but don't cross the line or we will be in trouble. The Nahdan's are very anti-social folks and it took a lot for them to let you in. We could need their co-operation in the future."

"Don't worry, I won't cross the line." I rang off and was so relieved I gave a whoop of triumph, before grabbing my stuff and heading out to hail a cab back to the military base and my ship.

Teesho Pretik peered at me and frowned at my request. I knew he could not refuse me access to Nahda 3, but I guessed he intended to grill me as to why I wanted to go there. I expected this and rehearsed some lies during the cab journey from the museum.

"Why do you want to go to The Old World Mr Sinclair?"

"Well Sir. I've discovered that Zaavi Dhilam went there many times on research missions from the museum. I also know that he was somewhat obsessed with your ancestors and their way of life, culture and so on. There are various sites that he visited more than once, and I feel it would be prudent to search those areas, just in case he should be hiding out there. It's standard procedure in a case like this; search the target's home, work, any places they habitually frequent and any locations known to be special to them in some way. The vast majority of cases of this nature end up with the target hiding out in a favourite place; somewhere they know well and feel comfortable."

"That makes sense I suppose. Do you have a list of those locations? Just in case you don't return and we need to get your bosses to send someone to look for you. Nahda 3 is a dangerous environment now."

I knew he would ask me this, so I had prepared a list of half a dozen locations Zaavi had been to on more than one occasion, all except the Temple Circle Fusion Reactor of course, and I handed it over. "Of course, here."

He took the list and perused it. "Okay, that's not a problem. You will have to wear a breather unit though. Teams have been down there since we emigrated, scrubbing the toxins from the atmosphere, replanting vegetation to create new clean air, filtering the oceans etcetera, but it's going to be a long job as you can imagine. The air is nowhere near safe to breathe yet."

"I have one in my ship and enough spare scrub filters to give me three hundred hours of breathable air. That should be more than enough for what I need to do and if not, I'll hop back here and beg some more."

"Right then. When do you want to leave?"

"As soon as possible. The quicker I do this legwork, the quicker I narrow down his likely location. If I could impose upon you to refuel my ship before I go, I'd like to get on with it."

"I'll get a refuelling tanker out to you within the hour. Meanwhile, I'll call up the Air Security Force and let them know you'll be heading over there and to allow you passage unhindered. You should be away within a couple of hours."

"Thank you, that's very helpful." I stood and offered my hand, which he shook with a nod.

I spent some time checking my breather unit and scrub filters. I had enough to last me much longer than the three hundred hours I mentioned to Pretik; I thought it prudent to allow myself some leeway, should the need arise for me to linger a little longer. After eating a tasteless mid afternoon snack from my nutri-vend machine, I went to the cockpit and set in the co-ordinates Tinnias gave me for the Temple Circle reactor, and noticed that the promised two hours had been and gone. Before I could set out to find someone to ask for an update, the tanker arrived. I was eager to get on with the chase now that I had a definite direction to follow, and this deliberate hold up annoyed me.

One of the tanker crew was apologetic when I asked what the holdup was. "Sorry. We had to run and refuel several military ships for some kind of exercise they're going on."

"That's okay. Not a problem." I swore under my breath, knowing that Pretik had sent his heavies on the trail of Zaavi from the list of bogus locations I gave him, and was thankful that I had no need to visit any of them. I was happy to let them go on a wild goose chase, and if it meant there would be no one tailing me, all the better. It was obvious that they intended to get there before me, find Zaavi, and let me spend a few days wandering around scratching my balls while they dealt with him in their own way. If they had been open with me about it, and asked to join the hunt from the start, I might have been happy to let them tag along. Going about things in such a furtive way was childish and it angered me. I could not avoid handing Zaavi over to them in the end; I could not keep them out of it forever, and you could say why not let them do the work. The trouble is, it was my job and once I put my energy into my work, I like to see it through to the end and come out with whatever result I can. Good or bad, at least I have done my job. To have these lying assholes steal my target from under my nose, and deliberately fuck me around for no good reason was more than my personal code of honour could take. They were no better than the unregistered Mercs that often tail me and try to relieve me of my catch after watching me do the hard work, and I had no intention of playing ball with them.

In my job, Mercs are a hazard we all have to endure. Unlike me, they are not registered with the Inter-Galactic Law Enforcement Agency. There is no code of conduct with them, no adherence to any of the proper laws and regulations regarding the treatment of prisoners. It is illegal to operate as an unregistered law enforcer, or bounty hunter as some of them still call themselves, but no matter how many of them we apprehend, there are always more ready to take their place. They regard it as easy money without having to operate under the control of the Agency, but deaths among Mercs is far higher than it is amongst us registered freelancers. They take more risks, with their own lives and those of their prisoners, and too many times, they bring in a dead prisoner when there was no need. I have even known a few occasions when they have brought in the wrong prisoner who happened to resemble the real one, and run off with the money before the Agency people found out. I hate them, but folks tend to lump all of us freelancers under that same unflattering label, and although I find it insulting, I do understand.

I used to work as a Law Enforcer until a few years ago. I had an untidy desk in a small office back home in the Sigma Prime Agency Headquarters, excellent pay, good conditions and nice colleagues. I joined the Agency around twenty years ago, after doing my statutory ten years in the military and I have always loved my job. One day I woke up and knew that although I loved the job, I was bored, irritated by the sometimes-petty rules and regulations that we had to operate under. Too often, I had to let a prisoner walk because of some technicality, and after a while, it got to me. I reached the point where something had to change, and as I could not change the laws the Agency worked under, I had to change myself. Tinnias was surprised the day I entered his office and announced I wanted to go freelance, but he was all for it and backed me all the way. I spent a good deal of my life savings on my ship, took possession of an official Agency Tag that identifies me as a licenced Law

Enforcer, and began work as a chase, catch and deliver guy. My job is simple; I have a specific target to find, apprehend and deliver into the care of the relevant law enforcement agency and although it may seem simple, no two days are ever the same. Over the years I have been freelance, I have been shot at, chased by all manner of horrific creatures, hunted by Mercs, and at one time had an underworld bounty on my head for upsetting a legendary Merc called Spillner, by not letting him take my prisoner from me. I have come close to losing my life on many occasions, and lost those close to me more than once, but I would not change it for anything. My job is me; it is what I am good at and what I live for.

As I waited for the tanker to refuel my ship's cells, I let my thoughts drift to Zaavi Dhilam, the Singing Sword, and the alleged powers bestowed upon its handler. I was quick to disregard any notion of superpowers like those possessed by the heroes of the science fiction movies I had seen. That was ridiculous of course; no one has those kinds of abilities, and there is no magic, sorcery or anything of such a fantastical nature. I have met many different races of beings and some of them have abilities that are strange to me. There are the Xerosians of course; they must be the nearest thing to a being with fantastical powers. They are natural psychics and telepaths, and meeting them is an unnerving experience. I've yet to meet any being that can conjure fire from their fingers, disappear into thin air or fire bolts of energy by the power of will, and as I sat waiting for my ship to be refuelled, all such thoughts were pushed to the back of my mind. I felt sure that the sword's power was no more than symbolic, and referred to the power its owner had over his people. Zaavi obviously thought otherwise, and was hoping to find himself endowed with immense power, and I was impatient to witness the disappointing awakening I felt sure he was due.

The tanker finished as I was packing a stash of tranquiliser darts into my backpack, and I was relieved to be able to get on with the job after so many unnecessary hold ups. The tanker driver waved as he flew off and I set about getting the ship ready for take-off. The intercom crackled.

"SC257, this is Nahda Air Security, you are cleared for take-off."

"Nahda Air Security, this is SC257, thank you."

"You have permission to enter Nahda 3 airspace, and all security personnel on the ground are aware of your intentions. You should not encounter problems from our staff."

The Trials of Nahda

"Thank you guys. I appreciate your co-operation and hope to bring this unfortunate matter to a close, very soon. Space Cop 257 out." With a whoop of relief, I gunned the engines and lifted the ship, whom I named Essy, off the ground and away from the military base. There was no hurry; I wanted to allow the Nahdan Security Force plenty of time to get way ahead of me so there was less chance of them noticing that I was not following. It crossed my mind that I might have someone tailing me, but that did not worry me. Once out of Nahda 4 airspace, I flipped Essy into covert mode, happy in the knowledge that I was now invisible to everyone.

The planet was serene from up there, as they always are, and I allowed myself several minutes to watch it. No matter how many different systems and planets I visit, every single one of them is beautiful from space. Whatever hardships the people down there might be enduring, however hard they may be fighting for survival, nor whatever dangers lurk in their forgotten dark places, nothing spoils their beauty as seen from this vantage point. That sight never fails to move me and remind me of my position in this vast universe, and believe me it is vast. I count myself very lucky to have been born at the time I was. To be able to see and experience all that I have during my life, is something I feel privileged to enjoy. I spend a long time in space travel, it is like home to me and I feel comfortable there, but there is always that scary feeling somewhere deep inside that never goes away. The knowledge that if something went wrong out here in the void, rescue is a very long way away is always at the forefront of my mind. Death in space is the coldest, loneliest and most frightening I can imagine, and the time I boarded a becalmed ship to apprehend my target, to find the whole crew dead from a hull breach five millimetres in diameter, gave me nightmares for a time. For weeks I would wake, sure I could hear their screams echoing through the cosmos, their frozen, distorted faces haunting my mind to the point where I found myself hesitant to look into a mirror to shave one morning. The fear of death in space, although always present, is something I never allow to interfere with my capability though, and as I acknowledged the blip of fear that flittered through my consciousness, I tore my eyes away from Nahda 4 and headed for Nahda Old World.

Well I need to break off for a bit. I have to go meet with a contact who I hope has some information for me. This is Sinclair V-Log PA884/R, data log reference point 1957365/7985.

The Trials of Nahda

CHAPTER FOUR

Hey there, I'm back. This is Sinclair V-Log PA884/R, data log reference point 1957365/7986, continuing report.

Nahda 3 was very different from the beautiful world I left behind a few hours before. It was a mixture of grey, muddy brown and sickly green and reminded me of a mouldy piece of fruit left to fester in the gutter. As I gazed down at the stricken planet, I understood why the Nahda 4 Security Forces were so strict about their laws. Having so recently caused a tragedy of such epic proportions, the Nahdan people must carry a heavy burden of guilt, and with nowhere else in their system to run, the worry must weigh on their minds. It showed me how easy it is for people's opinion to change when they are away from the problem, and how important it is to make objective judgements for the good of all. I would not make a good politician. It occurred to me that I may have been a little hasty in my decision to keep things from Pretik and his men, and I felt guilty at allowing my personal feelings to influence my actions. There was no way to change my course now though, with Pretik's men already hours ahead of me. They were on their way to search locations I felt sure would yield no sign of Zaavi Dhilam, so the best thing to do was to continue as planned.

I keyed in the co-ordinates of Temple Circle Fusion Reactor and headed down through the poisonous fog. As the city came into focus beneath me, images of Vidicom movies flashed through my mind. I love science fiction movies and have an impressive collection back home, and the city below me reminded me of all the global catastrophe movies I had seen. Abandoned for over three hundred years, everything was crumbling and tattered. A browny grey filth covered every surface like a blotchy plague; the single visible species of vegetation a stringy brown grass that even I knew would never be green again. I marvelled at the strength with which nature is able to hang on in the face of unimaginable odds. Even though the air was too toxic to breathe and no animal life had survived, this tough brown grass still clung to life on this devastated world. It made me feel confident that one day, the planet would be healthy enough to support an abundance of life again, and I hoped that when it happened, the new inhabitants would take more care than the last ones did.

The Trials of Nahda

After taking my time to circle around the area a few times to get my bearings, I spied what appeared to be an old parking lot, and came in to land. The rusting hulks of several personal shuttlecraft lay at the eastern end and I shuddered, spooked by the sight. My backpack sat waiting for me, already packed with my data recorder, DNA sampler, sedative darts, a couple of sets of restraints, laser bullet clips, basic med kit, and filters for my breather unit. After a little debate with myself, I decided to take a pair of laser pistols and leave the bulky laser rifle in the ship. I had enough of a burden already with my loaded backpack and the bulky breather unit to wear.

Temple Circle Fusion Reactor was a huge site and as I stood at the entrance and studied the now fading information board that lay on the ground at my feet, I saw that it was a self-contained community for the reactor workers. Covering three square miles, there were restaurants, bars, stores and entertainment centres, alongside apartment blocks for the workers. A park with a lake, swimming pool, a school for the worker's children, healthcare centre and even a memorial garden for the deceased, it all ensured the workers wanted for nothing. Generations of Nahdans worked at the reactor and they had every facility they could wish for on their doorstep in return for their labours. I took a scan of the signboard so I would be able to find my way about without retracing my steps, and entered Temple Circle.

Three hundred years of accumulated dust and toxic particles softened my boot steps, which left a clear trail behind me in the soft blanket that no doubt enveloped the entire planet, and I was both pleased and annoyed. The fact that the dust rendered my footsteps silent was a blessing, but the obvious trail I was leaving gave testament to my presence for anyone to see. There was no way I could cover my trail even if I did have the time, so I had to hope that Zaavi did not see them before I caught sight of his. The breather unit I wore made my face hot and sweaty but I did not fancy poisoning myself for the sake of a cool breeze on my skin. No amount of time spent in a dermal optimiser could repair that kind of damage so I suffered without complaint. I checked the readout on my air quality monitor and found that it was indeed extremely toxic. One day of breathing this atmosphere would ensure I would not reach my next birthday and my death would be slow and painful. No thank you.

As I walked the silent streets and examined the shops, bars and entertainment facilities, I thought about this Temple of Power and its possible location. Now, I am not a history buff but even I understood that with the Temple belonging in the time of the ancient Nahdans, its likely location would be underneath what I saw around me. Subsequent generations tend to build on top of previous buildings, the layers of occupation being of great interest to archaeologists. I had no idea if anything of this Temple of Power was still in existence, but I concluded that anything left would be underground. Had Zaavi found it yet? Common sense told me that if not, he would be camping out in whatever vessel he had used to travel here. He would not be safe in any of the residential apartments, the poisonous air and toxic dust that lay everywhere would make living and sleeping there impossible. My obvious first task was to find his ship, so I retrieved my scanner and studied the map for anywhere suitable to land a ship. I made a conscious choice to land outside of the Temple Circle complex; I did not want to alert Zaavi to my presence before I was ready, so I set off for the park that lay to the northern end of the complex.

For some weird reason, wandering around a deserted city was far more unsettling for me than one filled with unfriendly locals. All those empty shops, the accusing glare of their sightless eyes creeped me out. Those windows were hiding all manner of unknown horrors within their poisonous depths, and I found myself imagining all sorts of things that a grown man should not fear. I guess we all have a frightened child within somewhere, and mine was awake that day and wanting comfort that I struggled to provide. If the ancient Temple was underground, as I reckoned it had to be, any one of these empty buildings could hide the entrance and unless I found Zaavi before he found it, I would have to search each one. I shuddered at the thought and found myself questioning the wisdom of watching all those scary vidicom movies I love so much.

The Park entrance lay ahead of me and I entered, hoping that a garden labourer's tool shed would conceal an entrance to the old Temple, to save me having to search all those other buildings. Dead trees surrounded me as I walked over the stringy brown grass that fought its way through the layer of toxic waste and I felt guilty at treading on it. It had enough to cope with here without my boot steps adding to its problems, so I kept to what was left of the path and found myself within a forest of dead trees, their blackened corpses still standing around me despite the passage of time. It was strange being here where there should be green leaves, flowers, birds singing and wildlife. Instead, I was in the middle of a nightmare. Everything around me was dead and I, the single survivor. This was the loneliest place I had ever been to, and one I hope never to revisit.

The Trials of Nahda

Thirty minutes later, I emerged from the forest and found myself at the edge of the lake I remembered from the map. There was no water, just a thick browny grey sludge that I guessed must stink of something indescribable, and I was glad I was wearing a breather unit. I noticed the skull of some creature near the toe of my left boot and I stepped back, not wanting to hear it crunch beneath my feet. A jetty still stood, a few hundred yards to my left, but its boards were rotten through and I was glad I did not have to traverse it. As I scanned the opposite shore, a brand new shuttlecraft met my gaze, and I ducked back behind a blackened tree trunk while I fished for my scope.

The ship leapt into view and I watched for over an hour, but saw nothing of Zaavi. I presumed he was out searching for an entrance to the old temple, if he was not already down there gaining superpowers. With great care, I made my way around the edge of the lake to check it out. It was obvious as soon as I approached that the ship was locked down and the pilot, absent. This was not a problem, I rooted in my backpack for a neat little gizmo I was given by one of my contacts on Lamoriol 7 a couple of years before, and one I never travel anywhere without. About the size of a cigarette pack, I attached its magnetic back to the locking mechanism of the ship's hatch and switched it on. Four minutes later, with a loud click, the hatch descended. I approached with caution, my laser pistol at the ready, and entered.

This was a short haul vessel, that much was obvious right away. No more than a cockpit and small storage area behind, it would not allow anyone to travel long distances in any comfort. A toilet cubicle had been fitted at the rear, a bunk lay along one wall and a nutri-vend was attached to a bulkhead by a clumsy array of chains and thick gauge wire. There was a box containing several breather units and hundreds of hours' worth of scrub filters under the bunk, along with a bag that contained several changes of men's clothes and washing necessities. I saw several drums of water chained to the back wall and I noticed that there was no water treatment unit. This meant that the owner had to carry all the water he intended to use and could not filter and re-use any of it, further confirming that this vessel was not something you would want to use for long journeys.

I scanned the whole vessel into my recorder, together with the co-ordinates of its location and sent the file to Tinnias, back on Sigma Prime. At least if something unfortunate happened to me here, someone would know my true whereabouts. I found DNA on several items within the wash bag and within a couple of minutes I had confirmation that they belonged to Zaavi

42

Dhilam. I bagged and tagged the dental cleanser that gave me the DNA and stored it in my backpack. Once I completed the official process, I searched the large black bag of clothes and found something interesting.

Within the folds of a shirt, I found several sheets of paper, one of which showed the symbol I had seen on Zaavi's encrypted video. The three circles at the points of a triangle, all joined by lines emanating from a central point, seemed to mock me as I scanned it into my recorder. A thought hit me at the exact moment my Unicom beeped, and I almost jumped out of my skin.

"Hey Sam. I just got the file you sent."

"Hi Boss."

"Hey, are you okay? You sound funny."

"Yeah I'm fine. I'm wearing a breather unit and you startled me nearly out of my wits."

"Sorry. Don't you go taking that breather off though; the atmosphere on Nahda 3 is deadly."

"I don't intend to, don't worry."

"Have you confirmed that the vessel belongs to Zaavi Dhilam?"

"Yes. I got DNA from a dental cleanser, which matched that from the file you gave me. I'm sending you that file now."

"Okay good, any evidence you find, no matter how trivial or tenuous, bag it, tag it, and record it."

"Always do Boss. By the way, since you're here, can you do something for me?"

"Sure."

"That symbol from Zaavi's encrypted video, the three circles that mean a fusion reactor?"

"Yeah, what about it?"

"Can you scale it up and lay it over a map of the location I'm in now and tell me what you find?"

"Of course, I'm doing it now as we speak. What's your hunch?"

"That dot in the middle, where the lines come from. I reckon they indicate the entrance to the old Temple of Power, whatever may be left of it anyway. I figured that since the place is ancient, it must be underground by now and will have been built over, maybe several times in the intervening centuries, so anything left will be underground."

"Good thinking Sam. When you think about it, it's obvious really isn't it?"

"Yeah, I almost kicked myself when the thought occurred to me."

"Okay here is what I have. When I scaled up the symbol to match the map of your location, there is only one way to arrange the symbol so all three circles are within the Temple Circle Fusion Reactor complex. I'm sending you this file now, so you can see for yourself. There may be a problem though."

I almost swore aloud. "How?"

"That centre dot lies right in the middle of the reactor core itself."

"Shit and fuck."

"Yeah, exactly. Even after all these years, you cannot safely enter the reactor itself unless it's been properly dismantled, and I'm officially forbidding you from trying okay?"

"I got you Boss. There's no way I'm dying of radiation poisoning just for a petty thief."

"Good. But wait, your point about this old temple being underground is pertinent here. The actual temple itself may be right underneath the centre of the reactor core, but there may be an entrance nearby there."

"Right. I intend to search the place thoroughly. I have my radiation monitor with me, so I'll be okay. I just have to hope to either find Zaavi before he finds it, or to find it easily myself so I can chase the asshole down."

"Okay, take care Sam. What's it like down there anyway?"

"Spooky. Like all those nightmares you ever had about being the only guy left alive on the planet after they dropped the bomb. It's creeping me out."

"Nice. Remind me never to visit."

"I'll do that if you'll do it for me."

"Keep in touch Sam."

"I will as long as I'm able. If I do get underground, I might not be able to."

"Then we agree now that you call me the moment before you head underground. If I don't hear from you within seventy two hours, I'm sending in the troops."

"Okay. I'll call you as soon as I have anything more for you."

I studied the map of the complex before leaving the ship and heading for the reactor building. As I jogged along, I prayed that I would find Zaavi soon, so that I could leave this festering place and allow it to continue its healing.

The Trials of Nahda

What I assumed to be Zaavi's clear trail of footprints led me along the lonely streets, and fifteen minutes later, I saw the remains of the reactor building come into view ahead as I rounded a corner by a rotting clothes store. The footprints continued right down the street towards the reactor building, so I followed them at a run, eager to catch up with Zaavi and get away from Nahda 3. I had to make several more detours around the rusting hulks of abandoned hover vehicles and assorted debris left behind as the people fled the complex. Piles of now rotting garments, bags, a child's doll and all manner of other discarded domestic flotsam lay everywhere, and it occurred to me how fast one is able to decide what is important in life when a real emergency happens. Everything was the same grey brown and covered in dust and blotchy grime and I mentally shrank as the doll's lifeless eyes gazed up at me.

Around another corner I saw the entrance to the reactor building before me; its four stone pillars still standing, whatever they supported long since having fallen. Peering from the safety of a shop doorway, I followed the trail of footprints with my eyes. I took out my scope and scanned the area, but saw no movement to indicate a man was hiding out, waiting to shoot at me the moment I broke cover. Between my hiding place and the doorway into the reactor building, there was no cover whatsoever and I cursed with frustration. I now had two awful choices. I could take a risk and run for it, or stay and risk losing my target. Neither of those choices appealed to me, but having come this far, I could not call it a day yet. Before I changed my mind, I took a deep breath and ran for the door as fast as I could.

The breather unit hampered me as I flattened myself against the wall beside the door, and I heaved deep breaths. The units filter the air very well, but you have to make more of an effort to breathe in when using them. It means your chest muscles ache after a while, and if you exert yourself too much you can find yourself unable to get enough air and can pass out. My first priority was my own health, so I allowed myself the time to get my breath before moving on. The last thing I needed was to pass out on this poisonous planet and maybe lose my breather unit as I fell, or worse, have it ripped off by a crazed thief on the hunt for superpowers. I love my job, but hell there are limits.

Once my chest calmed, I peered around the door and into the darkness within. I heard nothing, so I stepped inside. Empty offices surrounded me on all sides, an elevator and staircase to my right, and a short corridor straight ahead. The roof had long since fallen in or been dismantled, and I saw grey sky overhead. Upstairs was of little interest to me, so I decided to leave the stairs for a last resort and concentrate on searching the ground floor for an entrance underground. None of the offices yielded anything of value, so I stepped towards the door at the end of the corridor and listened. For several seconds I heard nothing and was about to open the door, when I heard a faint metallic clink from somewhere on the other side.

With my audio enhancer plugged into one ear, I placed the other end on the door and listened. Every few seconds there was a metallic clink and twice, the sound of stone or rocks knocking together. I checked the readout, and was pleased to find that the noise was forty-five degrees to my right, which told me I could open the door and use it as a shield if necessary. Counting the seconds between the clinks, I timed it so I opened the door at the same moment as the noise. I hoped this would mask any sound the door might make as it opened, thus enabling me to retain the element of surprise.

The door opened no more than a crack, and the metallic clinking continued louder. I took a moment to prepare my laser pistol with tranquiliser darts, before pushing the door open an inch. The open sky above did little to illuminate the room within, but I was able to make out the remains of computer consoles in three banks curving away and around to the right. I assumed this must be the control centre, and guessed the reactor core itself might be no more than a couple of rooms ahead. The clinking continued every few seconds, accompanied by the occasional sounds of rocks falling and I pushed the door open further. When it was open enough for me to get through, I crouched down and took a deep breath before poking my head around to the right.

Zaavi held the massive hammer above his head, and with practised ease, brought it smashing down onto the metal wedge jammed between two rocks. The smaller of the two fell and rolled away to join the bottom of a large heap of others that stood to the left. The larger boulder, no longer propped there by its companion, came away from where it had been wedged for the past three hundred or so years, and all those above that depended upon it for support, came tumbling down. Zaavi leapt out of the way like an athlete and avoided getting his foot crushed, the Singing Sword that hung from his waist, clanking against rocks. I swore to myself as he chose the very same moment to make his leap, which I almost chose to shoot him in the neck with a dart.

With the offending rock pile now out of the way, Zaavi dropped the huge hammer and approached the wall. I almost swore aloud as he disappeared behind the pile of rocks and I scanned the room for a new vantage point. A bank of computer consoles lay to my right, so I made a dash for them. This gave me an uninterrupted view straight ahead, to where I heard Zaavi muttering to himself in Nahdan. Risking a peek over the top of the bank of consoles, I saw him studying symbols carved into the wall. Knowing I needed evidence, I took some footage of him with my scanner, and noticed the same symbol of three circles joined to a centre dot, carved into the wall. There was a bank of carved tiles, nine of them in three rows of three, six feet off the ground and I saw Zaavi bent over, peering at them. As he touched one, it sank into the surface of the wall, and I remembered a movie I saw. They must be some sort of ancient locking mechanism. I could not risk waiting any longer, so I took aim with my laser dart gun and stood.

"Zaavi Dhilam." My voice caught him unawares, and he spun around, the shock in his wide eyes and his open mouth invisible to me behind the breather unit he wore, which served to make him appear even stranger than he did normally. "I represent the Inter-Galactic Law Enforcement Agency, and I'm arresting you for the theft of the Singing Sword. Get down on your knees and put your hands behind your head."

"Never." We locked eyes. "I've come too far to stop now. I'm too close to my destiny. You've no idea of the power that awaits me, and you can't stop me. No one can stop me." He touched another of the tiles and I stepped forward, gun aimed at his neck.

"Get down on your knees or I will shoot you."

"Go away little man." He touched a third tile.

The dart hit him square in the neck and he gasped in pain. His left hand ripped the dart from his skin, while his right touched a fourth tile, causing a portion of the wall to slide back into itself and to the left. He staggered and I took a step towards him, but instead of falling to the ground unconscious, he stumbled like a drunkard towards the now open portion of wall. I fired again, hitting him right in the back of the neck and he arched his back in shock, before stumbling forwards and out of my sight. I ran for the wall and leapt through into darkness, one hand holding my laser pistol ahead while the other grappled with the loop from which my flashlight hung off my belt.

No more than five feet of stone corridor lay ahead of me, before a stone stairway led down into blackness, halfway down which was the body of Zaavi Dhilam. It had taken two darts to bring him down and I berated myself for underestimating the amount of sedative with which to load the darts. Being seven feet three inches tall and of corresponding breadth, I estimated it would take one and a half times the amount I use for someone of my own size, but it had taken three times as much to bring this man down. I hoped I had not killed him with so much sedative; he could even have landed on the sword and run himself through. Panicking, I leapt down the steps to check him out.

He had landed with his head lower than his feet, so I stepped down a couple of further steps to check his pulse, and as I stepped down, the step beneath me gave way a little. The sound of stone grinding against stone reached my ears as the dim light from the open doorway above us shrank and disappeared.

Panic erupted within and spewed out in my startled cry. "Oh fuck no." We were entombed and despite my years of experience, fear leapt from my heart and coursed through me. I will admit I was afraid of dying down there in the dark. I grabbed my Unicom but sure enough, there was no signal and another flash of panic swept over me.

"Shit. Shit, shit, shit."

After I had allowed myself a moment of panic, I forced myself back into cop mode and checked Zaavi's pulse. I was delighted to find he was very much alive, and hoped that both his superior strength and his knowledge of this ancient Nahdan stuff would be able to get us both out of here. Struggling to shift his body around was no mean feat I can tell you now. A man of his size with the added weight of the sword in that confined space proved very awkward for me, but I got him into a position where he could recover and I was breathing hard by the time I finished. There was no way I would be able to carry him back to my ship, but a man of his size and strength could prove awkward if he chose not to co-operate with me. It occurred to me that because of his size and weight, I might have to shoot him and bring him in dead, and that thought did not please me at all. Although I am licenced to use deadly force where I believe it necessary, I would always choose an alternative if there is one. There are times however when I have no choice, but it never gives me pleasure to end someone's life no matter what their crime. After trying and failing to unlock the clasp that held the sword to his waist belt, I turned him on his side, cuffed his hands behind his back, then sat and waited for him to wake up.

While I waited, I swung my flashlight around and found that we were trapped inside a stone staircase that led down into total darkness, beyond the reach of my flashlight. Nothing could persuade me to go and investigate, only to return and find him having woken up, let himself out and re-locked me inside. I sat down and cursed. My ass was cold and numb within minutes and although I am not scared of the dark, being trapped inside that place meant I had a constant fight with the urge to panic. Several times, I went back up the steps and felt around the wall but there were no tiles on this side and I found no hidden mechanism with which to open it again. Despite stepping on the loose step several hundred times, it slid down but nothing happened. It was a locking mechanism, not an unlocking one.

Two hours later, my air purity monitor beeped. I held it to my flashlight and was surprised to find it registering the air as safe to breathe. I tapped it a few times and assumed it was broken, so checked to see if Zaavi's breather unit had a monitor. It did, and like mine, it said the air was safe but I did not want to trust it, so I kept mine on. Down there in the stone staircase, it was much colder than it was on the surface and I was glad of the breather unit that at least kept my face warm. Another hour went by without incident, and I had just taken a pee when I heard a low hum that reverberated through the whole space.

Touching my hands to the wall, I felt the slight vibration and frowned. "What the fuck?" I concentrated hard to try to locate the possible direction from which the vibration originated, but it felt as if it came from the very fabric of the stone building itself, from within the stones themselves. A vibration meant an engine of some sort, and an engine needs people to run and maintain it. Generators can be programmed to switch on automatically given certain triggers, but with this planet having been abandoned for more than three hundred years, I found it hard to believe that any such delicate machinery would still be operational. I allowed myself to dare to hope that people were down here; maybe some archaeologists or even some of Pretik's security men he might have sent here in secret to search for Zaavi. I called out several times but got no reply, so rather than yell myself hoarse, I sat down and sulked.

Four hours and thirty-eight minutes after Zaavi succumbed to my sedative darts, he showed signs of waking up. A groan from beside me, followed by a weak cough, told me my prisoner was now back in the land of the living and I was surprised to find myself very relieved at not being alone anymore. Within a few more minutes he opened his eyes, squeezed them shut and turned away from my flashlight.

Another cough and he levelled a curse at me. "Get that light out of my eyes you idiot. You trying to blind me now since you failed to kill me?"

"It's dark down here, in case you hadn't noticed."

He coughed again. "For you maybe."

I frowned, then realised that those vertical pupils that made his eyes so strange would give him excellent night vision, giving him yet another advantage over me. "Sorry. I just realised about your eyes. Guess you can see in the dark huh?"

"Yeah. What the hell happened? Oh my head."

"Sedative dart. You refused to give yourself up so I had no choice. You have a cut over your right eye and you might have a bruise or two. I have some painkillers if you need them."

"So why am I not locked inside a security force transporter on my way to a government prison?"

"Because the door closed behind us and we're locked in here. I'm hoping you know another secret code to get us the fuck out of here so I can then haul your ass back to a lock up."

He struggled into a sitting position. "One of us must've tripped a secret locking mechanism."

"Yeah umm, that would be me." I pointed to the step and showed him how it lowered with the slightest pressure.

He grinned. "Well done buddy. Guess that means we go forward then."

"Can't we get out up here?"

"No. It's move forward or sit here and starve to death. That door was strictly one way."

"Shit. Then let's get on with it."

"Hey, how about letting me out of these cuffs huh? It's not as if I can run away is it?"

I reached towards him and let his right hand free, then locked his left to my right. "No, but just in case you do, we run together."

"Typical law enforcer." He struggled to his feet. "No trust."

"You're a thief. You teach me about trust huh?"

CHAPTER FIVE

We made our way down the stairs, my flashlight guiding the way, for me anyway. I tried to cover my fear with conversation. "So you can see in the dark?"

"Not in total darkness no." He was gracious and slowed his descent down the steps so as not to make me fall. "We think that the humanoids we evolved from were largely nocturnal, probably due to the predators around at that time, and they would've had these eyes. Maybe whatever creature they evolved from had them. We don't know for sure. It seems that the Nahdan's as we are today, evolved very quickly, like almost overnight in geological terms. We don't yet know why that is."

"That's interesting, but those eyes would be awesome in my job. Having to rely on a flashlight or night goggles is a drag sometimes."

"Well, you might not believe this, but amongst our young people, there is a growing trend for surgery to change their eyes to round pupils like off worlders have."

I gaped at him. "Really? Why?"

"Because what someone else has is always thought of as better than what you have yourself."

"I guess that's one humanoid trait that crosses all racial boundaries."

"Yeah, I guess it is."

"Why did you steal the sword?"

He did not seem at all fazed by my sudden and deliberate change in the direction of the conversation. "I didn't steal it. It's my destiny to bear it."

"Your destiny? Are you serious?"

"I wouldn't expect you to understand such things umm, what did you say your name was?"

"I didn't. Sam Sinclair. Inter-Galactic Law Enforcement Agency."

He stopped mid stride and frowned at me. "My people called off world law enforcers on me?"

"Yes. Destiny or no destiny, they want their sword back and you have to answer for stealing it."

"Everything that is known about it is because of my work. The hours I spent deciphering the inscriptions and pictographs makes me the only expert

51

on it. I am the one person alive who knows what the sword says, and that makes it my destiny to bear it."

"So what does it say?"

"It says many things, the most important of which is that the first to understand the message is the one to bear the sword."

"It actually says that?"

"It does."

"So where does that leave Cristik Noya? He spent many hours helping you decipher it. Doesn't he get to hold it sometime?"

"No. He does not have the right qualities to bear it."

"What qualities are those?"

"Courage, resilience, wisdom and self-knowledge."

"And you do?" I left the question hanging between us and he did not bother to reply for long moments.

"You do realise I'm not going to allow you to take me back." We reached the bottom of the stairs and found ourselves in a corridor that stretched away in front of us beyond the reach of my flashlight.

I peered into the darkness. "I'd be surprised if you didn't make some kind of attempt to prevent it."

"And neither am I going to let you take my sword from me."

"We'll see."

"Sam. I'm probably twice as strong as you. I could break your neck without raising a sweat. You think these handcuffs are going to stop me?"

"Try and get out of them." He stared at me and snickered. "Go on." He took hold of the cuffs and tried everything to break them, and failed. He twisted, pulled, pushed and all to no avail. With all of his superior strength, those cuffs were staying on his wrist until this little guy decided to take them off.

He gave up with a sigh and looked at me, his eyebrows raised in surprise. "What the heck are they made of?"

"Dalshin Tin, alloyed with Morgolium."

"Never heard of either of them. But I have to give you that one Sam. If I'm not going back with you, then you're staying here with me until I convince you to let me out of them. Once you witness the power the sword gives me, you'll come around to my way of thinking."

I started forward along the corridor. "I doubt that."

The Trials of Nahda

The corridor seemed to crush in on me more the further we walked and although I have never thought of myself as claustrophobic, this tunnel bothered me. Maybe it was having the breather unit on while being in such a narrow and confined space, or maybe it was having such a big person beside me to give the impression that the tunnel was smaller than it was, I do not know but I struggled with it. Zaavi had to stoop a little to avoid banging his head on the roof, and his hair no longer stood up in the same regimental stripe as Nahdan men normally wear it. I wanted to ask about that hair, but I did not want to be rude. It was the wildest hairstyle I had ever seen, and being dead white as well, made the Nahdan men an impressive sight.

Before long, I was unable to contain myself. "Zaavi. I just have to say, that hair is the most amazing sight I've ever seen."

He stopped and swung around to face me, a frown creasing his brow. "Thank you, I guess. I choose to assume you meant it as a compliment."

"Oh I did. Does it naturally grow like that or what?"

"Our hair does naturally grow longer in the strip from front to back, than it does on the sides, but we style it to enhance it."

"So does it grow? If you left it, would the sides grow longer too?"

"No. It grows to half an inch or so on the sides and then stops. The centre strip would grow to a couple of feet if we let it, but then it hangs everywhere and gets untidy, so we cut it to three or four inches. The action of cutting our hair stimulates the release of some chemical that encourages it to start growing again until it reaches its maximum, and then it stops again."

"And all the men have white hair?"

"Yes, although some of the younger men dye their hair, and some keep it all the same length. Our younger generation are trying to make themselves more like some of our galactic neighbours."

I nodded. "All young people want to make themselves unique from the older generation. That's the same on every planet. Where I come from, the men traditionally kept their hair very short, but when I was growing up, my friends and I grew it long just to shock everyone and be different."

"I would never have thought an off worlder would take such an interest in our appearance. We are stared at; our size alone ensures that, but people seldom actually talk about it with us like you are doing."

"Well I umm, personal grooming is important to me. I notice these things." People who know me well, tease me sometimes about the way I like to take care of my appearance. Yes, I do have regular treatments in a dermal optimiser, and I visit the hairdresser on a regular basis, but I would never describe myself as vain. I wanted to get to know Zaavi, and having something in common with him made it easier for me to show him that I am more than the man who is out to take away his liberty. Some freelancers do not care what their prisoners think of them, but I like to make sure they know that I am a good person at heart, someone with values who is not going to screw them. I do have to be the bad guy sometimes, it is inevitable in this job, but I do have a personal code, and I manage to stick to it ninety percent of the time.

Zaavi changed the subject, catching me unawares. "I suppose you talked to Shyola."

"Yes, and your mother, Cristik and Briel too."

"Briel. That man is more narrow minded than I ever thought it possible for someone to be."

"I admit that I found him very evasive, and he is a very bad actor."

"What did he say about me?"

"The same as almost everyone else. That you're extremely clever, knowledgeable about your subject and passionate about your work. He told me how lucky the museum is to have you working there and how worried he is about why you suddenly took off with the sword."

Zaavi laughed aloud. "He said that? Makes me sound like a paragon of virtue doesn't it? You said almost everyone, who ratted me out as being a trouble maker?"

"Cristik. He told me about your anti-government feelings and how you almost lost your job for trying to form some kind of pressure group."

"I might have known. I always guessed he was jealous of my position and knowledge."

"Or maybe he cares about you and wanted to help me find you before you got yourself deeper into a situation that isn't healthy for you?" Zaavi did not reply and we walked on in silence.

The tunnel ahead turned through ninety degrees and we found ourselves staring at a wall. I swore and swept my flashlight around, but found nothing that resembled a door handle, not even a bank of carved tiles like the ones that led us in there.

Without warning Zaavi grabbed my arm and fixed my flashlight on the floor ten feet ahead. "Look."

The Trials of Nahda

I looked, and saw a four-inch square of black, which stood out amongst the uniform grey that surrounded us. "A black square in a sea of grey. Another booby trap. Wonderful."

He fixed me with a stare. "This time you go in first and fall headlong."

"Listen, you're the destined Sword Bearer endowed with courage, resilience, and umm, what were the other two?"

"Wisdom and self-knowledge."

"Yeah, them too. So you be courageous and go first."

"I'd rather be wise and let you go first."

I unholstered my laser pistol. "Funny. I'm the guy with the gun, so you go first."

"You want to shoot me and be stuck in here with a corpse that's twice your weight, and no idea how to get out?"

I swore at his logic. "Oh for fuck's sake." I strode forwards, dragging him along behind and hesitated for no more than a nanosecond before banging a heel onto the black square.

The sound of rock grinding against rock filled the tunnel, the acoustics making the sound echo from all directions. I leapt back and with considerable strength of mind, managed to stop myself from hiding behind Zaavi in fright.

He pointed into the gloom. "Look." I swung the flashlight ahead and saw the wall that blocked our way, sliding to the right, revealing an uninviting black hole.

"Oh great, another tunnel."

"You don't like confined spaces?"

"They never used to bother me. It's probably having this breather unit on."

"Well we can't stand here, let's get moving." He walked forwards, dragging me along.

We found ourselves in a room, around twenty feet square. A domed roof rose above us and I craned my neck to look. The entire surface was covered in paintings. Zaavi gazed at it and exclaimed in awe. "Wow, look at that. The complete history of the ancient Nahdans. I must come back here and document this." Apart from a raised dais a foot square in one corner, the room was empty and no doorway was evident to us.

"Welcome." A voice boomed behind us and we both jumped out of our skins. Pure instinct drove my hand to my laser pistol as we swung around and found ourselves now joined by a hologram Nahdan man of advanced years. The same orange eyes with vertical pupils as Zaavi possessed, held us, the same hairstyle atop his head, which was not a lot higher off the ground than my own head.

I recognised what I was seeing, and frowned. "A hologram. And he's not much taller than me."

Zaavi nodded. "Our height is obviously a recent evolutionary development."

"My name is Vaylon, and I am Temple Keeper number 43852382693. This is the third month of my watch, and I welcome you Sword Bearer."

Zaavi grinned at me. "So this is the Temple of Power."

"It is indeed."

I gaped. "What the fuck? It's a hologram. How can it answer you like that?"

"Search me."

"I am a he, not an it. My name is Vaylon and I can see and hear you just as you can see and hear me. You can speak and I can respond to you. You may remove your masks gentlemen. The air down here is quite safe for you."

His direct response surprised me and I did not know how to reply at first. "I apologise." I removed my breather unit and took a deep lungful of air. "I didn't mean to offend. I didn't know holograms existed that were able to respond so naturally."

"This is the magic of the Temple. I, and all the Temple Keepers, have been waiting to welcome the Sword Bearer."

This was getting more and more weird by the second, and I was finding it difficult to understand. "You talk as if you're a real person rather than a hologram."

"The Temple is able to detect intruders and summons the spirit of the Temple Keepers. Each one of us guards this magical place for two years while the others sleep. We have waited for millennia for the Sword Bearer to find his way here so we can endow him with the true power of the universe, and I am proud to be the Keeper to welcome you."

Zaavi interrupted before I could ask any more questions. "Thank you. I am ready to receive the true power of the universe now."

"In order to find your way here, you will have deciphered the inscription we placed upon the sword."

He nodded. "Indeed I have."

The Trials of Nahda

"Then you will also know that you must prove yourself to be the true Sword Bearer and not an imposter."

"I am not an imposter."

"Then you may continue to the trials of Nahda. I will wake the other Keepers and we will be watching you at all times, but we cannot assist you in the coming trials. You must survive what follows by demonstrating that you are indeed, the true bearer of the Singing Sword of Nahda."

I could not believe what I was hearing. "Hey. What's this about trials, and what did you mean when you said we have to survive what follows?"

Zaavi watched the image of Vaylon vanish before turning to face me. "The Trials of Nahda. I have to display the four qualities of the Sword Bearer before I can be endowed with the true power of the universe."

"Four qualities?"

"Sam. Have you forgotten so quickly? You truly have the mind of a law enforcer. Courage, resilience, wisdom and self-knowledge. I, that is we," he raised his wrist and rattled the handcuffs, "must endure four trials, each of which will call for one of the qualities of the Sword Bearer in order for me to survive."

I cursed aloud. "Oh for fuck's sake." Another portion of wall slid back, the blackness yawning at us with tangible menace.

To say I was annoyed would be putting it mildly. Zaavi must have known there were some kind of trials up ahead, and yet he decided not to mention it. I was so angry that thoughts of shooting him right there and then did float across my mind. If it were not for the fact that we were trapped down there, and that he was so heavy, I might have been tempted. What lay ahead for us? We entered, and I hoped that his size and strength would prove useful.

I was spooked, but tried not to show it. "So what's first?"

"Courage."

"And how are you required to demonstrate that?"

"I don't know."

"But I thought you knew about these trials."

"I knew I would be required to go through them yes, but not exactly what they entail. We shall see, won't we?"

"I should've just shot you."

"Oh come on Sam. Where's your sense of adventure?"

The Trials of Nahda

"There's nothing wrong with it, thank you, but that doesn't mean I have a death wish."

The sound of stone grinding against stone told us the door behind us was closing, and my heart sank a little further as the silence wrapped itself around us once again. With every step we took, we were getting deeper underground and it spooked me. Would I ever see daylight again? I do not mind dying, if it is meant to happen, but if I were to die deep underground, my body might never be found. I guess it does not matter when you are dead, but thinking as a living person, I would want my body found and disposed of in a decent way. I consoled myself with the knowledge that at least Tinnias knew where I was and would send someone to search for me if I did not call within seventy-two hours.

From out of nowhere, an orange glow dispelled the darkness and with open mouths, Zaavi and I saw what lay ahead. An immense maze spread out in front and away beyond the reaches of the dull orange glow that appeared to emanate from the very bedrock of this enormous cavern. From our vantage point, we saw the passageways and corridors, the dead ends and crossing points, flaming torches positioned at intervals to light the way. A flight of rough stone steps led down from the ledge on which we stood, and we saw Vaylon waiting for us at the entrance to the maze.

"Hey Zaavi. There's that hologram guy, see?"

"Come on then." He stepped forward, pulling me along behind. "He will probably give us instructions or a map or something."

I struggled to keep up down the steep steps. "Oh let's pray for a map."

We reached the bottom and approached Vaylon. He smiled at us, his expression benign, and indicated the entrance in front. "This is the Labyrinth of Conmithlas. You must reach the other side in order to pass the first trial. Tread with care, for you will not be alone as you traverse its corridors, and they who dwell there are already aware of the blood that courses through your veins. It is this life giving fluid that they crave, and which they will do anything to acquire."

Now it was Zaavi's turn to look scared. His voice had an audible tremble as he questioned Vaylon. "What manner of creature are they?"

"They are the mind benders of Conmithlas. They are creatures of ancient Nahdan myth, and are endowed with magical powers with which to lure their unfortunate victims into their trap."

I sniggered. "Magical powers? Oh come on guys."

Vaylon fixed his eyes on my own. "There are many more things in our universe than those you have personally experienced Samelan Sinclair. You would do well to open your mind as you step into the labyrinth, for that may be the one thing that ensures your survival."

Zaavi spoke with the conviction of someone who accepted the prospect of beings with magical powers as commonplace. "What powers do they possess?"

"Through them, the distinction between truth and untruth becomes blurred."

The cryptic nature of his reply annoyed me. "What the heck does that mean? Can't you be a little clearer?" Before he could reply, he vanished into thin air and left us alone, the entrance to the Labyrinth standing before us. Zaavi and I exchanged glances, then as one, we both regarded the open doorway ahead.

"What do you reckon he meant?"

Zaavi shrugged. "I don't know. He said the distinction between truth and untruth becomes blurred, so I suppose it means we'll see things that aren't real."

"Possibly. He called them mind benders didn't he? So they'll play with our minds maybe, make us believe stuff that isn't real."

"They may even turn us against each other. It might be a good idea to unlock these handcuffs. If they make me believe you've done something awful, you could be in trouble."

I thought about that and I admit, for a moment I was tempted. If he decided to get violent with me, I would be chopped liver unless I kept a gun in my hand. I did not want to run the risk of him running off and finding the way out, leaving me there alone, so I shook my head. "All the more reason to remain cuffed together. How can either of us do anything against the other if we're cuffed?"

"You have a point."

"Just keep what we know to be true at the front of our minds all the time. Look, right here, right now, you and I are cuffed together underneath Temple Circle Fusion Reactor. I'm Sam Sinclair, Freelance Law Enforcer with the Inter-Galactic Law Enforcement Agency. You're Zaavi Dhilam from the museum in Lanis, Nahda 4. We met a little while ago, a few hours, less than a day anyway. Those are facts. We know them to be true. Whenever either one of us starts getting confused, we remind each other of those few facts okay? Forcefully if necessary."

Zaavi nodded. "Okay. Hold on to what we know to be true, despite whatever may be going on around us."

"Yeah."

"Right, let's get on with it."

"Shame he didn't give us a map though."

We crept along, the walls rising twenty feet into the air on either side. The flickering of the flaming torches spaced at regular intervals, made fearful shadows jump and leap all around us, the menacing faces reaching for us, and then gone as we jumped in terror. Zaavi took the sword from his belt and held it out in front, ready for whatever might strike at us without warning. I took out my laser pistol and checked the clip. There was no need to check it, I already knew it was full, but the familiar action gave me something else to focus on.

A junction lay ahead of us and for a moment, we were too scared to turn and check down each of the paths. Zaavi indicated for me to take the left and I nodded. We leapt forward, backs together and weapons at the ready, but nothing leapt at us.

I was breathing hard and fighting to remain calm. "So which way do we go?"

"I've no idea. From what I remember, seeing it from above before we came down the steps, the entrance was roughly in the middle, so I would assume that we should try to keep going straight ahead. The way out is most likely to be on the far side, wouldn't you think?"

"I guess it could be anywhere. It might be just around the next corner, and Vaylon could be allowing us to wander around in here for the pleasure of seeing us chase our butts."

Zaavi frowned. "But why send us into this huge labyrinth if the exit is just ten minutes from the entrance? What call is there for courage then?"

I glared at him. "Well I can assure you I'm using plenty of courage right now, and we've been in here no more than a few minutes." I heard Zaavi snigger in the dark and was pleased that he had something resembling a sense of humour.

The Trials of Nahda

"Well I vote we turn right here, then left, then right and so on. That way we should keep a roughly straight path and end up somewhere opposite where we are now. What's your idea Sam?"

"That sounds okay to me I guess. But whichever way we go, I don't want to go around in circles." I leaned up to grab the nearest flaming torch and lifted it from its hook. After stamping out the flame, I laid it on the floor with the torch end pointing to the right.

"Clever."

"At least if we do end up going back on ourselves, we'll know right away."

We continued on, turning left and right alternately, in the hope of maintaining something resembling a straight path to whatever lay at the far end of the labyrinth. We neither heard nor saw anything out of the ordinary for over an hour, and when Zaavi complained about being hungry, we stopped and sat down. Grateful for the rest, I put my back into a corner so nothing could creep up on me as we ate the provisions Zaavi had thought to pack. As we sat and ate, I asked him about himself and we were soon swapping life stories. In any other situation, I would say he was a nice person and I found we had much in common. Like me, he valued independence and freedom of choice, but unlike me, he was never able to exercise it as much as he would like. I did not want to get into an argument about his government, so I took care to avoid the subject. I remembered watching Nahda 4 from above as I left, and how different the planet appeared from up there. I did not want to tell him that those laws might be the only thing keeping them all alive, so I asked him what he knew about the upcoming trials.

"All I know is that this first one calls for me, us, to demonstrate courage. The next, resilience, then wisdom and lastly, self-knowledge. Once the four are over, and I'm hopefully still alive, the sword will sing for me and I will gain the true power of the universe."

"And just what is this true power of the universe?"

"The power of creation by thought and will. The ability to bring something into being just by thinking about it, or get rid of it the same way. The power to use my will to rule the universe."

I frowned. "How do you know?"

"Because I translated the inscription on the sword and it says so."

"It actually says you get to rule the universe and gain magical powers?"

"It says the Sword Bearer will understand the true law of the universe, and will be the living embodiment of that rule. It says that no other rules will hold sway over he who has the true power of the universe, and the whole of creation will bow down to this rule, as demonstrated by the Sword Bearer's existence. In short, it means I will become someone with godlike power."

I could not believe he really thought he would transform into an all-knowing deity by waving a sword around. He had to be crazy, I decided. "Well when that happens, perhaps you could will me twenty years younger but with the knowledge and experience I have right now huh?"

"If that is your wish Sam, then it will be so."

"Thanks."

He stood and looked down at me. "I guess we'd better get going."

I went to rise but something shocked us into silence and we both froze on the spot. Zaavi reached for the sword and I grabbed my laser pistol. The roar filled the entire space and sounded like a thousand Maktolian Emps, and very angry ones at that. The sound reverberated along the corridors, bounced off the dead ends and came from every direction at once.

When silence once again embraced us, I could still hear my heart thudding in my ears. I stood and shot a look at Zaavi. "What the fuck was that? Oh shit, what was that?"

He rubbed a hand over his face and I noticed it tremble slightly. "I've no idea."

"Whatever it is, it sounds like we're in trouble. Come on, let's move."

We got to our feet and ran as fast as we could. All our careful plans blew away as panic seized hold of our minds and controlled our feet. The roar came every few seconds, the ground vibrated with it, the echoes bouncing off the tall grey walls and coming at us from all directions. Every time we flew round a corner, we expected to meet them head on, but neither of us knew what sort of creature to expect. Our flight came to a dead stop as we flew around a corner and went smack into a wall. It was a dead end and we had allowed our panic to make us forget which way we had come. I had not bothered to lay down any torches to point the way, and how many lefts or rights we had taken was anyone's guess. We were lost, with creatures chasing us and a dead end in front. I could have cried.

We took some time to get our breath back, before retracing our steps and taking a right. We had no idea how we had arrived at our present location, but I was determined to be methodical, so I continued laying down torches as pointers whenever we turned. The roars of the creatures followed us, but it was not until another hour had passed that something occurred to me. I had a niggling feeling about the sound of the roaring for a while before it came forward in my mind and formed a coherent opinion, but when it did, I could not let it go.

"Zaavi. Stop, just a minute."

"What's up Sam?"

"That sound. Those creatures. There's something that's bothering me about it."

"What?"

I found his lack of insight irritating and struggled not to show it. "Haven't you noticed?"

"Noticed what? Whatever they are, there are lots of them and they sound hungry to me. What else is there to notice? Does anything else matter?"

"But the sound is always the same. It always sounds the same distance away, no matter which way we go, and it always lasts for exactly four seconds. Something is niggling me about it and as sure as I stand here, I know it stinks."

"Well I umm," Zaavi began then shrugged at me. "What are you saying?"

Before I could reply, the roar came again, forcing me to yell. "I'm saying there are no creatures." We listened and silence fell upon us like a blanket. "There are no creatures after our blood. They don't exist."

Zaavi gaped at me. "They sound pretty real to me."

"Don't you remember what Vaylon said? He called them mind benders. He said that they blur the line between truth and untruth. They want us to believe that creatures are chasing us, that we're the next thing on their dinner menu, but they're just fucking with our minds. I tell you what. If I'm proved wrong, I swear I'll uncuff you, no questions asked."

"He did say that. If what you say is true, then we are going to have to question everything that happens to us in here. Everything we see, hear or experience."

I nodded. "Exactly. Question everything and take nothing for granted."

"Okay, let's keep going then."

The Trials of Nahda

CHAPTER SIX

We continued on, and heard no more roaring of creatures and I must admit that I was feeling pretty pleased with myself. Zaavi, reluctant to admit I was right, added that he would have realised eventually himself and I chose not to argue with him about it. For the twentieth time, I tried my Unicom but got no signal and groaned in frustration as I put it away.

"Your gadgets won't work down here Sam." He shook his head, as if saddened by my lack of basic intelligence.

His obvious gesture of superiority annoyed me and I almost snapped in response. "No harm in trying."

"Okay, so which way? Do we go left or carry on ahead? You choose this time."

I opened my mouth to reply, when we both heard the unmistakeable sound of stone grinding on stone. We looked at each other in surprise, wondering where this new door was revealing itself.

Zaavi took a step back the way we had come. "That sounded as if it was back around that last corner." I nodded and allowed the cuffs that bound us to pull me along. We turned through ninety degrees into the corridor along which we had so recently travelled, hoping this new door led out of the maze and into somewhere warm, dry and comfortable.

I could not believe what I was seeing. "What the fuck?"

Zaavi scratched his head. "This can't be right."

"We just walked down this corridor. Didn't we? I didn't imagine it did I?"

Zaavi shook his head. "No, definitely not."

"Then maybe we're imagining this." I pointed at the solid wall that now faced us where seconds before, a corridor had been. We ran to the wall and examined it. There was no doubt that it felt real to me. We thumped the stone, kicked and pushed but that wall felt as solid as any of the others around us.

I stepped back a pace and examined it, scratching my head. "So this labyrinth moves now?"

His mouth flapped a couple of times as he struggled to put the strangeness into words, and had to settle for a bemused shrug. "I guess so. It certainly seems like it doesn't it?"

"So this whole place is moving and shifting around us, which means the exit, wherever it is, is also moving."

"Maybe the exit doesn't move. How can we know until we find it?"

I was reaching a point where I knew I would not be able to understand this weirdness for much longer. "We can't. We may never find it at all. We may be stuck in here forever until we die of starvation or thirst, and all because of that fucking sword." The raised pitch of my own voice, together with the sudden thumping in my chest told me that panic was trying to claim me. I let out an angry yell and thumped the wall. With a deep sigh, I closed my eyes and waited for calm.

"Feel better for that outburst Sam? Forgive me my sense of humour, but I thought you said there was nothing wrong with your sense of adventure."

"There isn't." I leaned on the wall, my head on my arm. "It's just that I prefer to decide when to be adventurous, rather than have it thrust upon me. I like it to be my choice, not someone else's."

"Then that isn't a sense of adventure. That's planning, which is the antithesis of adventure and spontaneity. That's meekness, cowardice."

"Excuse me?" This blatant insult inflamed me. Anger drove my hand to the laser pistol on my hip, which found itself pointing right at Zaavi's chest.

He put up his hands in a placating gesture. "Now Sam, just relax and think about what I said before you shoot me. Be honest now, how often do you relish and enjoy an experience that just lands on you without warning and completely throws your plans out the window? Well? Do you enjoy such experiences, do you seek them out, welcome them with open arms? Or do you try to avoid them at all costs and think of them as a nuisance?" He gazed down at me, his eyes challenging me.

I pursed my lips, a petulant gesture I know but I could not help it, and put my pistol away. "Adventure can be planned sometimes."

"If it's planned, it's not true adventure. Nor does it always have to be positive and enjoyable. It can be fearful and challenging too. That kind of adventure is often the most life changing and beneficial to your personal growth."

"So you're a psychiatrist as well as an archaeologist now?"

"If you need me to be."

My reply was instant and heartfelt. "I don't. Come on, let's keep going."

We walked on; the sound of stone grinding on stone telling us that the labyrinth was moving all around us as we walked. Like a living thing it breathed in and out, the walls of its lungs moving as it inhaled and exhaled, the corridors its veins and arteries, and the two of us foreign bodies within its bloodstream. I felt lost and trapped within some hitherto unknown leviathan and I went cold to the bone as the thought that I may never escape embraced me.

Around one corner, a piece of wall shot out from the wall to our right, turning what had been yet another long corridor, into a dead end. Without responding, we retraced our steps back to the last junction. We had long since stopped talking, or at least I had. This situation was causing me to feel stuff I had no business feeling. I had a good job, decent pay, the respect and trust of my colleagues and a healthy self-esteem up to this point. Now here I was feeling scared and trapped. I hated being at the mercy of someone or something else and I hated my own fear more.

Zaavi cut through my moment of self-loathing. "I wonder if that happens when we're near the exit."

"Huh?"

"When a wall suddenly shoots out in front of us and cuts us off like that. I wonder if it does that because we're near an exit."

"If that's true we're seriously fucked. All we can do is hope that hologram guy, whatever his name is, gets bored with the game before old age claims my hair, bladder control, and libido."

He grinned. "Let's hope so."

"There is also another possibility. Maybe it's a way of guiding us along when we take the wrong route."

Zaavi stared at me open mouthed. "So you're not a total cynic after all."

"Well I," I began but the sound cut me off.

"What the hell is that?" Zaavi's voice was a terrified whisper, as if fear had cut off control to his vocal chords. He glared at me wide eyed.

"It's umm," I began, not wanting to express it aloud in the hope that by denying it, it would cease to be true.

He looked into the distant gloom as he hefted the sword in both hands. "Oh please tell me I'm imagining it."

The Trials of Nahda

I yelled at him and took off, dragging him into action. "Run." Together we set off down the corridor, Zaavi's strides almost twice the length of mine and before we had gone a hundred yards, I fell. Unable to keep up with my giant companion, his panicked flight ensured I had no hope of matching his speed. For a few seconds he dragged me along, until the sudden weight of my body cut through his panic. He stopped and yanked me to my feet, thrust an arm around my shoulders and under my left armpit, and took off like a Slimpit Beetle. Despite Zaavi's speed, the thudding of what sounded like a large four legged creature, got closer and louder and I tried not to think about what it was that chased us. The thought that we might die in the most gruesome manner on the horns of some dread creature, fought for dominance with the memory of what the hologram had said about truth being blurred. I was desperate to believe that this too was make believe, but as yet, I did not have the courage. This knowledge cut through everything like a knife and I yelled at Zaavi.

"Zaavi, stop. Zaavi."

He was puffing with the extra weight of dragging me along. "What?"

"Stop, for fuck's sake just stop."

"Are you crazy Sam?"

"Please just trust me, stop." I tried to wriggle free. He clung to me, dug his fingers into my side painfully as he flew around a bend and sent us both smack into a dead end that flew out from the left hand side wall. I managed to get my arm up in time to prevent getting my nose smashed.

He put me down. "Okay, so I stopped." The thundering of hooves continued to approach, and it was the most terrifying sound I had heard in a very long time.

"This trial. It's about courage isn't it?" He nodded. "When we were running, I suddenly wondered if this was make believe, like that roaring we heard earlier. I decided I didn't have the courage to believe that just yet, and then it hit me."

Zaavi frowned, his eyes darting to the corner behind us, and the sound of the ever-approaching creature. "When what hit you?"

"Courage. It all comes back to courage again. Not knowing what is chasing us, the fearful imaginings that sound brings to my mind, the knowledge that we can't get away. It's all about courage, or lack of it. How easily we discard what courage we possess when faced with something we can't control huh? It's so instinctive for us to let fear drive us when we're in a hole, even when we have no proof that what we fear actually exists."

The Trials of Nahda

"It sounds pretty real to me." The clattering of the creature's feet was closer, echoing around the stone labyrinth's lofty corners.

I raised my voice over the sound of the creature's thudding feet. "But the hologram guy distinctly told us that truth and untruth is blurred in here. Remember what we said when we started? We remind each other of the facts we know to be true." Zaavi nodded and the floor vibrated in time with the animal's thudding feet.

"I'm Sam Sinclair. Freelance Law Enforcer with the Inter-Galactic Law Enforcement Agency." The sound lessened a tiny bit and I continued, encouraged. "My tag code is Sinclair 27593-4/167AZP." I nodded encouragement to Zaavi.

"I umm," he began, faltering as his eyes darted back and forth. The sound got louder so I slapped his face to get his attention away from his fear. He looked at me, gasping quick breaths as his body readied itself for fight or flight. "I'm Zaavi Dhilam. Head of Ancient Nahdan Languages at the museum in Lanis, Nahda 4." The sound quietened enough for him to notice this time, and he risked a fearful grin. "I'm thirty five years old, my girlfriend is called Shyola Mastak and we're due to marry next year." He stopped and we both held our breath as we listened to the silence.

"Shit." I heaved a breath as we flopped down to the floor. "I haven't been that terrified in a long time."

Zaavi closed his eyes and wiped a hand down his face. "I don't think I've ever been that terrified." He rested his head back against the wall and I watched his chest moving as his heart thudded in fear.

We sat for several minutes before continuing. After a drink, we got up and made our way back along the corridor, our nerves on high alert. I made a point of talking, about anything and everything in an effort to distract my mind from my fear, and Zaavi was happy to join in. I told him some of the funnier of my experiences as a law enforcer, and he told me about some of the artefacts he discovered and worked on. From time to time, we heard roars, grunts, thudding of many feet, and the fear would rear up beside us once more. Coping with the fear was hard work, both mentally and emotionally and as we rounded yet another corner, I knew I was reaching the end of my endurance.

I stopped walking, exhausted by the mental stress as much as the physical, and checked my Unicom. It told me that it was early morning. I thought back to the day before, and remembered having found Zaavi in the late afternoon. After waiting several hours for him to awaken, we had spent the entire night traversing the labyrinth, and I had been awake for a day and a half. "I need to rest. I'm sorry; can we take a few minutes?"

Zaavi nodded and sat down. "Sure. It's not exactly physically taxing so far but my head feels like it's been kicked and stamped on by a herd of Lopmylers."

"Mine too." I tried to make myself comfortable on the stone floor. "I don't know about you, but I'm going to need some sleep soon. Just a couple of hours will do, but I'll need some. I can't go on forever without my ability to function being compromised, and I reckon this situation needs us both to be alert, don't you? It's morning now up top, and we've missed a whole night's sleep."

"Yeah, I agree. I've been digging my way into this place for the past two weeks and existing on just a few hours' sleep a night. The excitement of my new discovery somehow gave me the energy, but now I'm beginning to flag."

"If I get too tired, I'll be so spaced out from lack of sleep that I won't feel fear, I'll be too tired to feel anything."

Zaavi grinned. "Maybe we shouldn't be too quick to get some sleep then. Maybe we should just drag ourselves along without sleep." I laughed aloud and he frowned. "What?"

"It's just the mental image of us dragging ourselves along, hallucinating through lack of sleep, with all sorts of dangers around us and we're totally oblivious. Like a couple of junkies on the best high ever." Before long, we were both laughing our heads off, exhaustion making us lose our inhibitions as we shared our hysterical mental imagery. We both soon agreed that no matter what form of creature should appear around the corner at us, we were too tired to give a fuck.

I opened my eyes and grimaced as pain shot up through my shoulder and neck. Recognition embraced me and I blinked in the gloom of the corridor and lifted my head. Hissing in pain, I sat upright and rolled my neck around. Exhaustion had claimed both of us and we had fallen asleep where we sat, my head falling sideways onto Zaavi's shoulder. I shifted my weight, my ass was numb, and I tried to move enough to get some feeling back into it. A soft groan from beside me told me that Zaavi was waking up.

He opened his eyes and moaned. "What's going on?"

"Sorry, I tried not to wake you. My ass is numb and I have a crick in my neck."

"That's okay." He yawned and sat up, grimacing in discomfort. "Oh my ass."

I grinned and rummaged in my backpack for my water bottle and a snack. I found a couple of protein bars and offered one to Zaavi. "It's not much but you're welcome to it."

"Thank you." After unwrapping it, he disposed of it in two bites. With such a large body mass to sustain, he must be starving. My Unicom did not work but it was able to tell me that we had been down there for almost twenty-four hours with almost no food and very little water.

I knew we would need food and water soon. "I wonder if there's any food or water supply down here. I have one full bottle of water left, and four protein bars. That won't sustain us for long. We could go without food for a while but water is essential."

"I have two bottles of water in my pack and some Blaxno."

"Blaxno? What's that?"

"It's a highly fortified, dried and reconstituted nutrient puree. It's used in our spaceships for those who don't like nutri-vend, and by anyone needing easily packed and carried nutrition. We always take it on our archaeological digs."

I made a face. "It sounds horrible."

He grinned. "It's not bad actually. Next time we eat, I'll let you try some. You're right though, we will need extra water if we're to remain down here longer than another day. Maybe we should start rationing what we have?"

"Agreed. Now I gotta stand up, I need to pee."

Once we had relieved ourselves, stretched, yawned, and scratched our bellies, we set off up the corridor. For hours we trudged, the sound of stone grinding against stone coming to our ears from time to time, sometimes carried faintly on an underground breeze, at other times fearfully close. The vastness of the cavern in which this immense labyrinth sat, weighed down upon me and I shivered at the realisation that I was trapped in an enormous underground tomb that had a life of its own. In a bid to stem the creeping loneliness, I hummed the tune to a bawdy song I learned years ago from a friendly Merc from Earth named Harry, and before long, I was singing aloud, much to Zaavi's amusement.

"Oh, when I was down in Haskrey Bay,
I met a gal named Daisy May.

She made me laugh, she made me cry,
She sucked my dick and bled me dry.
Oh Daisy, yes Daisy, I know you are wise,
So lift up ya skirt and show me the prize."

Zaavi roared with laughter and before long, was joining in with the chorus.

"Daisy May, Daisy May,
The loveliest whore from Haskrey Bay.
She'll love you, she'll hate you,
She'll always fellate you.
She's the loveliest whore from Haskrey Bay."

Just as I finished the eighteenth verse, we reached a junction and found ourselves with three options. Left, right, or straight ahead.

Zaavi swept his arm from left to right and looked at me. "So which way?"

"Let's go left." I headed towards the open doorway. Zaavi came up behind me and I had just enough time to register that my foot had not found solid ground, before I felt myself falling. I yelled in surprise as empty air embraced me and I fell into the darkness below. My heart leapt in my chest as terror coursed through me, but my progress came to an abrupt halt as I found myself dangling from my right wrist, the handcuff cutting painfully into my skin. Zaavi grimaced as the sudden weight almost brought him down after me. Crying out with the effort, he leaned back into the wall, grabbed my wrist with his free hand and hauled me up. I shrank back into the wall, my chest heaving as terror washed over me.

I gasped in terror until I could talk. "Oh shit. Fuck."

"Yeah, I agree." Zaavi massaged his wrist.

"Thank you. I owe ya one for that."

"I hope for my own sake I don't make you repay the debt in the same manner."

"Hell no, for fuck's sake don't fall off anything or we're both screwed."

"I'll try not to. Unless of course you fancy uncuffing me now."

"What? But then next time I fall, I might break my neck. Hell no, the cuffs just saved my ass. They're staying."

"Well at least let me suggest that while we're down here in the dark, you let me go first."

I nodded. "Deal. I've no problem with that at all."

Zaavi described what he saw, and it did not make me happy. We were in a large oblong chamber, the only other door being several hundred feet away across a chasm that descended below the reach of even his sensitive eyes. A narrow ledge ran all the way around the walls, upon which both of us balanced, and joined with the door opposite.

My heart fell as I realised how we were to make the journey around the room. "So we shimmy our way around. Nice. Real nice."

Zaavi peered into the gloom. "There is a problem with that."

I almost laughed. "Why am I not surprised."

"Halfway around the room, the ledge is partially blocked by a huge block of stone that sticks out from the wall. It's the same whichever way around we go. I could make it, my legs are long enough to reach around, but I doubt that yours are."

"Shit."

"This place was built for Nahdans Sam,"

I was about to nod in reply when a thought occurred to me. "But wait. The hologram is not a lot taller than me. We both commented on that when we first saw him. We agreed that your height must be a recent evolution. Remember?"

"Yeah, I remember. I can't explain that, but since we can't make it around the edge, we'll have to cross the bridge."

I gaped at him. "There's a bridge? You got me all worried about shimmying around this ledge and all the time there's a fucking bridge?"

"There's a bridge."

"And just when were you planning on mentioning that?"

He snapped back at me, his own anger raised by my own. "I just did." I noticed an edge to his voice that I had not heard before. "But you won't like it any more than you like this ledge."

"Why not?"

"Because it's four inches wide."

I stared at him, my mouth falling open in disbelief. I was lost for words and my mouth flapped, any effort at communicating my feelings was useless for many moments. Many thoughts raced around inside my head and for a while, everything was a blur as I waited for them to slow. I have been in tight spots many times and I recognise panic when it happens. I've learned over the years to stop, close my eyes, breathe, and wait for my mind to slow, so that I can think straight again.

When I felt the stillness within my head, I opened my eyes. "Okay, let's think this through. We have a ledge that I can't get round because it's blocked, and we have a bridge that's four inches wide but isn't blocked."

"Correct."

"Well I have no choice but to take the bridge."

"I'd rather take the ledge. My size will not be my friend when I'm trying to balance on that tiny bridge."

"I'm not going to walk across it. I'm going to sit astride it and scoot across like a girl. Undignified perhaps but I have a greater chance of staying alive."

He sighed and nodded. "Okay. Let's do that then. Anything rather than stand here till we fall asleep and fall to our deaths. Unless of course you want to go back into the labyrinth and take the other corridor."

I considered it for a few moments before shaking my head. "No. This is the first, and maybe the only opportunity to get out of there and I don't want to be walking those corridors forever. Let's at least try to get across here before we give up huh? If it gets too dangerous, then we'll consider going back into the labyrinth."

"Okay."

We made our way back to the door and over to the bridge. I sat down and scooted my ass onto it. The cuffs binding our hands forced me to hold my right hand behind my back. This made me lean back slightly, which unbalanced me and I swore. "Shit. Okay look." I reached for the key in my pocket. "You take the ledge if you want, but I can't balance with my arm behind my back."

"I won't run away and leave you Sam, I give you my word."

"I have little choice but to trust you." I glared into his eyes, a nagging doubt filling my mind. There was no other choice but to uncuff him and hope he waited for me. It was so dark in there that I could not see to shoot him if he ran away, so I had to take the chance. His footsteps echoed in the chamber as he made his way back to the ledge for the difficult shuffle around to the door opposite. With a huge effort of sheer will, I forced my mind to forget him and concentrate on the task at hand. With great care, I shuffled my way onto the bridge on my ass. I did not care if I looked ridiculous; I was effectively blind and knew I would be doing the whole thing by feel. I heard Zaavi's footsteps far off to my right as he shuffled along the ledge, and by the sound of it, he was making better progress than I was. Worry about being left alone encouraged me to try to hurry up but I almost lost my balance and panicked, my shouts echoing around the chamber as I slowed down.

"How are you doing Sam?" The acoustics of the room making his voice echo all around me.

"I'm okay now thanks. How far across am I?"

"Just over halfway."

I was surprised and pleased. "Oh, that's further than I thought. How are you doing?"

"I'm reaching the block now."

"Be careful."

"I can just about step round it. It's huge, you'd never make it." I heard a grunt, some scrapes and a sigh, so I guessed he had made it. Several times, I had to stop and rest, my whole body shaking with terror knowing a soul-chilling drop ached all around me. The narrow four-inch wide strip I was shuffling across was digging into my ass, but I did not dare try moving into a more comfortable position. Every so often, I had to open my thighs a little, as the fabric of my pants kept bunching up and pinching my balls as I shuffled. During this inelegant manoeuvre, I felt more vulnerable than I could remember in years, and several times wished I had tried the ledge instead. I even wished we had gone back into the labyrinth at one point, but knowing Zaavi would make it across without too much of a problem meant that I would be going back alone. There was no way I was going back into those endless corridors alone. I forced my mind back onto the task.

It felt as if I was shuffling across that bridge for hours before my knees knocked into the rock wall of the far side, and I was able to get up. I found myself on a ten-foot wide ledge, with the door facing me, and Zaavi absent.

I called out but got no reply. "Zaavi? Hey Zaavi." Silence greeted my calls and I cursed aloud. My hunch had been right; the asshole had run off and left me alone.

I yelled into the dark, all the bottled up fear from my terror-filled journey across the room, spewing out at once. "You fucking asshole." Fate had given me no choice but to let him out of the cuffs, I had known there was a good chance he would run off and leave me, and he did. Now here was I, all alone and trapped underneath a fusion reactor on a planet that was too poisonous to survive. Fuck you universe.

The Trials of Nahda

CHAPTER SEVEN

I took some consolation in the knowledge that even when my life was hanging by a thread, my people reading skills were as sharp as ever, so I brushed myself down before heading towards the door. I took one step through the door when arms encircled my chest, a hand covered my mouth and a voice whispered in my ear.

"Be quiet you idiot. You want to get us both eaten alive? See, up the passage to your left." I swivelled my head around, and what I saw almost made me lose control of my bowels. Now, I have been around more than most people my age. I have seen all sorts of things, many of which defy description, many of which are extremely dangerous, but only one of which I will admit to being terrified. I had my first encounter with a snake on Caprima Prime when my parents took me, aged six, on my first ever holiday. I awoke one night to find this snake, as big as I was, curled up on my chest, one of its coils resting across my neck as it slept, my body heat providing it with life giving warmth on that winter night. I screamed the place down, and my parents came rushing in to find the snake, frightened out of its wits by my yelling, rearing up in a defensive gesture. I will remember the sight of that snake forever, gazing down at me, its fangs glinting in the moonlight and although I have since found them on many of the worlds I visit, they always terrify me.

The one that lay to my left coiled up and apparently asleep, was as thick as me around and I guessed its length to be at least thirty feet stretched out. There was no way in hell I was going anywhere near it. I did not care what the alternative was.

"Oh fuck. I can't. Anything but snakes. I'll even go back and try the ledge. I can't do the snake." I grappled with Zaavi, the terror flooding through me with a power I had not felt in a long time, and ended up on his back, my legs wrapped around his waist. I was in full panic mode, but despite my cries of anguish, he eventually soothed me down from his back.

"Come down Sam, take control remember? Tell me your name and tag number again huh?"

"I uh, I can't." My insides turned to mush as the breath left my lungs. I tried to listen to Zaavi, my eyes never leaving the snake. He grabbed hold of my head and forced me round to face him.

78

"Name and number Sam, now."

"Sinclair." I felt vulnerable; I knew the snake was there but now I could not see it, and I tried to peer as far around as my eyes would go. "Tag code Sinclair 27593-4/167AZP. I'm from Sigma Prime, single and happy to remain that way." The initial wave of panic washed away as I verbalised these basic truths and I breathed hard.

Zaavi smiled. "Good job. It's a Mandour, and they don't bite."

"Don't tell me. They're squeezers."

"Yeah. How did you know? I thought you'd never been to Nahda before."

"They're on every planet I've been to." I stood behind him, my body trembling with abject terror. "All different sizes, colours and names. Back home we call them Slowns."

"You called it Snake."

"Yeah, I had a buddy from Earth in the military and we were together on Sahlon 5 one time when we saw one and he was as scared as me. He kept yelling snake, snake, at the top of his voice and it was so funny that it made me laugh despite being scared. He even had one tattooed around his body, and the other guys nicknamed him Snake after that. I guess it's my way of remembering him."

"Well I vote we go in the opposite direction to the snake."

As silently as we could, we made our way along the passage to the right and round the corner, to find a dead end. I was horror-stricken and swore. "Shit. Shit and fuck."

"Yeah, I agree with you Sam."

I reached for my laser pistol and turned around. Leaning against the corner, I peered through the scope attached to the barrel and saw the tail of the snake disappear around the corner. "It's gone."

Zaavi frowned. "Gone? But it was just there."

"It woke up. I just caught sight of its tail going around the far corner. C'mon, let's go."

We tiptoed back up the passageway to the corner, where we pressed ourselves against the wall. I took a deep breath, counted to three and peered around the corner through the scope. It slid through a doorway to its left and out of sight.

The Trials of Nahda

I felt the familiar wave of terror as my eyes caught sight of it, but managed to stem the rising panic as I gave Zaavi a running commentary. "It's gone through a doorway on the left, about halfway along."

"Okay, so we go straight up."

"Yeah, and quietly okay? By the way, thanks for saving my dick back there, again."

"You're welcome Sam. This is becoming a habit. You're going to owe me when I rule the universe."

"Yeah well don't be too hasty. This is the first trial. We may end up with you owing me by the time we get out of this hole."

"Name your price. Whatever you want, it will be yours. I will be able to shower you with riches, power, and fame, anything you want. I will even be able to raise the dead."

I stopped, the memory flitting through my mind uninvited. Of all the gifts anyone could offer me, this is the one I would not hesitate to accept. I remembered my ex-partner Ren and how he died when we were so close to finishing the job on Deligon 2. I would love to have him back, alive and healthy again and ready for a day's work. Next, I thought of Merellia Gilden, the girl I loved when I first joined the Law Enforcement Agency twenty years ago. We were to be married when she was kidnapped and murdered by someone I was investigating. He recorded himself raping and murdering her, then called me and played the recording to me, before telling me where I could find her body. The memory was still painful, but I had finally come to terms with it in a healthy way, thanks to Ren's influence.

A dig in the back roused me from my memories. "What's up Sam?"

"Huh? Oh nothing. I was remembering someone that's all."

"We better get going."

We crept along the passageway, being extra careful as we passed the open doorway to our left, through which I saw the snake disappear. As we came abreast of the opening, a new bit of wall rose up from the floor and closed it. I was greatly relieved to know that a solid wall now lay between the snake and myself and I leaned on it and breathed hard.

Zaavi frowned. "That is one heck of a fear Sam."

"Yeah, I know it's silly but I can't help it. It started when I was a kid and had a scary encounter with one."

"You've not tried to deal with it since?"

The Trials of Nahda

"I've never had to I suppose."

"You were really scared. I'm sorry to laugh, but you were so funny." He bent over and guffawed, his hands on his knees with the effort and I blushed.

"Laugh all you want. You wait until you display your greatest fear."

Once we both finished laughing, we continued down the corridor for several more hours, taking lefts and rights as the fancy took us. After almost two days, the constant sound of the wall configurations changing all around us no longer bothered us. The knowledge that the labyrinth was constantly reconfiguring itself told me it was useless trying to keep to any kind of plan, so we wandered where our feet took us. As we rounded yet another corner, we met a dead end. This was no ordinary dead end though; this was very different from every other one we had encountered so far. A series of tiles adorned this wall, the same kind of tiles I saw on the wall when I first encountered Zaavi, the ones that unlocked the entrance.

I pointed them out to Zaavi. "Oh, more tiles. I wonder what they do."

He took off his backpack and peered at them. "So do I."

"They must open something. Maybe the exit is beyond this bit of wall."

"Not necessarily. They might indeed open the wall, but they could also trigger something else to happen."

Now it was my turn to frown. "Like what? Like something unpleasant?"

"It's possible, yeah."

I cursed aloud as I took off my own backpack and sat down. "Shit. So what do they say?"

"Well." He rummaged in his backpack for a notebook and flipped pages. "This tile here means journey or quest. Give me a few minutes to study the rest huh?"

"Okay, sorry. I didn't mean to rush you or anything. I just thought you could read this stuff as easy as you can read your own language."

"No way. Look at this for instance. What do you see?"

I leaned forward. "Well. It looks like a face. A face grinning or maybe snarling. It's showing teeth so it could be either."

"Good. Yes, it's a face. Notice anything about the face that might tell you more?" I shook my head and he gave me a clue. "See the eyes?"

"Oh yes. They're not like your eyes. It's not the face of a Nahdan."

"Right. This face is something that is found on many artefacts, and we think it means danger, or to be more precise, the spirit of danger."

"The spirit of danger?"

"Our ancestors believed that things like danger, fear, luck, anger, love, and other concepts of that nature, were forces outside of ourselves. They believed we could be influenced by these outside forces, and saw them as totally separate non corporeal beings."

"Interesting concept."

Zaavi nodded. "Very. Now chill for a few minutes and let me concentrate huh?"

Fifteen minutes later, he sat back on his heels and scratched his chin. He read the notes he had made, then lifted his head and sniffed. "Okay, I think I know what it says."

"Great."

"It goes something like this. The Temple of Power awaits the Sword Bearer." He touched each tile in turn as he translated, and my eyes followed. "Beyond, a quest invites. The spirit of danger talks to you. The spirit of fear walks beside you. The great enemy, doubt, dwells in the dark. The door opens. The big place becomes small, the small man becomes big. The sun blinds the eye. The moon brings the dark. Be awake in death. Be asleep in life. The Temple of Power awaits the Sword Bearer."

"Right. So that means what exactly?"

"Well." He ran a hand through his hair. He was in his element, and his knowledge impressed me. "It means that we press this tile here to start whatever process this thing does. Once we do that, we're in danger from something. We then make a choice from either of these two tiles here. One will kill us, the other will save us."

"Any idea what the danger is?"

"It says the big place becomes small. I guess the big place means this entire space we're in down here. This labyrinth or maybe even just this corridor. Then it says the small man becomes big. I'm not totally sure what that means."

I scratched my head. "Well if the place gets smaller, then the man will appear bigger. Won't he?"

"Umm, yeah. I guess so."

I shrugged. "Okay, so what then?"

"Then we have the sun blinds the eye and the moon brings the dark."

The Trials of Nahda

"If you look at the sun you will hurt your eyes."

Zaavi nodded. "And the moon is around at night, in the dark."

"So which ones do we choose from?"

"The sun and moon ones. Once whatever happens, is happening, we then press either the sun or the moon. One will kill us, the other umm, won't. I guess."

I looked at him, hoping he knew the answer to my next question. "So which do we choose?"

"Hell, both have good points and bad. It's dark down here so we could press the sun and find it lets us out of the dark and into the blinding light of day. Or we could press the moon and umm." He scratched his head. "I haven't the faintest idea."

"Oh great. Okay, so we have the sun and the moon right? Well the sun is good. It means light, warmth, plants can grow and everything loves warm summer days. But it can also burn you, blind you, kill plants, dry up the water so you have nothing to drink, and totally sterilise the whole fucking planet."

"Right Sam, that's all correct but it doesn't help us to choose does it."

"No but I'm just getting my head around it so run with me okay? Now we also have the moon. Now the moon is good too y'know. It rules the tides and keeps the water moving, which keeps the water from going stagnant. It stabilises the planet's orbit, it lights up the dark of the night, many animals are nocturnal, and some plants only flower in moonlight. Come to think of it, I can't think of anything bad about the moon. How does the moon cause harm?"

"Umm, I can't think of any way in which it would."

"Neither can I."

"So do we choose the moon then?"

I nodded. "I would, given what we've come up with so far."

Zaavi did not seem convinced. "The only argument I can bring is that the ancient Nahdans worshipped the sun. They thought all that was good came from the sun, and without it, they would die."

He had a valid point, and I could not argue with him. "Which is technically true. Without a sun, a planet cannot sustain any life at all."

"Right. So at the most basic level, the very existence of life depends upon the sun. Maybe our lives depend on the sun on this tile."

"True. Let's go with the sun then. It makes sense, and it fits with your ancestors' beliefs, and they're the ones who built this place."

"But what you said about the moon is also relevant. Everything you said makes total sense."

"Well back home on Sigma we used to revere the moon millions of years ago when we were first evolving. The majority of the planet at that time was desert, and it was so inhospitable to life that the evolving humanoids could only survive by remaining in the cooler regions. They learned to fear the sun as it made the land turn to dust on which they couldn't survive. They believed that every night, the moon fought the sun to rule the land, so they came to think of the moon as their guardian, fighting for their survival. As the land and climate changed over time, the desert receded and jungle took over. The ancient people assumed the moon was winning the fight with the sun. That's why all Sigma dwellings have moons carved above the entrances, to guard the people from death."

"That's amazing Sam. Worship of the sun or moon is such a common theme among developing people, you find it on the vast majority of planets when you delve into their far history. It's like it's a natural part of humanoid nature or something."

"Possibly. As this place was built by Nahdans, and as you're the Nahdan Sword Bearer, I would say go with your people's belief system."

"So we go with the sun then yes?"

I raised both arms to the side. "I guess so." I put on my backpack and mentally readied myself for, something. Zaavi put his backpack on, crouched down, hesitated for no more than a second, and pressed the tile to set things in motion. The effect was immediate as the sound of stone grinding upon stone filled our ears. A portion of wall shot up from the floor with a loud bang, blocking us in from behind and we both jumped in terror.

"Holy shit." I yelped in surprise and jumped backwards, banging my elbow on the wall to my right. Zaavi pressed himself into the corner and crouched. We were boxed into a space roughly four feet wide by six long, with the tiled wall still blocking the way ahead, and the new portion of wall blocking the way behind.

As quiet once again reigned, we took a moment to breathe, before Zaavi reached for the tile with the sun on it. "Are we sure?"

"Well no, not totally. But it makes the most sense, doesn't it?"

He nodded. "Yeah, it does." He pushed the tile. For a second or two nothing happened and we looked at each other expectantly. Before either of us could express irritation, the familiar grinding sound rang out as a brand new slab of stone slid across above us. Up until this point, there was no ceiling to the labyrinth, the domed roof of the cavern rose above us somewhere in the darkness beyond the reach of my flashlight or Zaavi's eyesight. Now trapped inside a little box, I felt the familiar flush of panic come to life inside.

I shrieked in panic. "Holy fuck, what the hell is happening here?"

"I don't know." Zaavi's eyes were wide with terror.

"I am so gonna bust Tinnias' balls for giving me this job." I thumped the wall beside me in anger. Once the brand new ceiling to our prison fully engaged with an audible clonk, it descended towards us, and I noticed for the first time the engraving of the sun carved into its surface. Zaavi and I exchanged another horrified glance and utter terror passed between us. I was about to scream when a new sound reached us. A sound like metal scraping on stone filled our chamber, and we both saw holes appear in the stone surface of the sun carved ceiling. Plugs of stone disappeared from view, their places immediately taken by sharpened metal spikes.

I pointed towards the ceiling. "The sun blinds the eye." Zaavi nodded, his mouth flapping uselessly. I yelled at him as we crouched to avoid the rapidly descending spikes, my own panic rising. "Press the moon, quickly. This little man is getting awfully big and this place is becoming uncomfortably small." My voice was now almost an octave higher. "Press the fucking moon." I shook my fist in Zaavi's direction and he dropped to his knees in front of what remained of the tiled wall. Stone ground on stone as the tiled wall slid aside and we scrabbled through the gap as soon as it was big enough. I was lying on my side by the time Zaavi got through and unceremoniously yanked me through the gap with inches to spare before I was impaled.

We lay and breathed for long moments before getting up. We were in an identical section of the labyrinth to the one we had left. I brushed myself down, glad that I was still in one piece and trembling with fear at having experienced such a narrow escape.

Zaavi's shrieks continued for several moments until he calmed himself. "I've never been so terrified for my life."

I gasped at the thought of how my life could have ended and squeezed my eyes shut to block out the image. "Me neither. I hope to fuck never to have to go through anything like that ever again."

After a much-needed drink, we set off. The corridors were identical to those we had left, but this time there was no sound of the labyrinth changing around us. There was no sound of stone grinding upon stone as the walls reconfigured themselves. All was still and quiet as we traversed the corridors.

After a couple of hours, we rounded a corner to find a doorway in the end wall that led into a small room, roughly ten foot square. There was a door in the far wall, which led into an identical passageway to all the others.

I could not face yet another passageway without having a rest, so I stopped walking and turned to face Zaavi. "I'm tired. Can we rest for a bit?"

"Yes, let's rest. I'm exhausted too. I have some food left, let's eat."

"That's okay, you have it. I'm fine going without for a while. I'll just have some water."

"You have to eat Sam."

"Your body is bigger than mine. You need it more than I do. We may very well need your strength before we get out of here, so eat up. I'm the guy with the gun, so don't argue."

"Okay, but don't moan later when your stomach is grumbling."

"I won't."

We sat in a corner and Zaavi ate, while I tried my Unicom again and swore when it refused to work. It was lighter in here, the flaming torches giving off a soft orange glow and giving a decent amount of heat to the small room. I was so busy turning the situation over in my mind, that it was not until a head flopped onto my shoulder that I noticed Zaavi had fallen asleep. I nudged him gently and he stirred.

"Huh? Oh sorry Sam."

"It's okay. Lie down and get some sleep, I'll watch."

"Thank you. I'm so tired. Wake me when you want to sleep."

I looked at him and acknowledged the truth that I owed him an apology. He had not run away when we were crossing the room with the bridge. He could easily have made a run for it and left me to the snake, but no, he saved my life yet again. I know I am a law enforcer and I always meet people when I am trying to take away their liberty, but I do have a code, and when I owe someone, I always like to deliver. I have known many people who would not know what a promise was, let alone how to keep one and I have been let down more times than I care to remember. I will not be one of those assholes, even when the person I owe is a criminal. I thought about Zaavi, as I sat there in the small room and tried to get comfortable. He was confident that he was the one destined for superpowers, to rule the universe like a deity, but at the same time, he seemed to need me down there. Not physically, I admit I was probably more of a hindrance than a help. I mean mentally, emotionally. It was almost as if this quest of his was showing up his shortcomings rather than his strengths. He was an enigma, even if he was crazy.

Despite promising to wake Zaavi when I got tired, I fell asleep without realising it, and when I awoke no more than two hours later, my back stiff from lying on the stone floor and a painful crick in my neck, I leapt up to find myself alone. Zaavi was gone and so was the sword and my first thought was that he had run off. I shook myself fully awake and as my mind cleared from the fuzz of sleep, I decided not to call out. Remembering what almost happened last time when I yelled my head off, made me keep quiet this time, despite my annoyance. If only I had not fallen asleep, or if I had put the cuffs back on him, this would not have happened. There are always a lot of if only this or if only that moments in my job, but I have to work with the situation I'm in at the time, and at that moment, I was alone, locked in an underground labyrinth with who knows what kind of creatures, and a hologram guy who said much but told us nothing. I swore under my breath as I took a pee, put my backpack on and checked my laser pistol. At least he had not stolen that, I thought to myself as I headed towards the door.

The doorway revealed a left turn and a short passageway that ended in a right turn. I stole quietly along the passageway and listened before peering around the corner, to find a longer passageway that was lost in darkness up ahead. There were no flaming torches here, so I took out my flashlight and shone it up the passageway ahead. I saw a junction, left and right options, so I tried to remember the journey I had taken so far, and decided to take the right. At least that would prevent me from going around in circles, and as I had no idea where any exit was, I thought a nearly straight course was probably sensible.

I walked the passageways for several hours, taking left and right turns alternately to try to maintain a straight course, and at no time did I encounter any creature. It was not until I found myself at another junction, that I heard the noise and froze on the spot, leg in mid stride. I strained my ears and heard the unmistakable sound of slithering from somewhere up ahead. I knew what that meant. My heart sank and the blood froze in my veins. For a moment, I panicked. On the one hand, instinct told me to run. On the other hand, I knew going back would get me nowhere useful. I had to keep going, but that meant facing the source of that slithering, which terrified me beyond anything else in creation. Thoughts raced around in my head and I mentally swore at my predicament. Should I run or should I stay and face the snake? Why was I so scared? I hate myself for being so scared. All these stupid thoughts and many more raced around my mind and because of them, I was unable to do anything but stand on that spot, shaking with terror and wishing I was anywhere but there.

I wished I had refused the job when Tinnias offered it to me, I wished I had taken the time to call him before chasing Zaavi through the door in the wall, I wished I had stayed awake, and I even wished the hologram guy was here to advise me. At the memory of him, I got angry. Even if he did appear, he would make some cryptic comment about the line between truth and untruth being blurred. He might even remind me to avoid the mind benders, but then I was not the Sword Bearer so he would not give a fuck about what might happen to me. Just as this last thought found its way to the front of my mind, something happened that silenced my thoughts. For a second, my mind was still as things fell into place. Truth and untruth, he said. They can make you believe anything, he said. At this moment, that sound had me fully convinced that the giant snake was around the next corner, but now, my belief faltered. I stopped trembling and stood up straight, raised my flashlight, gritted my jaw in determination and strode around the corner.

The empty passageway stretched out before me and I grinned. I almost leapt into the air and whooped, but decided not to take anything for granted yet. Maybe it was a coincidence; maybe the snake had been there but disappeared round the corner at the far end the moment before I stepped around my corner. I caught myself just before I fell back into disbelief again and reminded myself of the facts as I now knew them. Truth and untruth can occupy the same time and space down here, and the more you believe something, the more real it becomes. Maybe the ancient Nahdans were psychic or telepathic, and picked up my fear of snakes. Maybe they used it to make the show more interesting. This thought led to another that brought me to a stop. The hologram was exactly that, a hologram, that much was obvious. I have seen enough of them to recognise one and even Zaavi did not argue with me on that. This hologram was far different from any I had ever seen though. He could respond, but holograms can never respond. They are pre-programmed with responses to specific questions, and if you ask it something it does not recognise, either it does not respond at all, or you get a standard reply asking for a more specific question. Not only could this one respond, he knew my name.

"You're no damned hologram are you asshole? We don't have to take care to avoid the mind benders down here. You're the mind bender, whatever your damned name is. It's you we have to avoid isn't it?" I laughed as the pieces finally fitted together and I will admit now, that I felt proud of having deduced this all on my own. I may be a law enforcer with a logical mind who works within very strict guidelines of absolute and provable truths, but I can think outside the box when I need to. I walked on, turning left and right and wondered just how far the line between truth and untruth really was blurred down here. Did I really fall in that room with the bridge, or was that a fabrication too? Maybe this whole labyrinth was not real either. I turned to face the wall to my left.

I strode forward. "You're not real."

I carried on up the passageway, the bump on my forehead stinging painfully and felt glad that Zaavi had not been there to witness my moment of idiocy. The image of the hologram, tears streaming down his face with laughter, filled my mind as my cheeks reddened with embarrassment.

A doorway to my left revealed another small room like the one Zaavi and I had fallen asleep in, so I entered and sat down for a rest. After a drink and a pee, I took the door opposite and found two flights of steps. One leading up, one leading down. On the small square between the two, stood the hologram.

"Well if it isn't the mind bender. How ya doing old man?"

"Congratulations Samelan Sinclair." He bowed his head in affirmation of my achievement. "My name is Vaylon, and you have successfully traversed the Labyrinth of Conmithlas."

"Where's Zaavi?" Before he could answer, a scream came wafting up from the depths below, followed by what sounded like grunts and snarls. I leapt down the stairs, pistol in hand and Vaylon already forgotten. I did not give a shit about Zaavi's destiny, or his perception of it, and whether he was going to gain superpowers or not, he was my prisoner and I was not about to let him elude me. Besides, being stuck underground is less fun on your own, than with someone else, even if he is nuts.

The stairs wound around and down for an eternity, the noise of a struggle getting louder with each step. I leapt down them two at a time and almost stumbled several times before I found myself in a large room. Zaavi was at the far end, fighting a losing battle with a large group of dark, hairy, four legged creatures. Each one was the size of me, with shaggy dark fur, a large head and a long curved horn with which they were trying to impale him. His shirt was torn and blood covered his abdomen, but he fought on regardless, slashing and jabbing with the heavy sword. I yelled but he either could not hear me, or chose to ignore me, so I swung my flashlight to catch his attention.

The relief at seeing me was evident in his expression. "A little help Sam?"

"You don't need help."

"Look, I'm sorry I left you okay. This is my destiny after all and you should know by now that I do not intend to let you take me to jail for stealing that which is my destiny to bear. Just help me out here and we can talk about this."

"You don't need help."

"Oh come on Sam, can't we fight about this after you've helped me kill these things?"

"Listen to me Zaavi. They aren't real. You're imagining them. It's the mind bender doing it. Remember what he said about truth and untruth being blurred? The roaring things weren't real, the thundering hoof thing wasn't real, the snake might not be real, and these aren't real either. Why aren't they attacking me if they're real?"

"But, that's crazy." He jabbed with the sword and managed to dodge getting a horn through the chest.

"Trust me. Just believe me, they're not real and your injuries aren't real. Stop fighting and look down at yourself."

The moment I first saw the scene before me, I thought it was real, believed it. For a moment, it was real to me, and in that moment, I saw the creatures, their wicked horns, their pungent fur and Zaavi's injuries. As soon as I reminded myself that this was a fabrication, the creatures disappeared and Zaavi's wounds healed before my eyes. He still believed though, as he continued leaping, ducking, slashing and swiping at thin air. I walked towards him, through what he believed was a crowd of the creatures and stopped just out of reach of the sword.

"See? They aren't attacking me because they're not real. You see them because you believe they're real. Stop believing what you're seeing. Trust me, for once huh?"

Zaavi frowned, looked down at himself and was shocked to find no blood, no torn shirt and no injuries. "You mean this is all in my mind?"

"Yeah. Remember what Vaylon said about truth and untruth? He wasn't just talking about some weird creatures that live down here; he was talking about this whole place." Zaavi sat down on the floor, his chest heaving in deep breaths after his exertions. I sat down next to him and waited while he calmed down.

"Of course. It makes sense when you think about it doesn't it? Thank you Sam."

"I said I would probably find a way to pay you back before we got out of here, didn't I?" I grinned and he nodded. "Oh, and I've found the way out too."

We hauled ourselves back up the steps to find Vaylon still stood where I had left him. He smiled as we approached, breathing hard from our climb. "You have more than exceeded the requirements for successful completion of the first trial Sword Bearer." He bowed his head.

Zaavi puffed out his chest with pride. "Thank you. I am ready for the second trial now."

"Can we get something to eat and drink first. I only got a couple of hours sleep last night, and I've been without food for over a day. I'm reaching the end of my endurance here." Vaylon nodded. He pointed behind us, back towards the small room I had come from earlier. I ducked through the door and almost yelped in surprise.

I gaped as my eyes beheld the sight that lay before me. "Wow." Zaavi pressed in behind me and gasped. A woven rug lay on the floor, on which was a whole roast animal of some kind, bowls of some steamed grain, vegetables, fruit, bread and jugs of liquid that had a vaguely fruity taste.

Zaavi pushed past me. "Oh please say that it's real."

Vaylon was still standing behind me. "It's real. Eat your fill, drink and rest for as long as you wish. The second trial will be ready for you, when you are ready."

We sat down and for a moment, all I could do was gaze at the feast. I was so hungry and thirsty, that it was all a little too much to take in. Once my nostrils registered the smell of the meat however, my stomach took over and I fell upon it like a mad thing. Zaavi and I ate until we were stuffed, and when we could eat no more, we sat back, belching and farting. We both agreed that was the most delicious meal either of us had ever eaten. I've been in situations where I've had to miss a meal or two a few times, but down in that hole, with what we were going through, the hunger was worse than any I've experienced before. Maybe the stress enhanced it, maybe naked survival needs took over when my mind was overwhelmed, I do not know but I never want to be that hungry again. We lay down and I knew I would fall asleep. Would I wake up alone again?

"I'm probably going to fall asleep." I tried to make it sound non-confrontational.

"Me too."

I wanted to say something more, but could not decide what without sounding as if I was sulking, so the silence hung between us for a few moments before Zaavi continued.

"I'll be here Sam, don't worry. Whatever the situation between us, down here, we're probably more effective if we stay together. With my strength and your brain, we stand a better chance of surviving if we do it together."

I yawned. "Okay." Within a few minutes, I heard soft snores from the body beside me, and within a few more, I was asleep. He kept his promise, and was still there when I woke, many hours later. After a pee, we finished the last of the drink, headed out and up the stairs to whatever was in store for us, in the second trial of Nahda.

The Trials of Nahda

CHAPTER EIGHT

Vaylon was waiting for us at the top of the stairs, which opened out onto a balcony overlooking a vast open cavern, the floor of which was lost in darkness. I peered into the gloom but could not make out anything that might give away what could be in store for us.

"Well at least there's no maze." I tried to make it sound light hearted.

"There is no labyrinth in the second trial. "Vaylon was smiling as he explained. "What awaits you is an experience that requires you to call upon your inner strength in order for you to triumph."

Zaavi stood tall, the same note of pride in his voice as I heard a few hours before. "I am the most resilient of all Nahdans."

"You will need that resilience, both of you. It is the only thing that will get you through. Do not underestimate how important it is during the coming trial. There may be times when other matters seem more pressing, but without that inner strength, that resilience, you will fail to survive."

I felt the need for reassurance. "Are there any creatures this time? Real or imaginary?" Vaylon did not answer, but indicated with his hand, for us to make our way down to the floor of the cavern by way of a perilous narrow ledge cut into the rock. Zaavi went first, his long legs taking the steps without a problem. I struggled along behind, having to jump down each step because they were so steep. All the time, I was aware of the aching chasm to my left, and at times, I would have sworn it was pulling me away from the rock wall, willing me to fall. By the time we found ourselves on the floor of the huge cavern, my knuckles were white from grasping the rock. We took a few minutes to get our breath and calm our nerves.

"Well here we go Sam. Are you ready for round two?"

"As much as I'll ever be." With a nod of agreement, we headed into the gloom, my flashlight making little impression in such a huge space.

We walked for two hours without incident before we came upon a wall of rock that must have been forty feet high, which halted our progress through the cavern, and decided to scout along in both directions before climbing. Thirty minutes to the left, we found the boundary wall of the cavern and no sign of any doorway, stairway or tunnel to indicate a possible route. What we did find however, was the skeleton of what must have been a Nahdan, judging by its size.

"A previous contender for your title Zaavi?"

He looked and nodded. "It would seem so. Come on, let's go back and try the other way."

I went to follow, but stopped. "Hey wait. Shouldn't we at least bury him or something? We're the first to find him in hell knows how long. He probably went through everything we've been through, and he was alone. He deserves a decent burial and a few words don't you think?"

"He failed the Trials of Nahda. He was not the destined Sword Bearer, so of course he was bound to fail. I have to complete all four of the trials so that I can attain my power, why do you want to waste time on ancient bones?"

I could not believe what I was hearing and my mouth fell open in shock. "Because it's the right thing to do, asshole. Besides, these ancient bones may have belonged to one of those ancient Nahdans you've been obsessing about all these years. He may have been one of those whose lifestyle and culture captivate you so much, and brought you here chasing your crazy ass destiny. He may even have been the one who forged that damned sword you worship so much. Have you brain enough to think about that?"

Zaavi lowered his eyes to the floor before meeting my gaze once again. "You're right. Okay, let's bring him over here and make a Laukol over him."

"A what?"

"A Laukol. It's a way of covering the body with stones when it can't be buried in the soil."

"Oh, okay. That sounds good. Let's do that."

We laid the bones out and Zaavi showed me how to construct a Laukol. He first outlined the body with the flattest stones we found, before building up in layers, each one offset a few millimetres from the layer below, so that the whole thing curved up and over the body. A final row of long, narrow stones sat over the remaining gap, until nothing more than a hole over the skull remained.

Zaavi stood and looked down at the Laukol. "I shall recite the passing song now." He took a breath and recited the song. Slow sombre words I could not understand, but whose message was clear by the tone of his voice and the effect they had upon my heart. I had no idea what he was saying, but those words moved me. Maybe it was the way his voice echoed around the chamber, or perhaps the desperate situation we were in, I do not know, but I would be more than happy to have those words spoken over my body, when the time comes. Once Zaavi finished reciting the words, he bent and laid the final stone on the Laukol, and we walked away in silence.

An hour later, we saw the other side wall of the cavern looming towards us and my heart sank. Unless there was a gap in the wall, a doorway, or something, we would have no choice but to climb. I examined the wall beside us, and was pleased that it was rough and rugged. There were plenty of hand and foot holds, and I have climbed before when circumstances demanded it, but it would not be my first choice.

I cursed under my breath and sighed in frustration. "Looks like we might be climbing after all."

"Yes. Are you going to be able to make it up there and down the other side?"

"I should be able to. But probably not nearly as fast as you will though, so be patient with me okay?"

"The climb will call for much resilience huh?"

We sat and rested when we reached the wall and found no helpful doorway or other means of passing beyond the barrier in front of us, and I swore under my breath. As I thought about it, it struck me that maybe we were regarding it in the wrong way.

"Hey Zaavi. You wanna hear something really crazy?"

"What's up Sam?"

"That wall. We're thinking of it as something to test our strength and resolve, yes?"

"Of course, what else could it be?"

"Well maybe, just maybe, it's there to prevent us from continuing further."

"I had managed to work that out for myself."

His continued lack of basic intelligence annoyed me more with each passing hour, and I worried about my ability to keep it hidden. "No, listen. Maybe it's there because whatever is on the other side, is something we really don't want to get involved with. Maybe it's not there to try to keep us out of whatever is over there. Maybe it's to keep whatever is over there, from coming over here and trashing our little party."

"Oh. You mean maybe it's keeping the monsters in?"

"Well if you have to put it that way, yeah."

"Umm, it could be, I guess. What other alternative do we have though? There is no way through from down here, and if we climb the side walls, we'll just end up at the ceiling with a very long way to fall. I don't think we have any other choice. And before you suggest it, even if we did go back, you know as well as I do that we can't get out the way we came in. Believe me, if there was a way, I'd let you out and come back here on my own."

He was right and I swore. "Shit. Shit and fuck. I'm hating this more and more with each minute that passes. Why the hell do I have to keep having myself tested to within an inch of my life, just for some jerkass thief?"

"I didn't exactly force you into it Sam. You have no one but yourself to blame."

"I'm a Law Enforcer you idiot. It's my job to chase assholes like you so decent people can live their lives and not have to worry. I don't get paid enough to have to justify what I think or how I feel every minute of the day, and I sure as hell don't get paid enough to have my mind infiltrated by some creature who gets his rocks off by watching me get scared and chase my tail." I sighed in frustration and put my head in my hands while I waited for my anger to disperse.

"This is not exactly a picnic for me either Sam. I've left my job, committed a crime, left my mate worried sick about me, all because of this conviction that what I'm doing is the right thing. I'm sorry I've made your life difficult. If it's any consolation, which I'm sure it isn't, I do think you're a nice guy. In any other circumstance, I would value your friendship."

I was surprised at this sudden burst of insight and shocked at my loss of control. "Thank you. I'm sorry; I shouldn't have insulted you. That was unprofessional of me and I know better. I guess this situation got to me more than I would have expected."

"It's okay. I had my moment of madness and managed to find my way back, and now you've had yours and got over it. That makes us even."

"Moment of madness?"

"When I left you alone while you slept. I was consumed with the need to fulfil my destiny and I failed to realise that I need you in this situation. It taught me that I have to learn to work with others, even when my natural inclination is to go my own way. I've always been a bit like that, so it was a valuable lesson. You came back for me, despite my having left you, and you helped me see the falsehood we were in. Now you've had your moment of panic and let some anguish out, which leaves room inside your mind for more

97

of that creative interpretation you are so good at. I accept your apology, and offer you mine."

"Okay."

"Whatever this situation has in store for us, we seem to function better when we work together." I nodded in agreement. Much as I hated to admit it, I would have to forget he was my prisoner while entombed down there and make use of his skills.

"You're right"

"So let's make a pact now. Whatever anger or frustrations come up between us, we let it out, let it go and move on. We don't let anything cloud our judgement okay? When this is over, however it ends, we can fight about it if you want, but until then, we're a team."

It was the most sensible plan, so I nodded. "Okay. Sounds like a plan to me."

After tightening the straps on my backpack, I set out on the climb. Zaavi climbed to my right, and I was surprised that he was struggling to keep pace with me. After joking about him slowing down to make me feel better, he told me that sometimes his size is not of benefit to him. Climbing is for the strong and lean, not the big and bulky. I was glad to know there was at least one physical activity in which I had a fighting chance of beating him. I thought back to Tinnias and guessed he would call this a pissing contest. It must be a man thing.

It felt like many hours later when we sat on top of the wall and surveyed the huge space that surrounded us. I discovered nothing, my eyesight being almost useless down there and I cursed at my vulnerability. Every muscle in my body trembled with exhaustion, and I knew I would be aching the next day. We both peered into the gloom, but the cavern was too dark to afford us much of a view. I was glad too because I was once again aware of aching emptiness on all sides, and it made me nervous. We took our time up there, sitting and getting our strength back enough to make the climb down the other side. I was about to suggest we get going, when my Unicom beeped and made me jump so hard I wobbled as I straddled the wall and for a moment I thought I might fall.

I struggled to get it out of my pocket. "What the fuck? I have a signal? Oh my god." I gaped at the display, saw Tinnias' number and exclaimed aloud as relief flooded through me. "Hey Boss. Man am I ever glad to hear your voice. You have no idea what's going on here."

"Hey Sam." The moment he spoke my name, I detected a tone in his voice that worried me. I have known Tinnias for twenty years, and he is like a father to me, so I knew something was wrong.

"What's wrong?"

"Sam. I don't even know where or how to begin to tell you what I have to tell you."

"Hey come on, we've known each other forever. Just say it."

"There's a problem with Ambassador Stell from Abastra 7."

My heart sank. This was the last job I had before being landed with babysitting Zaavi, and it was one of those rare jobs when everything that could have gone wrong, did. To cut a long story short, I found out too late that a new contact of mine was a double agent. He laid a trap for us and we walked right into it. Eight people ended up dead. Two of them were law enforcers, working with me to make final arrests, and one of the others was Ambassador Stell's daughter. The whole job was a total fuck up from beginning to end and although the man who was my target was among the dead, the damage was too big to hide.

I knew this meant big trouble for me, and I swore. "Oh shit."

"He's after your blood Sam."

"But his daughter was working with that murderer, which made her party to everything he did. She knew all about his activities. She told me herself. Just because her father didn't know that, doesn't mean she was an innocent bystander. Her chosen career path meant there was always the risk she could end up getting herself killed."

"I know, but he's pulled a few chains and a warrant has been issued for your arrest."

"What the fuck? That's ridiculous."

"I know, but this has been done by those way above my pay grade, and I have no choice but to go along with it, or become a target myself. If I was a single guy like you, I wouldn't hesitate to stand by you, but I have Grellina and Ambella to think of. I can't risk them getting hurt."

"You mean you've been threatened?"

"Yeah."

"Fuck. I'm sorry. What the fuck can I say or do to make this better?"

"I don't know. I've been forced to take a few week's holiday while they deal with this in their own way, and I'm taking a day trip into the country with the family and calling you to warn you. They know you're on Nahda 3, and they know your location at Temple Circle. They're already on their way. If you move now, you can get a couple of day's head start and with your contacts, you should be able to disappear."

"I can't. I'm trapped underground. There's no way out of here that we can find yet. We're in some sort of huge cavern. I've been trying to call you but couldn't get a signal. There must be something in the rock here that helped get your signal through to me. If I get out of this hole alive, I'll just have to call in a few favours and get some decent witnesses."

"Damn. I was hoping you could get away and start fresh somewhere far away. Remember, whatever happens, I'll do whatever I can to help, even though it may not be much."

"Thanks Boss. Tell the family I love them will you? And thank you, for everything. You've been a good friend to me."

"I'm sorry for this Sam, I love you buddy." Before I could reply, a crackle and a hiss cut off the signal and my Unicom died, my mind still trying, and failing, to digest the shock of his revelations. I closed my eyes as the realisation that it was now official; I was in the shit, settled inside my mind and knocked the breath from my lungs. Never in my life have I been the subject of an arrest warrant, and the irony of the situation was not lost on me. For the first time, I now knew how each one of my targets felt, and it was not good. Adrenalin flooded through me, my heart raced and I almost dropped my Unicom as my sweaty palms fumbled to get it back into my pocket. My world, my life, stopped at that moment and all my years of experience vanished as one single thought filled my mind. I did not know what to do.

"Sam? What's up?"

"Huh?"

"You look terrible. What's wrong?"

"Everything's wrong. That was my boss. Something went wrong on my last job and some people got killed. We had a double agent that we didn't know about and he blew my cover. One of the people who died was the daughter of someone important and now he wants my balls. He's pulled a few chains and got a warrant issued for my arrest."

Zaavi stared at me, wide eyed. "Wow, umm."

"Yeah. I guessed you'd be thrilled."

The Trials of Nahda

"Well I suppose that means I'm not your prisoner anymore then."

"Technically, I don't know about any of this going on, so actually you are still my prisoner."

"But you just said."

"My boss called me unofficially. Besides, your warrant is still valid and you are still wanted for your crime. Sorry, you don't get off. If the Agency guys are waiting for us when and if we get out of here, it just means they'll be arresting you on behalf of the Agency, instead of me."

Zaavi shrugged. "I tell you what Sam. They can't get down here, for the same reason we can't get out, so when I've completed all four trials and gained my powers, I'll do something to help you out. Give you a new identity or wipe the whole business from the universal mind. I'll think of something, don't worry."

"You're all heart Zaavi." I shifted around for the climb down the wall. I did not want to offend him by telling him that I would sooner take my chances with law enforcement, despite Ambassador Stell's personal agenda. As I descended the wall, my heart felt torn between the urge to run and faith in my innocence that told me to stay and fight. Tinnias was right about one thing; with my contacts and friends, It would be easy for me to disappear off the galactic map forever, and although I knew it would be easy to do, my instinct as a law enforcer fought the other side. I knew I had not done anything wrong, and my reports, data and witness statements should prove that beyond doubt. My law enforcement experience has taught me something else though; mud sticks and when someone with power gets it into their mind that they want to take you down, they tend to get what they want in the end. Even if I didn't lose my job, my reputation would be soiled and Tinnias would be advised to farm me out somewhere where I wouldn't be seen too often. Knowing Tinnias had been forced into that position was very upsetting for me, but the idea of not being able to do anything to prevent it, was worse. By the time I reached the floor of the cavern and sat down to rest, I was in mental turmoil.

"Okay." I tried to force the source of my anguish from my mind by concentrating on other things. "After a drink and a rest, onward."

"I have a solution to your problem Samelan Sinclair." The voice of Vaylon made us both jump, and we spun around to find him smiling at us.

"You were listening in on my call? I guess I should've known; it's what you people do."

The Trials of Nahda

"However much it angers you, I do have a solution."

"And that would be what?"

"I can get you out of here, right now. You could leave and do whatever you need to do in order to prevent yourself from being wrongfully detained."

"You can get us out? We've been stuck down here for hell knows how many days and you've known how to get us out all along?"

"Of course I know. I'm the Temple Keeper. As I said, I am willing to get you out so you can attend to your own personal problems."

Zaavi cut in before I could reply. "Do it Sam. What's more important really, your own liberty or a petty thief as you call me? This is probably your only chance. You really should take it."

I knew he was right, but it hurt me to have to admit it. To have to change my whole life without more than a moment's preparation was something I had no desire to do, despite knowing it made sense to run. Everything in my life was now different, I would never meet any of the people I love ever again, and never be able to do the job I enjoy again, and I was scared for the first time in ages. Not scared in the way my job scares me sometimes. I get scared when my life is in danger or when some creature wants to kill me, but this was not that kind of normal healthy fear. This time I was scared because I did not have a life I could rely on any more. The years rolled away and I was like a kid again when my parents died, alone in the world and no one to help me. In that moment, I could have cried, I felt so alone and afraid.

Vaylon smiled at me. "Follow me Samelan, and before you know it, we will be on the surface and you can go to safety."

"You have the power to do that?"

"I have many powers. You don't believe in magic do you?"

"No."

"Well you should, because it is all around you here. Where do you think all those folk tales and fireside stories of magical lands, mystical beings and strange powers came from? Why do you really think the Nahdans are so paranoid as you put it? Just because of Esplonite TX5? Oh come on, credit us with a little more intelligence please."

"I believe what I can see and experience."

Vaylon nodded, and pointed behind me. I spun around to see a point of light hovering in the air, about twenty feet away. He chanted some words that even Zaavi did not understand, and as the words echoed around the chamber,

102

the light grew in size until it was a bright pulsating ball fifty feet in diameter. As we watched, the ball exploded into a thousand tiny luminescent birds that flew as one around the chamber. Higher and higher they climbed until they reached the arched ceiling, whereupon they changed direction and descended towards me. As they closed the gap between us, I saw them changing, coalescing, reforming, and my mouth fell open as a huge dragon, trailing flames from its wing tips, soared towards me. I stepped back in terror, but when it was ten feet from me, Vaylon yelled a word and it exploded noiselessly and vanished.

"Did you see and experience that my friend?" I could not speak, but nodded my head, my mouth hanging open in both disbelief and awe.

Zaavi was as amazed as I was. "Will I be able to do that when I complete the trials?"

"The Sword Bearer who earns the true power of the universe will do far more than that."

I scratched my head and grinned at Vaylon. "That was awesome. I still can't quite believe it, but it was awesome."

"Just a party trick, as your people might say. Are you ready to leave now?"

"Be safe Sam." Zaavi came towards me and shook my hand. "I guess I'll probably never meet you again, but I will remember you with a smile. Thank you for helping me when I needed it. I will never forget it."

Vaylon took a step away, then turned and looked at me. I took a step towards him and almost followed, then stopped and shook my head. "I'm not leaving."

Zaavi was shocked. "Why not? This is your only chance. Why throw it away just because of me? Especially when you know I will never allow you to take me away to your justice system. This is crazy."

"It just doesn't feel right. I know myself too well, and running for the rest of my life is something I wouldn't be able to maintain. I'm a law enforcer, and fair justice is what my job means, what my life means. This time it's fair justice for me I'll be fighting for, but I can't run when I know I haven't done anything wrong. It's not my way. I'd rather go to prison as an innocent man, than run away and not even try to prove myself. Looks like you're stuck with me."

Vaylon nodded and smiled. "Then you may continue with the trial."

The Trials of Nahda

We had been walking for over an hour before I noticed we were going downhill. The descent was gentle enough, but the temperature was dropping fast. The rock floor upon which we walked was slippery, and more than once, we lost our footing on the damp stone beneath our feet. We trudged with as much care as we could, our breath forming white clouds that glinted in the light of my flashlight as the moisture droplets turned to ice and drifted away.

"There's ice underfoot here Sam. Be careful."

"I see it."

Slowing to a crawl meant we made very slow progress through the immense cavern, and all the time I was aware of the huge empty space around me. It was odd, but the sheer scale of the place made me uneasy as I crept over the icy floor in near total darkness. All of that empty darkness weighing down on me creeped me out, and I was delighted when the far wall of the cavern loomed into view.

"Oh, thank heavens it's the end wall."

"You okay Sam?"

"Yeah I'm okay. It's just a bit creepy being in such a huge empty dark space."

"I know. I keep trying not to wonder what may be creeping up behind us."

I glared at him. "Shit, did you have to say that?"

He grinned. "Sorry. Hey, there's a doorway."

We found that the door led into a tunnel, wide enough for us both to walk side by side and tall enough for Zaavi to walk upright. Rivulets of icy water ran down the walls and dripped from the ceiling, and no matter what we tried, it dripped down our necks and soaked us through. A hundred yards along, an almost right-angled turn brought me face to face with a steep downward slope that disappeared into darkness.

My heart fell as I looked at it. "Oh fuck. Can this possibly get any worse?"

Zaavi gave it a tentative poke with a toe. "It's a sheet of ice."

"How the hell do we get down without being smashed to bits?"

"On our asses. Hug our backpacks to our front, cross our legs with our feet tucked under, and try to steer by leaning with the upper body."

"Umm, yeah, I guess that sounds doable." His idea impressed me, and my surprise must have been evident in my voice as he grinned at me.

The Trials of Nahda

"One thing Shyola and my mother obviously never told you about me, is that I'm three times champion for Lanis City in the Bideong Descent."

"The what?"

"The Bideong Descent. Outside the southern end of Lanis is a range of mountains called The Bideongs. Their peaks are permanently snow-capped and we use one of them for a popular sport we call Descending. You slide down an icy slope carrying a container of water. There are various slopes for the various skill levels, the most difficult being very twisty and winding. The water containers are large; you need both arms to hold them, which means you must use your body and thighs to steer. The winner is the one who gets down to the bottom quickest and with most water in his container. I'm the best in the whole area and have been for the past three years."

"That's awesome. So what do I do?"

"Okay, so sit down and cross your legs. Tuck your feet as far under as you can, you don't want toes sticking out; they can be lost easily on rocks. Hold your backpack in front and scoot up right behind me. The backpack will act as a buffer should we crash. Wrap your arms around my middle and grab hold of my backpack straps. That will keep us together, so the only time you should let go is if your arms get ripped clean off. Okay?"

The image of my arms flying off did nothing to endear me to his idea, and it was funny in a dark sort of way, but it was all we had. "Right." I reached around him, encircling my wrists in the straps of his backpack. "Okay, I'm secure."

"Whenever you feel me lean left or right, lean with me. We must work as a single unit or I won't be able to steer us properly."

"Right, gotcha."

"Okay, here we go." He edged us forward onto the top of the slope. Icy wind caught my ears as we flew downhill and although I was terrified, it was exhilarating at the same time. I clasped my eyes shut, not daring to look for fear of what I might see. My imagination was bad enough; I had no desire to find out how much worse the reality of it was. My ass quickly became wet and freezing and I decided there and then that if my balls froze solid, I would shoot Zaavi. He leaned a little to the left and I went with him. Next came a series of lefts and rights in quick succession and I almost could not keep up. Then another long straight, before Zaavi's voice floated back to me.

"Very sharp left coming Sam, lean with me."

"Okay."

The Trials of Nahda

I hung on for all I was worth, Zaavi leaned almost flat over his left knee, and I followed suit. I found that leaning on my left knee forced the heel of my right foot that was snuggling underneath it into the ice, which acted like a brake. This slowing of our left side, forced our right side to move faster, thereby taking us around the bend. Zaavi sat up straight and I followed as we flew down another long straight. This was fun and I could not help but whoop aloud, which echoed along the tunnel and reverberated around us. Zaavi joined in and I imagined Vaylon watching and grinning at us. Another long section of quick flips to either side, followed by a sharp left and two sharp rights, the last of which had us almost lying flat on our right thighs. My body was hurting by this time and I was not sure how much longer I would be able to cope, when I heard a startled cry from Zaavi.

"Oh fuck, there's," was all I heard before something knocked into my ass from underneath and I flew through the air, yelling in surprise. Zaavi flew ahead of me and we ended up in a heap thirty feet or so away. For long moments I lay there, not daring to move in case I found broken bones and smashed limbs.

I groaned as I tentatively moved an arm, then a leg. "Oh shit, what happened?"

"We ran out of ice."

"Holy fuck." I dared a wriggle and winced as hot pain coursed its way up the backs of my thighs and across my buttocks. "Oh my ass."

"And mine. I think I've lost some skin."

"Yeah, tell me about it." I tried to move and winced in agony. Like aged men whose bodies no longer enjoyed the normal range of movement, with many ooh's and ahh's of pain, we managed to get up. Sitting was too painful, so we knelt on our knees and waited for our bodies and minds to recover. Our descent stopped dead for three reasons. First, the downward sloped levelled off. Second, the ice covering the slope vanished at the point where it levelled off. Third, a thick layer of small stones covered the floor. I touched my ass as I saw those stones, expecting to find bare and bloodied skin where once was fabric, but was surprised to find my clothing still intact. The image of us two guys walking along with our asses hanging out of our pants, leapt over my mind, and I burst out laughing. Zaavi soon joined me and the small space filled with our guffaws.

I grinned. "Man that was fucking awesome."

"Wanna go again?"

"It wasn't that fucking awesome."

"You were a good passenger Sam."

"Thanks."

Once we recovered our composure, we got up and gathered our belongings. The small spherical chamber was thankfully free of ice. This was strange, as we were much lower into the ground than we had been, and it was icy up there, so I reckoned it should be icy down there too.

"Funny how it was icy up there but not down here."

Zaavi nodded. "I was thinking that too. It's probably just another fabrication to test us out. We can't know until this is over, so why worry about it?"

"Well I'm not worried exactly, but understanding it might just help us out later on."

"True. So what do you make of it?"

I shrugged. "I haven't a clue. The only thing I know is that it ensures we go forward with this."

"How do you work that one out?"

"I feel pretty confident when I say that I would not be able to climb back up that slope. We've no choice but to continue now."

"Oh I see. Yes, it does rather force our hands doesn't it?"

"Yeah. So let's just hope there's a door huh?"

"Now that would be unfortunate wouldn't it?"

"Don't even think it Zaavi. Don't even think it."

He grinned. "Okay. Ahh, there's an opening over there, look."

We entered another tunnel, wide enough to walk side by side, and I noticed that Zaavi was limping and in obvious pain.

"Hey, you're hurt."

"My ankle. It isn't broken but it is sore. I think I pulled a muscle during our descent or maybe during our less than elegant stop."

"You wanna stop and rest for a while?"

"Not here. Maybe if we find somewhere that's not so cold and wet."

"Okay, but take it as slow as you need to."

We trudged on, getting colder and wetter with each minute that passed, the icy drips from the ceiling running down our necks and chilling us to the bone. Zaavi's limp was worse and I worried for him. I suggested he use the sword as a walking stick and it helped him a little. The last thing I needed was a cripple of his size expecting me to carry him through two more trials, just so he can get those damned superpowers he insisted on believing in. We needed somewhere safe to rest, food and warmth.

The tunnel curved to our right and I saw a doorway on the left. Peering in, we saw a small chamber filled with crates. On inspection, they were all empty, but I was delighted to find they were made of wood. I whooped with joy and urged Zaavi inside, sitting him down in the driest corner. Within minutes, I had a fire going by the entrance, and the draft from the tunnel took the smoke away and saved us from asphyxiating. Leaving Zaavi to warm up and dry off, I headed out into the tunnel to scout around, hoping to find some cave dwelling creature to roast, and returned after an hour with five small black things that reminded me a little of the Amfets we get back home on Sigma.

The smell of cooking meat woke Zaavi, who was by now, dry and warm. "You found something to eat?"

"Yeah. You're never gonna guess what lies up ahead along the tunnel."

"So long as it contains more of whatever smells so good, I don't care."

I grinned as I held one out for him. "It does, but they're assholes to catch. I haven't had to hunt for a meal in quite a while, so I feel justly proud of my haul today."

"I've never hunted, so I'm amazed by your skill." He took the creature, dodging it from hand to hand to avoid scalding himself and tore off a leg. "Tastes wonderful."

After we had eaten, I took out my water purifying kit and broke the top off one of the small phials. Dropping the contents into one of the water bottles, I shook it and offered it to Zaavi, before repeating the procedure with my own bottle.

"There's plenty of water there too, which is now guaranteed safe to drink." He took it, nodded his thanks and drank. Grubbing in my backpack, I found the pack of painkillers I always carry, and offered him four. "These will help with the pain. Four should be okay for a guy of your size."

"Thank you Sam, I appreciate this. I'm being a burden to you."

"Hey, you saved me twice remember? This makes us even now. I may be a law enforcer but I'm a good guy too y'know."

We decided to sleep before continuing. The cold, lack of decent food, and the constant exertion exhausted us, so after building up the fire with the remains of the crates, we laid down and slept. In my dreams, I was running, alone and terrified from men with angry faces. They cornered me and I awoke with a shout of fear that had Zaavi by my side in an instant.

"Hey Sam, wake up. What's up?"

"Oh, it's just a nightmare I guess." I sat up and tried to come to my senses. "Sorry, did I wake you?"

"No, I've been awake for a while. What was it about?"

"Being chased, men who caught me and wanted to chain me up. Regular nightmare type stuff. I tend to get them when shit happens in my life. A friend once told me they were my subconscious mind telling me I need to understand myself more."

"He sounds like a very wise man."

"He was."

"Was?"

"He died."

"I'm sorry for your pain."

"Thanks. It happened a while ago on a job we were working together." I remembered Ren, and the familiar feeling of bonding swept through me. I gave myself a mental shake and stood. "I'll just take a pee and then we'd better get going I guess. Are you feeling better?"

"Yeah I'm much better, thanks for the help."

I am going to stop here for now. I have to get something to eat and then I have some stuff to get done. I will pick it up tomorrow. This is Sinclair V-Log PA884/R data log reference point 1956365/7987.

CHAPTER NINE

Morning everyone, sorry for cutting off yesterday. Kind of a crazy day. This is Sinclair V-Log PA884/R data log reference point 1956365/7988, continuing report.

Zaavi and I felt much better after some food, warmth and a few hours' sleep, so we set off down the tunnel and I couldn't wait to show him what I'd found when I went to hunt for our dinner. His expression was amazing, and I laughed as his mouth fell open in shock. I guess I must have had that same expression when I saw it for the first time.

"Wow. Is this real?"

I grinned at his astonishment. "It tasted real when we ate it last night, didn't it?"

"I've never seen anything like this, anywhere, ever."

"Well I have actually. A couple of times but that doesn't stop it being amazing."

We stood at the end of the tunnel, the entrance to another, even more vast cavern ahead. Where the last one was cold, dark and inhospitable, this one was paradise. Lush vegetation grew everywhere, birds flew above us and the sounds of animals calling came to our ears. There was light above us; not sunlight but something contrived by people with amazing technology, and it felt warm on my skin, like a sunny day would do. As we made our way along the path that lay ahead of us, we saw a stream trickling by, all manner of fish, water creatures and plants living within its bubbling depths. An orchard of trees lay to our left and we noticed the trees were laden with huge ripe fruit.

Zaavi smiled as he reached to pluck one. "This is a Pornskwall." He bit into the large spherical orange fruit the size of his fist. "My mother used to make pies out of these when I was a young boy. I haven't had Pornskwall Pie in years."

I took one and bit into it, the tang refreshing but not too sharp, and nodded in appreciation. "It's delicious." The juice ran down my chin and stained my shirt.

Zaavi burst out laughing. "I remember my mother chastising me for staining a new shirt with Pornskwall juice on my first day at the education academy. I was eight years old and terrified of the new adventure."

We continued our exploration and as the hours wore on, an idea crept into my mind and refused to go away. With my life in tatters and my future unknown, this paradise had a strong influence on me. After several hours, I had to say something to Zaavi.

"Hey Zaavi. I've been thinking."

"What about?"

"This place." I waved an arm around.

"It's beautiful isn't it?"

"Oh, it is. It would make a nice place to make camp don't you think?"

"Sure. You want to pitch camp for a day before moving on?"

"I was thinking more along the lines of, umm," I hesitated, unsure all of a sudden.

"You mean stay here?"

"Well why not? My life has gone to shit, I have no family and no friends I dare call on anymore and no one would ever find me down here. There's food, water and what passes for sunshine."

"And you'd be just as alone here as you would up top. I can't stay with you. I have to complete the trials and gain my powers, and I've promised you that I'll make sure you're safe and happy. Trust me to keep my promise Sam. I may be a thief, but I'm not completely without morals you know. You saved my life, and helped me last night when I was hurt and suffering, and I don't want to forget that."

"I'm scared. Everything I knew and took for granted has gone. All the things that were real and solid, the supporting structure of my life has just been blown apart and for the first time in my life, I don't know where to go or what to do. Part of me says run, part of me says fight and part of me says curl up into a ball and hope it all goes away."

"You don't have to do any of those things. Try something else entirely."

"Like what?"

"Like trusting me, the sword, this place. I know you don't believe in magic, and I have to admit that it's not something I've ever really thought about until now, but we're here and the things we've seen and experienced, really happened. We weren't dreaming or hallucinating, they happened Sam,

111

and even if you can't trust it, I do. We are going to complete the trials, I'm going to get the true power of the universe, and then I'll make things all right for you. You have nothing more to lose, so take a chance and trust me, please."

I sighed and looked at the floor. "Okay." I was at the lowest point I can remember in many years, and any thread of hope, however tenuous, was more than acceptable to me.

"But it is a good idea to make camp for a day. It will give us time to eat well, get our strength back and some good sleep." I nodded in agreement.

We ended up staying for two days in the cavern. I hunted for food, whilst Zaavi built a fire and we ate well on meat and the many fruits the trees offered us. The water from the stream was cold and fresh, and the fish that swam in the depths, delicious. We washed our clothes and swam naked in the stream while they dried and slept on the soft grass as the artificial sunlight changed to a star filled sky above us. It was beautiful to watch it changing. This was the closest thing to heaven I could imagine, but on the third morning, something caught my eye and made me frown.

"Zaavi. Hey, wake up."

"What's up Sam?"

"Look." I pointed up at the tree under which we had slept. Zaavi squinted the sleep from his eyes, the sight snapping him awake at once. He leapt to his feet and gazed up at the tree, the bright green of its leaves now grey, and covered with mildew, the rich red fruits now lying rotten on the ground all around us.

"What's happened here?"

"I haven't the faintest idea, but it's dying. Look at the grass where we've been sleeping." I heard a sharp intake of breath as the new shock registered. The vibrant yellow of the grass was now brown where we had lain, and the now dead grass marked the shape of our sleeping bodies.

He frowned as he fought to understand what he was seeing. "But." He ran a hand over his head as he tried to work out what was happening, and the expression on his face told me he was failing.

I was having the same difficulty myself. "There's more, over here." I walked over to the stream and pointed to the now stagnant water on which hundreds of dead and rotting fish were floating. The smell made us both gag and we leapt away. As we walked back to where we had slept, I pointed back along the path, the way we had come. "Look." Behind us, paradise was dead. The lush vegetation was grey, brown and dead, the bodies of birds lay on the path and even the artificial sunlight felt much less warm.

He shook his head. "But, I don't understand."

"I do. At least I think I do. It's us. We're killing this place by being here. I've been thinking about it ever since I woke up and I reckon that our presence here has somehow upset the balance of things."

"How? We've taken no more than we need, and we haven't done any damage."

"Humanoids always do damage. Like your ancestors did on this very planet, and like all humanoids do, wherever they live. We take from our worlds like parasites, and like most parasites, we eventually kill our host. We however, always the strong ones, the resilient ones, survive to go somewhere else and do it all over again."

"Resilient." He repeated the word and I nodded.

"Yeah. You see, I reckon this trial was not just about us demonstrating our own resilience, but an understanding of our effect upon the resilience of everything else. Seeing as how you're trying to get the power of the whole universe, it stands to reason that you need to understand how what you do will affect the universe, so you can, hopefully, try to lessen that effect."

Zaavi nodded. "That makes sense Sam. And I suggest we move on right away, before the whole place dies."

"I agree we should probably get going, but I think this place is doomed now. It was here to teach you something and now you've learned the lesson, it's not needed anymore. Remember what Vaylon said at the beginning of all this? About truth and untruth."

"Yes, the first trial. The labyrinth and the make believe creatures."

"I think it would be a good idea for us not to forget what he said about truth and untruth, all the time we're down here."

"You think this is still make believe?"

I shrugged. "It could be. It certainly wouldn't hurt to bear it in mind anyway."

We continued on, and spent most of the journey in silence, each lost in our own thoughts. I felt a mixture of emotions; nervousness at the way my life had crumbled around me, insecurity at what might lie ahead for me, anger at the way people always try and fuck things up for you when things don't go right for them, and embarrassment at the way I had panicked over the snake a few days before. Oh, and there was also some gratitude towards Zaavi for having helped me. Now that the life I had known and enjoyed, for the most part, was effectively over, I spent some time remembering the people I have met over the years and tried to decide whether my influence on their lives had been positive or otherwise. I was in no doubt that the job I do is a good one. I help keep the crazies out of the general population and although there are always more waiting to take their place, I help to stop people getting hurt and give folks a chance for some closure on what is sometimes, the worst experience of their lives. There have been times, such as the one on Abastra 7, when things go wrong, but I am glad to say that they are in the minority. Throughout my years as a law enforcer, and even during my ten years in the military before joining the Agency, I have always tried to do what is right. Even when I had to kill, it was always a last resort, and I hated every single killing. Despite being a law enforcer, I hate killing. The reason I do this job is to prevent killings and for me, taking a life should never be done without knowing there is no other way. I feel I have that soul on my conscience, and only when I have had no other option, have I taken life.

I was so lost in my thoughts that it was not until I bumped into Zaavi's back, that I noticed we had reached the far side of the huge cavern. "Oh sorry buddy. I was miles away."

"No problem Sam, so was I. Look."

My eyes followed his pointing finger back the way we had come. Paradise was gone, as if it had never been. There were a few rotting tree trunks and the carcass of some animal visible in the rapidly failing light. As I watched the scene, something tried to happen inside my mind; a coming together of an idea, and I almost understood but it was gone before I grasped it. I was feeling much stronger in both my mind and emotions, but paradise was now dead and I knew the two were connected but I was unable to formulate the sequence of ideas that would cement my understanding of it and enable me to put it into words.

"This has been very significant Zaavi. That," I pointed to where paradise used to be, "is very significant. All the time we're alive, we're having an effect. On people, their lives, our environment. It may not seem so bad when you just think of yourself, but think of everyone on the planet and the collective effect they have. You know what happened here on Nahda 3, and why, so you should find this lesson easy."

Zaavi nodded. "Yeah, there is a large public feeling of shame at what happened here, and although we all know about this part of our history, that feeling of shame is something we're taught. We don't feel it through any tangible connection with it because it was so long ago and we've moved on. These past two days though, I understand it completely."

"That's good. You can also think of it in a smaller way."

"Huh?"

"Well, think of it more on a person to person basis. You can think of a person like a universe, and your interactions will affect them, as they affect you. So I guess you could say this is something you can take and integrate into every area of your life, whether you're ruling the universe or not."

"Yeah, that's true. Now, where do we go do you think?"

Just when I thought he was learning something valuable, he proved how shallow his understanding truly was. How anyone could change the subject so quickly, after such a profound experience, was beyond me. "Well umm." I craned my neck up at the wall facing us and saw it disappear into the darkness above. "I guess we search for some steps or something."

"You want to go right and I'll go left and see what we can find?"

"I umm," I hesitated, still not wanting to trust Zaavi. I still had a nagging doubt about his integrity, and I was not at all confident that if he found a way out, he would notify me about it.

"Come on Sam. It might be you that finds the door, and then you might be tempted to run away."

"But you want to stay here." I fixed him with a glare.

"And what is waiting for you up top? Men with guns and a prison cell? You want that?"

"No. No I don't want that, but I want to be stuck down here alone even less."

"We have more chance of surviving; I have more chance of surviving, with you helping me. You already showed me that twice. I'm going left, if you want to follow, it's up to you." He snorted in anger, turned his back, and walked off.

I hissed under my breath. "Shit." There was no way I wanted to trust him, but I had little choice, so I walked to the right, along the wall. The uniformly dark grey stone loomed with tangible menace. What would we do if we never found a way forward? Would we end up going crazy and killing each other? Would Zaavi kill me and eat me because of his crazy idea of gaining superpowers from an old sword? Worse still, would hunger drive me to do the same? I hoped not, and decided that I would sooner kill myself than end up like that. I was so lost in my thoughts that I almost missed seeing the crude stone steps cut into the face of the rock wall. My flashlight picked out the dark yawning maw of a doorway high above, and the stone steps had been cut so that only when viewed from one precise point, can they be seen at all. Stand in any other place, even a few inches away, and they are invisible. Clever, very clever. Was there a similar staircase carved into the previous wall that we had not seen? I would not be at all surprised. Maybe our climb had not been necessary. I yelled for Zaavi and within minutes, I heard his footsteps running towards me.

"What's up?"

I pointed. "Look."

"At what? I can't see anything."

I laughed aloud and stepped aside. "Stand here and try again." His expression told me he thought I had lost my mind. "Go on." With a shrug, he stepped to his left and looked at the wall, and I had the satisfaction of seeing his frown turn to astonishment. Three times, he stepped aside and back again to watch the steps come into view.

"That's incredible. If you don't stand in exactly this spot, you'll never notice them. Amazing. Well done Sam." He grinned and clapped me on the back.

"I have a cop's eye for detail."

"Thanks for not running away and leaving me."

I snorted in response. "Funny." After tightening the straps on my backpack, I took a deep breath and hauled myself up the steps, which I was delighted to find were my size instead of the giant ones I had seen so far on this planet.

The doorway revealed a short corridor that ended in another doorway to our left. What lay before us was like nothing either of us had ever seen. We took in the scene and when we realised what it meant for the two of us, we both cried out in shock and despair.

My heart fell through the floor. "Oh fuck, I'm gonna die in horrible agony." I put my backpack down and slumped to a heap beside it.

"For once, I don't feel like disagreeing with you."

The Trials of Nahda

We were in a large long room, a doorway visible at the far end. What lay in the space between, was a series of pendulums. Gigantic structures, fixed to the ceiling so that they swung freely from side to side, missing the side walls by no more than a couple of inches. Making my way to the far left, I focussed on them as they swung. There were nine in all; three pairs and three singles, and each was different. Some had blades; some were designed to crush and a couple had flails attached that swung from the back and forth motion of the pendulum itself. The first one had a single huge curved blade that swung through a groove cut into the floor and into similar grooves cut into the side walls. It was obvious that there could be no going under or hugging the walls. We had no choice but to dodge and run at the right moment. I then noticed something else that made my heart sink even lower. Within the range of the pendulums, the floor was dotted with the same black tiles as we encountered when we first entered this hellhole. They were far enough apart to avoid standing on, but our attention would be focussed on the pendulums, and the space available to us was limited. Try as I might to avoid it, I could not help but foresee one or both of us standing on them and bringing hell knows what down upon us.

I pointed them out to Zaavi. "Look. See the floor underneath the pendulums?"

He nodded. "So we have to avoid being sliced, diced and pulverised, and we have to avoid stepping on the black tiles. Well this is a real test of resilience, don't you think?"

"I do indeed. But I'm taking a rest first. Let's sit down for a while." I sat and watched, timing the swinging and trying to formulate some plan of action. I watched and made notes of the time taken for each of the pendulums to complete its swing back and forth. I was about to say something to Zaavi about the timings, when I noticed that during the last ten minutes, each of the pendulums was coming nearer and nearer to a point where they would all be in the middle of their swing downwards at the same moment. My eyebrows shot to the top of my head as the realisation hit me. If we ran at the right moment, we could cover half the room at once. All we had to do was wait until all the pendulums swung away from our direction in unison, and run as fast as we could.

I exclaimed in surprise when it hit me. "Oh shit. That's it, that's the answer."

"What?"

"I've been timing the swinging. Because they're all swinging at different speeds, we have to time our runs properly. I noticed when watching the swinging, that they seem to be approaching a moment when all of them will be at the lowest downward point at the same time. All of them will be pointing to the floor at the same moment, and if we run at that moment, we can get halfway across in one go, maybe even further. Then we just wait for it to happen again and do the other half."

"You're talking about synchronization."

"Am I?"

"Yes. The action of two or more systems that interact with each other and eventually come to move together."

"Huh?"

He pointed to the swinging pendulums. "That."

I nodded. "Ahh, okay."

"How long do we have?"

"A few minutes. It's difficult to be sure, I'm no scientist."

"Okay, then let's be ready to move. Any idea how long it will take to happen a second time?"

"Judging by how long it's taking now, I'd say between twenty to thirty minutes. I'll time them again while we're waiting and should be able to tell you more accurately. We may be sitting and waiting a while halfway through there."

"That doesn't matter, so long as I'm not getting turned into sliced meat, I don't mind waiting."

I stood and we walked towards the first of the pendulums. The huge blade swung by a foot from my nose and I felt the air disturbance brush my cheek. I reminded Zaavi about the black tiles on the floor and we noticed that the only trouble spot ahead was between the third and fourth pendulums. One of them lay right in the middle of the safe zone between the two swinging pendulums and I mentally rehearsed leaping a little to the right, as we waited for our moment.

I was worried that his size would be a problem for us. "It's a shame you've got such big feet. It's gonna be really easy for you to touch one of them without realising it."

"Hey I'm quite light on my feet y'know Sam, for a big guy."

Another theory occurred to me. "I suppose it's not beyond the realms of possibility that they could stop the swinging altogether."

"I guess not. Go ahead and try it if you dare. On second thoughts, don't."

I grinned. "Here it comes. Get ready to run. A couple more swings should do it. As soon as they start to swing away, run. That'll give us the maximum time okay?"

He nodded and rolled his neck around. "Okay."

Hugging the left wall, we ran forward as soon as the huge curved blade swung away from us. My heart was thumping in my chest, the fear of what those things would do to my body, keeping the adrenaline pumping and my feet moving. The third pendulum swung back towards us as I leapt the black tile and made for the gap between the fourth and fifth. The fifth pendulum was a giant spike covered ball, so I slumped down on my ass against the left wall, hoping the upswing would take the wicked spikes above us and out of harm's way. I yelled for Zaavi to hit the floor, his body crashing into mine as he allowed his legs to carry him into a prone position, his extra height being a major disadvantage. We had made it half way intact and we both breathed hard as the pendulums swung back and forth on both sides, the swooshing noise they made creeping us both out.

When Zaavi could speak, his voice was no more than a terrified whisper. "Oh man, I never thought I'd ever be doing this."

"Me neither. And I'm damned sure I won't ever be doing it again."

"I'm no expert on synchronization, but as far as I recall, they should stay in sync once they've reach the sync point. We should be able to make the other side right away."

"They would if they were operating at the same speed, but these are all going at slightly different speeds, so the time they spend in sync is short. They're now moving away from each other, and we have to wait for them to come back together again."

"Okay. In that case, they will keep going out of sync until the only way for them to go is back into sync again. As soon as you know when they are not moving away from each other anymore, you will know how long we have to wait. It's basic physics."

"Basic for you maybe. You're a scientist, you know about this shit. I'm just a law enforcer."

"Just keep timing and tell me when they're no longer getting away from each other. However long that takes, will be the same time it takes to move back into sync again."

I nodded. "Okay." Twenty-three minutes later, I noticed that for a couple of swings, the timings indicated there was no more movement away from sync and I nudged Zaavi. "I think they've reached the maximum point now. The last two swings have shown no difference in the timings."

"Great. How long?"

I took a quick glance at my notes and calculated again. "Twenty three minutes."

"Okay, that's not so bad. Better than twenty-three hours. By the way, do you still believe that none of this is real?"

"I don't know. Maybe."

"You wanna find out?"

I glared at him. "Nope."

"I thought not. Where's your conviction now then Sam?"

"It was just a thought, not a conviction. I have no desire to take it for granted and find out the hard way that I was wrong. I'm happy to err on the side of caution, thank you."

"You can't rule the universe if you always err on the side of caution."

I frowned. "Why ever not?"

"Because you need to be decisive, take action when it's needed and strike boldly."

"And what if your bold actions turn out to be the wrong ones? What then, screw the consequences?"

He shrugged. "It's a big universe."

"And what of the lives under your rule? I guess they're just collateral damage to you when you've a whole universe to play in."

"There will always be casualties when forcing change upon people."

I was shocked at his attitude. "It wasn't so long ago that change was forced upon you and your people. You don't like those changes and are actively trying to make changes of your own. How can you go from one extreme to the other so quickly?" I shook my head in astonishment. My question was irrelevant, as I already knew the answer. He was drunk on the power he believed lay ahead for him and the thought of being in a position of overall power was too much for him to resist. The thought of what he would do with such powers, if indeed they were to come, made me shudder.

"This is my destiny Sam. You cannot judge when destiny dictates change."

I groaned inside my mind. I was sick of hearing about his damned destiny. "Destiny may well dictate what happens to you, but how you choose to wield such power has fuck all to do with destiny. That is your own personal choice. If it's so right and just, then at least have the grace to own up to it and stop putting it down to destiny."

Zaavi did not reply, but glared at me before shrugging. I did not push the point; I could not afford to piss him off too much while we were still reliant upon each other. We sat in silence until the time for our next run approached.

"Get ready." I kept watch on the pendulums. "Another few swings and we can run. We should make the door this time."

"Great. I'm dying for a pee."

"There's a black tile in the gap between six and seven, so jump over it okay? There's also one right after nine, so jump that one too."

He nodded. "Jump after six and nine. Okay, I got it."

I was relieved to make it past the last pendulum and stopped to catch my breath. My relief was short lived though, as Zaavi misjudged his footing and caught the black tile. For a second, nothing happened and we stood holding our breath, our eyes darting around the room frantic with worry. The floor beneath my feet rumbled and a crack appeared at the far end of the room from which we had come. It snaked its way towards us and I went cold to the bone.

My mouth fell open as my eyes fixed on that crack as it came towards us. It was mesmerising and for a fraction of a second, I froze in place. Something snapped me out of it, naked survival instinct maybe, I do not know but I yelled at the top of my voice. "Run." The sound of rocks breaking reached me, and then a rumble and the crash as parts of the floor fell away into whatever abyss lay below the room. The blood froze in my veins, but I forced myself to concentrate on nothing but the doorway ahead, which seemed to get further away the faster I ran. Hands grasped me around the chest, and my feet left the ground as we swept towards the door, Zaavi's longer legs making short work of the distance despite my added weight. Together, we fell through the door and into a small square room, making an undignified heap on the floor. Instinct had me shunting backwards on my ass to the far wall and I hoped this room was safe. Zaavi joined me and we listened as the sounds of devastation died away and left us in silence, our heaving breaths the only sounds.

Zaavi put both hands over his ears and squeezed his eyes shut, the sheer terror evident on his face, the mirror of my own. "Oh shit, I'm so sorry. My ankle went over and I hit the tile as I stopped myself from falling. I'm sorry."

"It's okay. We made it, that's the important thing. Accidents can happen to anyone. Just be more fucking careful next time huh?" I was so scared and so relieved that I yelled at him, despite knowing it was an accident. He nodded and we sat in silence for several minutes waiting for our minds and hearts to calm. "I'm sorry for yelling. I was scared. I shouldn't have taken it out on you. Is it the same ankle you hurt the other day?"

"Yes. It's okay, no damage. Don't worry, I was scared too. Yell all you want."

"Thanks for saving me again."

"This is becoming something of a competition isn't it?"

A bright light exploded in front of us, and we put our hands up to shield our eyes. When the light dimmed, we found Vaylon standing there smiling.

"You have successfully completed the second trial of Nahda Sword Bearer." He bowed his head with a smile.

Zaavi stood. "Thank you. What is next?"

I stood and brushed myself down. "Hey. Hold up a second. How about a meal and a rest first huh? We earned it."

"Very well." Vaylon bowed his head and waved a hand. Like before, a fabulous meal appeared on the floor before us. "Take your time. When you are ready, call and I will come and guide you to your third trial."

I barely had time to thank him before he vanished into thin air. "Thanks." Zaavi looked at me with what I can only describe as frustration. "Hey I'm hungry and thirsty, even if you're not. I work better on a full stomach and when I've slept well, even if you don't."

"Of course, you're right. We must take care of ourselves or we could make a mistake. I'm just anxious to complete this and fulfil my destiny."

"I know, but destiny will still be there in a few hours."

The Trials of Nahda

CHAPTER TEN

After eating another fabulous meal, we slept. My own was fitful and troubled with nightmares. Each was of the same nature and I awoke every hour and a half or so, sweating and with a feeling of dread weighing upon my soul. In each of the dreams, people judged me. People whose hatred for me was obvious in their angry eyes and the spit that flew from their lips as they raged at me. They wanted me punished for something I knew I had not done. In one, they chased me through darkened streets, and every time I turned, a dead end was there to meet me and I had to back track and find another way. I could hear the shouts and taunts of those giving chase; they were catching me up and I knew that if I did not get away, I would never see the sun again. Another had them leading me down tunnels to a waiting prison cell, inside which was a filthy mattress to lie on and a bucket for a toilet. The door clanged shut behind me and I screamed, begged to be set free and protested my innocence but no one heard. I awoke from that one with the sounds of boot steps echoing as they retreated down the corridor. The last one before I got up was the worst of the whole bunch. I was in a courtroom for trial, but I did not know what I was supposed to have done wrong. Men with angry faces were yelling at me, asking me why I did it and what my motive was. I asked what it was they thought I had done, and they said I was a murderer. They slammed photographs down in front of me and I saw my ex-partner Ren lying dead on the ground in the tunnel, exactly as I remember from the last time I saw him.

I told them I did not kill him, that he was shot by one of the research station people, but my judges did not believe me. They said his death was my fault, that I put him in the situation that led to his death, and because of that, I was responsible. The next photographs showed Merellia Gilden, the woman I almost married over twenty years ago. They played the tape of the man raping and murdering her, and I heard the voice I had never forgotten, mocking me before telling me where I could find her body. I was distraught, and told them the story, begged them to understand that I never wanted her to get hurt. They asked me if I accepted any responsibility for her death, and I had no choice but to say yes. I do feel responsible for both of their deaths, but not because I caused them in any direct way. The responsibility for me lies in their connection to me, that knowing me got them killed. This is the main reason I do not mind how lonely this job can be. People I have loved and got close to have died because of that closeness to me, so I tend to keep a measure of detachment from people. Not because I am anti-social, but because I do not want them to get hurt. I guess there is also the fact that I do not want to feel the pain of that feeling of responsibility either, and in that respect, I guess it is selfish of me. No one is perfect, me included, and I have learned over the years to live with myself in the best way I can, for others and for me too. Yes, I am a bit of a loner, and yes, it may well be a self-protection mechanism, but it works for me and saves the lives of others, so do not knock it.

I jumped awake, dried my eyes and went for a pee before having a drink and thinking about our situation in the quiet. Zaavi was snoring beside me and I wanted him to remain asleep for a while longer so I could have some quiet time. The situation I had found myself in was unlike any other during the whole twenty years I have been working for the Inter-Galactic Law Enforcement Agency. Never before had I been forced to face up to my basic beliefs as to the nature of the universe that I call my home. My experience of life has taught me that no matter how far across the universe you travel, no matter what kind of people you meet; some things can be relied upon. People are the same across the whole universe; they eat, sleep, shit, have sex, go to work, get drunk, fight and want to be better than their neighbours. They want the best things in their homes, good jobs and plenty of money. Most people want a decent home, a flash car, nice clothes, a reason to party and sex at the weekend. No matter where I have gone nor whom I have met, those things are always a part of life, and it is because of those things that it is so easy to feel at home wherever I go.

Not once have I ever needed to entertain the idea of magic or anything mystical or fantastical. The closest I ever got was meeting the Xerosians. The mind is a source of electrical energy, and those with the ability to use that energy in a certain way can tap into that same energy within another mind. It is basic stuff that even I understand, but it is not magic. In my universe, no one waves a hand and a fabulous feast appears, no one can make you see huge snakes or dragons with fire on their wingtips, and pre-recorded holograms from thousands of years ago cannot interact with you. If everything I had so far experienced was true, my universe was a very different place than I had so far believed it to be. I had to admit to myself, it made it a place I would no longer feel as comfortable living in. Magical powers make people unpredictable, and my job relies on my being able to make predictions about people. The way they are likely to behave, and my ability to work that out, is the reason I am so good at my job and without that, the game reaches a whole new level of weird that would make me feel more inadequate than I am prepared to entertain.

There are some fantastical things I have learned to accept over the years. The Xerosians were a shock to me when I first heard about them, but once I learned about the process and understood it, I was able to fit it into my belief system without a problem. The physics of the process helped me with that. The other thing I had to learn to accept was life after death. Now, that was a biggie for me, but it happened in a natural way that made accepting it not too difficult. Also, the basic physical principles of energy transforming from one state of being to another state, is quantifiable and known science that I was able to grasp. I once did a job where I got to know and work with some people from the planet Lilea 4. They have a close working relationship with others of their kind who have died, and remain in contact with them throughout their own physical lives. At first, I thought this was crazy, another one of their beliefs. Once I understood that life force is another form of electrical and electro-magnetic energy, it became science rather than belief. They showed me that this energy is not destroyed by the death of the physical body, and it gave the whole thing a scientific basis I could accept. Working with them in close proximity for a significant amount of time, and seeing this relationship happening on a daily basis was both educational and amazing. I have no problem with the whole concept of life after death now; it is comforting to me to know there is something else waiting.

Magic though, that is a completely different arena of crazy. Waving your hands in front of someone and something appears out of nowhere? What is next, beams of light from the palms of your hands, flying without space ships maybe, teleportation by thought? No, I am sorry but I have a hard time with that, and I struggled with it as I sat in the small room waiting for Zaavi to wake up. It hit me that it was probably fear that trouble me. The fear of what it would mean for my life if everything became unpredictable overnight and without an order I could understand. Thoughts of Zaavi filled my mind. The thought of him gaining superpowers, what it meant for one man to have the powers he spoke of, terrified me. With all the normal emotions humanoids have, the anger, the jealousy, and the obsessional desires we all encounter from time to time, what manner of chaos could such a man cause? I went cold to the bone as I imagined all sorts of scenarios, and as he awoke and stretched, I knew that if it came to it, I could not let him gain such powers.

"Hey Sam. You been awake long?"

"A while."

He sat up and yawned again. "Any of that drink left?"

"Yeah, plenty." I handed him the jug. "I've filled our bottles and there's some left over."

"Thanks." He wiped his chin and put down the empty jug. "I'll go take a pee and we can be off I suppose."

"Where? The only door is back through the way we came, and I for one am not negotiating those pendulums again, especially as there is now no floor in there."

He shrugged as he zipped himself up. "Vaylon said to call when we're ready, so I guess we just yell."

I was opening my mouth to call, when Vaylon appeared before us and made us both jump. "You are ready to continue?"

I nodded. "I guess so."

"Then you may proceed." He pointed behind us. We turned and saw a doorway appear out of thin air in the wall, revealing a short corridor that ended in a junction about fifty yards ahead.

"Okay." I tried to sound excited as I strode forwards, but I do not think Zaavi was any more convinced by my act than I was myself.

The junction offered us one dead end, and a carved wooden door with a silver metallic knob. I hesitated before turning the knob and pushing the door, which swung inwards without a sound to reveal a huge library. There must have been a million or more books in there, stacked on shelves twenty feet high.

I was taken aback and did not know what to say for long moments. "What the hell? Books?"

"Well it looks like this trial will require mental exertion rather than physical. I'm so glad you have a good brain Sam."

"Hey man, don't put this all on me. These are your trials remember? I'm down here against my will."

"But you want to get out don't you? And in order to do that, I need to succeed and if your brain can help me do that, you get what you want too."

I snorted in response, angry at his logic. "Okay so what do we do?"

127

The Trials of Nahda

Vaylon was a little more forthcoming this time as he explained. "These volumes contain all the wisdom of Nahda. Your task is to find that one passage that you feel epitomises the true power of the universe. Find those few words that contain within them, the wisdom of that phrase. Once you have decided upon your chosen passage, call for me and I will guide you to the next part of the task."

Zaavi was as astonished as I was. "We have to read all these?" Vaylon said nothing.

I grinned. "Well it looks like it's down to you after all buddy. I can't read Nahdan, so wake me up when you're done." I flopped down into a comfortable armchair and helped myself from a flask of what appeared to be some kind of alcoholic spirit on a small table to my side.

Vaylon looked directly at me and smiled. "Whoever reads the books will find the words are written in his own mother tongue."

Zaavi laughed aloud. "Up off your ass Sam."

I snorted. "Magic. Damn how I hate magic."

Several hours later, I threw away a large tome giving an account of the financial income of the Nahdan Union of Transportation Workers, and yawned. My head ached, my neck ached, I wanted to pee, and I was bored out of my skull.

"I can't do this Zaavi. This will kill me quicker than anything. You have to find it soon or I'll go nuts."

He slammed shut a history of meteorological surveys. "You think I'm enjoying it?"

"I'm sorry." I got up and walked around to stretch my legs. "We need to think about this rationally. Rather than just going through the books one by one and waiting till we're both too old to be able to read anymore, we should find books that are likely to contain something relevant."

"And how do we do that?" He stretched his back and grimaced.

"Well umm." I scratched my chin. "We need some wisdom about power, about having power and using it wisely I guess. What sort of books might contain that? Nahdan history books maybe. Discover how they wielded power in the past and hope there's some nuggets of wisdom about how they could've done it better."

"Good point. Maybe poetry books too. They sometimes contain little phrases about being wise and good to your fellow man etc."

That was a good idea that I had not thought of. "Yeah, good thinking. Also political stuff might be good. The politicians had the power, they wielded the power, whether they did it well or not, and they might give us what we need."

Zaavi slapped the table and stood. "Right. I'll take the politics, I know about that stuff probably more than you do and will hopefully be able to stay awake longer while reading it."

"Okay. I'll take poetry for starters and if we come up against a dead end, we can both attack history."

We spent the entire day reading and by the time I knew I was ready for a meal and some sleep, I was beginning to hate Zaavi and his crazy scheme. This was torture unlike any other, and I knew if we did not find what we needed soon, my sanity would be in jeopardy.

Vaylon appeared when we called and provided another magical meal, which we ate and enjoyed while comparing notes on what we had read. I had trawled my way through thousands of poems, from exclamations of wonder at the colour of a flower, through outpourings of love from jilted lovers, and on to meaningless drivel about the meaning of life. None of it struck me as giving any wisdom about the true power of the universe and I read a couple to Zaavi. We laughed our way through several of them as we ate, and it felt good to laugh again after the stress of the situation. Zaavi had spent the day reading all about Nahdan politics and I felt sorry for him as he gave me a potted version of his day.

"It appears that before we emigrated to Nahda 4, the government was much more free and easy in the way they governed. Nahda 3 was very much a capitalistic society, and everyone was free to work their way up the corporate ladder and gain power if they wanted it. Once we emigrated, and the laws were changed, things were very different for Nahdans. Corporate power disappeared overnight and financial freedoms were reigned in. The people protested about it, and there were riots during the early stages of the change. Several corporations were expelled from Nahda altogether, and trade with other worlds was strictly controlled. Esplonite TX5 was banned from export and the people affected lost their entire wealth, and the power that went with it."

The notion that the answer to our predicament lay in the politics of the ancient Nahdans was still at the forefront of my mind, and I nodded. "Maybe that's where we'll find what we need. This whole power thing must be tied into Nahda and the way it thinks about the whole subject."

"Possibly. There is one phrase that I've marked as being a possible solution." He flipped the pages of a large book and read it to me. "This is a snippet from a speech given by a government minister two hundred and seventy six years ago."

'What we have learned, through our greed, and the suffering it brought down upon us as a people, is that power, and the want of it, will always corrupt. We must act now to avoid that corruption, and in so doing, ensure our survival and that of our children. It is only through limiting the power wielded by individuals and corporations that we may achieve the peace we desire.'

"That sounds like a definite candidate. Well done."

A smile spread across his lips at the possibility that he might have found our answer. "I vote we move on to history tomorrow and see what that brings us."

I nodded. "Okay, agreed."

He noticed me fingering a little book that nestled by my side. "What's that book?"

"It's empty." I picked it up and flipped blank pages. "Nothing in it at all."

"That's weird."

I nodded. "Very. Why would a book with no words be in a library? What wisdom can an empty book afford us?"

"None surely."

"That's what I thought too, but something about it keeps nagging me, so I'm keeping it by me and hoping I'll understand what that is, soon."

"You could always keep it and write your own journal of this adventure." He got up and went to pee.

I watched him walk away and I had that same feeling I had when looking back at the paradise cavern. Something struck my mind at that moment, a knowledge that those last few words had profound importance but I still could not put the ideas into a recognisable chain. The book with its blank pages sat in my lap, heavy with significance and as I swung my eyes around the library with its massive collection of words, I felt sure I had the answer we needed. What I did not know, was how to verbalise it when Vaylon asked.

The Trials of Nahda

The next day, we trawled our way through Nahdan history and although some of it was interesting, my mind was not on the job. Three and a half hours into our morning's reading marathon, I slammed the book shut and groaned aloud.

Zaavi frowned. "Bored already Sam? It's only been a day and a half."

"Well yeah. I am bored but that's not my problem now."

"So what's up?"

"I just feel we already have our answer. We're wasting time reading anymore."

"You think that passage I found yesterday is what we're after?"

"Actually no. I think this blank book is the answer. In fact, I'm convinced of it, but I don't know how or why."

He frowned. "The blank book? But that's nuts. How can a blank book paraphrase the meaning of the true power of the universe?"

"I don't know, but it's haunted me since I found it and my mind just won't let it go."

"Well then, let's discuss it." He put his book away. "It's a blank book, yes?"

"Yes. Totally blank." I looked down at it, benign but profoundly significant.

Zaavi continued, unaware of what I was feeling. "And we need an explanation of the true power of the universe."

"Yes."

"So umm," he faltered.

"So what do you think about the true power of the universe." I expected him to take time to consider the question, but his answer was immediate and direct.

"I think it's mine."

I groaned and rolled my eyes to the ceiling. "Yeah, I know that. I meant apart from that. Come on, help me out just a little huh?"

"Okay. The true power of the universe means umm, being in charge of everything everywhere. Being in ultimate control of everything that is. Making the decisions about everything. What does it mean for you?"

"I think it's going to be something a little less physical than that. Listen, why don't we both take some time and write down our thoughts on it, and then compare notes. Say, an hour, with no discussing. You go to one end of the room and I'll go to the other and we'll both think and write down our thoughts."

"Okay, if you want to try that, I'm willing. Can I have something to write on?"

"Here, take a few sheets out of this blank notebook." I tore out some sheets and handed them over. He took them, thanked me and walked to the other end of the library. As I watched him striding down the room, everything slowed down. Inside my head, my mind emptied and I was left sitting there, watching Zaavi walking across the room in slow motion, blank paper in his hands. My mind registered the paper in his hands, then the book in my lap, and clarity grabbed hold of my mind, shaking it to its foundations. The whole universe exploded inside my mind, and I had a moment of extreme awareness unlike anything I have experienced before. The true power of the universe cannot be explained away by anything other than one's own experience, views, and beliefs. The true power of the universe is unique and personal to everyone, and what it means to one, is as valid as what it means to another. In that moment, I knew why the blank book was the answer.

I whispered aloud as I continued watching Zaavi walking away. "That's it. You can't explain the true power of the universe in one sentence. It's unique to each individual, borne out of your experience, beliefs and character."

Before I could call out to Zaavi, Vaylon appeared in another bright flash and smiled at me before addressing us both.

"You have successfully completed the first part of this trial." Zaavi and I gaped at each other. "You can now proceed to your second task."

"We found the answer?" Zaavi asked.

Vaylon nodded. "The Sword Bearer has, once again, proven his worth to the Temple Keepers."

"So I guess my political quote was right after all." He grinned at me and raised his eyebrows.

"Now you have proved your understanding of the true power of the universe, it is time for you to put that wisdom into practice." He pointed to the far corner of the room, where a spiral staircase flashed into being, its ornate metalwork winding up to another carved wooden door like the one through which we had entered. We climbed and the door led us through into another small square stone room in which was a single table. On the table was a clear square jar containing some kind of insect colony. Thousands of tiny brown insects in one huge colony all working together, it was fascinating to watch them running along the tunnels, carrying bits of food, tending to their young and cleaning out unwanted mess.

"This is a universe," Vaylon continued, "and with it, you must prove your worthiness as possessor of the true power." Before either of us could ask questions, he vanished.

"This is awesome." I grinned as I bent to peer into the jar. "When I was a kid, I made something like this for a school science project. Back home on Sigma Prime, we have an insect called the Malionscar. They live in huge colonies just like this and they produce a substance that is a natural antibacterial. Many homes in the poorer regions have jar colonies like this in their homes. I can remember my mother smearing the stuff onto cuts I got while out playing with my friends."

Zaavi bent to look into the jar. "I can understand the resemblance to the universe, but what we're supposed to do is beyond me. They seem to have their world all sorted out nicely without our interference."

"Yeah. I can't understand how us fiddling with it is going to improve anything. Why don't we just sit and watch for a while and see if anything happens?"

"Okay." We sat and took turns watching the jar. For the rest of that day, nothing of interest happened and when Vaylon appeared and gave us another magical meal, no amount of questioning could prise an answer from him. We went to sleep and although my dreams were benign, I awoke several times. Once I got up to pee and glanced at the jar. To my horror, I saw a huge insect inside with the tiny ones, grabbing at the little ones as if trying to kill them. I yelled and Zaavi awoke, leaping up and grabbing the sword, startled out of his wits and stumbling around as wakefulness took its time to reach him.

"Look at this." I pointed to the jar.

He gasped as he saw the huge insect grabbing at the smaller ones. "Get out you asshole." He reached in and pulled it out, stamping it underfoot.

"Are you sure that's what we're supposed to do?"

"What? The big guy comes along to the little guy's world and tries to take over? Yeah I'm sure. Isn't that what a decent ruler does, stop the big guys from stamping out the little ones?"

I shrugged and turned my attention back to the jar. I understood Zaavi's logic but I felt it was interfering in the ways of nature a little too much. That is what nature is like, creatures eat each other, it is all teeth, claws, and blood out there. The survival of the fittest is nature's way and stamping out the big guy before finding out what he wants, seemed a little heavy handed to me. Worlds come and go, people make war with their neighbours, and it is the same wherever humanoids live. It was obvious to me that Zaavi was an act now and think later type of person, but I am more of a leave it and see what happens guy. I once met a race of people who taught me many things I will never forget, one of which is the conviction that the universe as a whole is a living being, and no one knows better how to maintain it than it does itself. They taught me that interfering in the ways of the universe and the cells that make up its body, the cells being individual worlds and their inhabitants, prevents it from maintaining itself at optimum. I will never forget those people, nor what they taught me, and their wisdom came back to me as I watched the jar.

Zaavi went back to sleep and I took a pee. When I returned, I glanced into the jar again and saw another large insect the same as the previous one. Instead of calling Zaavi, I decided to keep quiet and watch what happened. The big guy kept grabbing hold of the little guys by their rear ends, and appeared to bite at them, but there were no injuries occurring and none of the little guys died. I watched as it scuttled away to the very bottom of the colony and disappeared into a hole. With the tip of an auto injector I grabbed from my backpack, I scraped away the earth and saw the big insect tending to its eggs. It was regurgitating something and spreading it over them. I watched as it went back into the colony four times and grabbed at the little ones, and I noticed that when this happened, the little ones excreted a clear blob of fluid from their rear ends. The big one spread this over its eggs. On the fourth journey, a different insect appeared within the colony and set about killing the little ones. The huge insect immediately attacked and killed it, leaving the body for the little ones to dissect and carry away into the heart of the colony. I grinned and woke Zaavi, who screeched when he saw another big insect. Being much bigger and stronger than I am, I had a hard time preventing him from killing it, and almost had to threaten him with my laser pistol.

"For fuck's sake Zaavi will you stop?" I struggled against him. "Just stop for a second. Shit. Can't you use your brain just for once?" He bristled at my insult and I felt bad. "I'm sorry for insulting you, but please listen."

"Okay. So talk. I'm listening."

"What's it called when two creatures can't survive without each other?"

"You mean symbiosis? Where two different creatures need each other for their own survival. They often live in close proximity to each other and help defend each other's territory."

"That's it. Well that's what this is here. The big guy isn't killing the little guys, he's catching something they're excreting and putting it onto his own eggs. Actually, it must be a gal not a guy, but anyway, something the little ones shit out, is what she needs for her own eggs. I've been watching for ages, come and see." I showed him the big insect's hideout and her eggs.

He peered through the side of the jar. "Wow."

"Just now, another insect flew in and started killing the little guys. This big guy, umm I mean gal, she shows up and kills it, then leaves the body and the little ones cut it up and carted it somewhere deep inside. They're working together and helping each other, and our best course of action is to do nothing."

"You're right. Well done Sam. I guess sometimes there will be occasions when it would be better for me not to do anything."

"Yeah. I'm sorry for insulting you, but you're bigger than me and I needed your attention."

"I understand. You want to continue now or wait until we've had some more sleep?"

"Let's have some more sleep first. Brain work is tiring."

We slept on, my dreams weird but not frightening but when we awoke, I felt tired and heavy. There was food left from our meal the night before, so we ate some breakfast before calling for Vaylon, who appeared beside us and smiled.

"You have done well Sword Bearer."

Zaavi grinned. "Thank you. I understand that sometimes, my best course of action is one of non-interference."

"Are you ready to continue with the trial?"

"I am."

Vaylon indicated a door, which appeared behind him. "Then you may proceed."

CHAPTER ELEVEN

We found ourselves in another huge cavern, and our mouths dropped open at the sight of the busy primitive village that filled the space. Crude huts stood to the sides, pens containing animals behind, and all around, people rushed about their lives.

Vaylon appeared by my side. "You may spend as long as you like amongst these people. They will welcome you like family, you may eat and drink whatever they offer you and accept their hospitality. All you will be required to do in payment for their kindness is solve whatever problems they present to you."

"What sort of problems?" I asked, knowing that he was not going to tell me, but hey, if you don't ask, you don't get, right?

"That I cannot say. You must use your wisdom to bring a solution to their queries in a way that is acceptable to them, their culture and their beliefs."

Zaavi frowned as he looked around the village. "They aren't Nahdans. They're too small."

"You are correct."

"So I've no way of knowing what their culture or beliefs might be."

"That is true."

"So how will I know that my solution won't offend them?"

"They will show you."

"How?"

"Take as long as you need." Vaylon smiled at us both, looked at the villagers, and vanished.

By now, I was getting annoyed at the vanishing into thin air thing, and I swore. It was damned rude to vanish like that. If he had just walked away it would have been better, but to keep vanishing into thin air, it irritated me. My next thought was how silly to get irritated by something so weird.

Zaavi cut into my train of thought before I could verbalise how I felt. "Well at least we have some company while we work our brains this time."

I shrugged. "Maybe they know a way out of here that Vaylon isn't telling us about."

"You think he would let us stay in here if they did?"

136

The Trials of Nahda

I was once again irritated by Zaavi's unarguable logic. Most of the time he came across as single minded and selfish, and I have to admit, a little stupid. On occasion though he would come out with something so obvious and logical that I had not thought of, and could not argue with, and always when it meant we were screwed. I guess I am more of a hopeful type of person, always choosing to assume that luck is waiting to smile on me. This means that I tend to ignore, or not recognise, those obvious things that make it plain how dreadful a situation is. Maybe I do not like to admit defeat. Either way, he did it again.

I strode forwards. "Okay, let's get on with it."

The people smiled at us as we walked, and we smiled back, anxious for them not to take offence at our presence. Vaylon said they were to ask for our wisdom by giving us problems. So when were they going to present us with some horribly complicated problem that neither of us would have a clue how to solve? If we could not solve it, would we be stuck here forever? All these questions and many more raced around my head as we walked.

They were dressed in simple garments; just lengths of woven cloth wrapped around and tied at the shoulders. The small children were naked and played in the dirt floor of the cavern whilst the adults worked. Baskets of fruit, vegetables and grains were stacked against the walls of the huts and huge pots of water stood by their side. These people had everything to fulfil their basic needs and did not appear to be suffering from any lack of necessities. They looked happy enough.

Within a few minutes, we heard raised voices and I nudged Zaavi. "Okay, here we go."

"What?"

"I reckon our first problem is just about to present itself?"

"Oh. Okay well umm, wanna go another way before they notice us?"

I tried to catch him with his own logic. "You think that would work?"

"Probably not, I suppose."

"Just remember. Don't say anything without thinking about it first okay? Don't just say the first thing that comes into your head. Give me time to think."

"Are you trying to tell me something Sam?"

I noticed a tone in his voice and stopped walking. "Huh?"

"Are you saying I can't think before I act? You did it before, with the bugs yesterday."

"Well you can be a little umm, impulsive."

"Impulsive? You say that like it's a problem. Just because I can make quick decisions and carry them through when you can't, you have to disrespect me?"

"What?"

"You're always on about needing thinking time." He jabbed a finger towards my chest. "Just because your mind works slower than mine, you have to make me out to be the bad guy."

"Hey there's nothing slow about my mind asshole. Just because I choose to take the time to make sure my actions will be the right ones, doesn't make me slow or stupid. You're supposed to be the scientist with a brain, but it's me that's used my brain down here the most."

Zaavi grimaced, anger flashing in his eyes as he glared at me. He snarled, spreading his lips and showing his teeth as he clenched his fists, and I prayed he was not planning to punch me. If he was, I was going to be in serious pain.

"You're nothing but an insect compared to me. I'm the Sword Bearer, and it is me that destiny has chosen to receive the true power of the universe. What does that tell you about who is the better man here?"

"It tells me that destiny is fucked up." I spat the words at him, angry at having my intelligence questioned by a petty thief obsessed with magic and believing in superpowers. "I've met hundreds of guys like you, psychos and crazies with all sorts of fucked up ideas, and all of them convinced that they're the ones destined for greatness. They're all either dead or rotting in jail now. Remember, you're just a petty thief who doesn't like being told what to do by people with way more experience than you. You couldn't even organise a group to discuss your politics. Instead of bringing about an empowering revolution, you almost lost your job. And this is all destiny found to rule the universe? What does that tell you about destiny huh?"

Zaavi did not reply. He growled, his body shaking with anger, spit flying out of his mouth. He grabbed me by the arms and flung me aside with all his strength. I flew through the air, coming to a stop as I crashed through a wooden fence and hit some large domesticated creature square on the ass. It let out a surprised bellow and bolted, frightening its herd mates into action and together, they stampeded through the rear fence and off somewhere out of sight. I was thankful it had chosen not to crush me underfoot, but I heard surprised yells from the people and felt guilty. I hoped no one was injured from the stampede, and worry gripped my mind as the image of those little naked kids sitting on the dirt floor came to my mind. I leapt up and headed towards the back fence, but stopped dead as I heard a woman's anguished wail. Running through the gap in the fence, I saw a group of people huddled together a little way ahead and my heart sank. Through the gaps in their legs, I noticed a small shape lying on the ground. My mind emptied and time slowed to a stop as I recognised the shape and heard the woman's wailing. I was aware that my legs gave way and I fell to my knees as a dark empty hollow filled me inside.

A voice beside me caught my attention and I turned to see Zaavi standing by my side. "What happened?"

I stood and wiped my face on my sleeve. "A kid got trampled."

Zaavi's eyes widened as his jaw dropped open. "What? Oh fuck no."

"Yeah. What the hell are we to do now?"

"But, we've only been in here a couple of minutes."

"I guess it doesn't take long to totally fuck things up huh?"

"How are we supposed to deal with this?"

I pointed to the people. "The same way they're supposed to."

"But we didn't mean for this to happen, it was an accident."

"We didn't mean it and they didn't deserve it. It happened and we are just going to have to carry it, as are they."

Zaavi shook his head and paced as he wrestled to put into words what he was thinking. "No, I'm sorry but this isn't right Sam."

"Huh? What do you mean it isn't right? Of course it isn't right; the kid is probably dead because of us. How can that ever be right?"

"Stop yelling and listen."

I was surprised to hear Zaavi taking this tone with me. "Excuse me? You're telling me to shut up?"

"Yes, please listen for a minute. You can yell later, but please listen now. This whole thing stinks, as you would say. We aren't here for more than a minute before circumstances take over and run away with us. How many times have you argued with someone, in a public place even, and had someone die as a result? Well? How many?"

I frowned. "None."

"Me neither. Now we also know that Vaylon told us truth and untruth is blurred down here right?"

I was beginning to understand where this was going. "Yes, he did."

139

The Trials of Nahda

"So I reckon that no matter what we could've done, a tragedy was bound to take place because it was designed that way. We could've come in here smiling and happy and still something bad would've happened."

"You might just be right there Zaavi."

"The only thing I can't get is why?"

"Well bad things do happen. Sometimes you get to witness it; sometimes you have a hand in bringing it about, other times you know nothing about it. I guess he wanted to show us that umm."

"That what? You almost had an answer there Sam."

"I know, but it's gone."

"Try again. Go back to that place in your head."

I closed my eyes and went through the whole scenario again, through our conversation word by word. My eyes snapped open when it hit me, and I smiled. "Things don't always go your way. Sometimes, things happen that you have zero control over. Most of the time you're not aware of the consequences of every little action, of just your presence even, and you get on with your life. Every now and then though, you do get to be aware that something happened just because you were in a certain place, said a certain thing, did something, or didn't do something. Maybe even it was just because you exist. Whatever, sometimes you see the shit that happens because of you. What happens then?"

Now it was Zaavi's turn to frown. "Huh?" You've lost me Sam."

"What happens is that you worry about it, feel guilty perhaps, angry maybe. Whatever is appropriate for the circumstance. You have all these feelings and emotional consequences for something you had no hand in causing. You carry the emotional baggage for something you didn't do. You believe in destiny, call it that if you want. Destiny writes the plan, makes the decisions, and watches us cope with the backlash."

Zaavi nodded. "I think I understand you. Sometimes we don't control bad things that happen around us, so why carry the emotional baggage for it? That kid did die though, and we did cause it. How does that fact fit in with your explanation?"

"Because all this down here is not real, we can learn the lesson without anyone actually having to die. We can be made to realise consciously that sometimes, we do cause the shit that happens but not always. Sometimes, we cause it simply by existing, without having to do anything. Most of the time

140

though, shit just happens and we don't ever realise it. I think the moral of this is to understand that some things are out of your control, and always will be."

"Even a deity can't get away from destiny."

I nodded. "Or just pure chance."

We walked down the path towards the crowd, both of us still expecting the people to react with anger. It seemed odd that they chose not to.

Zaavi appeared beside me again. "Why aren't they angry at us?"

I shook my head. "I've no idea. Remember this can't be real, no group of people could live and survive down here forever. There aren't enough of them for a start, they would die out within a generation or two."

"I know but I would have thought Vaylon would've made it a bit more realistic wouldn't you? People naturally would be angry with us. He wouldn't make such a mistake."

I stopped walking as I realised he was right. Why would Vaylon engineer these people to react this way? The obvious lack of anger had to be the key. "He didn't make a mistake."

"What do you mean?"

"It's not a mistake Zaavi, he meant it this way. These people are not being angry towards us because Vaylon wants us to learn something about anger and the way we display it. Maybe guilt too."

"These people are being friendly towards us at a time when they have every right to be angry. What is that teaching us Sam?"

"You just said it; they're choosing a non anger response. They're making a conscious choice not to react angrily, even when they have the right. That's extreme compassion."

"Compassion that I would find hard to display."

"Right, but now you know, you can try to learn it. You're obviously meant to. Why else would this be pointed out unless you're supposed to change something about yourself?

Zaavi looked at the village around us and nodded. "Yeah, and that will be the most difficult lesson of all four trials, you mark my words Sam."

"Well look." I indicated the village around us. "This is the universe in miniature. This village represents the universe. We just affected the universe in a negative way; the kid probably represents a world or a race of people perhaps, and we snuffed it out due to our fight. It happened, even though we didn't mean it to."

"Yeah." Zaavi ran his hands through his hair. "That's correct."

The Trials of Nahda

"So you just showed how good you are at managing the universe. Within five minutes, you wipe out a world because you can't take constructive criticism without getting angry. I tell you, if you want to win this true power of the universe and get superpowers or whatever other crap you're expecting to be endowed with, you're gonna have to do better than this."

Zaavi stopped, took a deep breath, and closed his eyes. For a moment, I thought he was going to blow again, but he gave a quick nod and moved on. "Let's keep moving and hope this doesn't scupper the whole thing. We are allowed one mistake surely? How else do you learn than by making mistakes?"

After retracing our steps and gathering our belongings, we continued through the village. The people smiled, waved and said hello when we passed and several times, we were given a drink, some fruit, and one man sat us down and asked us to smoke with him. He hand rolled a huge cigarette, wrapped in a large brown leaf that had been soaking in some liquid, lit it, and offered it to me. I coughed for twenty minutes solid, and Zaavi told me later that my face went bright green. There was no way I was going to argue with him, for I felt decidedly green for hours afterwards.

While we were enjoying a delicious but basic lunch, offered to us by a man and his family, his oldest son came over to where we were sitting. In his hand he held a sack, and under each arm was a pot. He put the pots down and crouched down beside us.

"Friends. I have lived in this village my whole life and have never known the world beyond our village border. You are from outside and therefore must be wise. I have to go to the market today to sell the beans we grow." He removed the lids from the pots and we saw one contained red beans, the other contained yellow. "The red beans are favoured by the women of the village, while the men prefer the yellow." He opened the sack and poured the red beans in. Taking a length of cord, he tied the sack around the middle, above the level of the red beans, before pouring the yellow beans into the top half of the sack and tying the top. "What do I do if a woman comes to me and wants to buy my red beans before I sell my yellow beans? How do I get the red beans from the bottom of the sack?"

"Put the yellow beans in first," I said and Zaavi nodded.

"But then what if a man comes to me first and wants to buy the yellow beans before I sell the red beans?"

"Tip the yellow beans out," Zaavi suggested. "Sell the red beans, then put the yellow beans back in the sack."

"I cannot tip them out. They would be soiled and I cannot sell soiled beans."

"Cut a hole in the bottom of the sack?" I offered.

"Then the sack could not be used again and we have no other sack. Without a sack, we could never go to market again."

I scratched my head.

Zaavi shrugged. "You're the one with the brain Sam."

"Thanks buddy. You're a great help."

Zaavi and I spent the rest of the afternoon playing with the sack and pots of beans and as the hours dragged on, my mind clogged with fuzz. I shook with frustration. Several times, we lost our tempers with each other and it was not until I smelled meat roasting for dinner that I slapped Zaavi's hand away and found the answer.

"Get your damned hand away," I snapped for the fiftieth time. "I'm trying something out."

"But my way is better, watch." He demonstrated, before slapping the sack down and swearing. I picked it up and fiddled for a few minutes before whooping aloud with joy and relief.

"Holy shit, that's it." I called the boy over. He sat before us, expectation clear in his expression. "Here's what you do," I said as I demonstrated. Having persuaded Zaavi to hold the sack open for me, I poured in the red beans and tied the sack in the middle as he had done earlier. Next, I turned the sack inside out, the tied portion now at the bottom inside the sack, under the red beans. Zaavi yelped as understanding took hold and grinned from ear to ear. I poured the yellow beans into the top portion of the sack and tied the top, and handed the whole thing back to him.

I grinned. "Please Sir, I'd like to buy the red beans please."

"No problem at all my friend." He untied the top, put his hand down to the very bottom of the sack, and untied the binding. The red beans tumbled out as the sack turned itself inside out, allowing the yellow beans inside to fall to the bottom.

The boy laughed so hard he fell onto his back and held his sides. "You are very wise"

The father beckoned us over. "And now you must eat with us."

"I thought we would never get it," Zaavi said as we ate the rich but delicious meat.

"Same here. I never thought I would be saying this, but I would sooner face those pendulums than do much more of this. I'm feeling old and tired with all this brain work."

"I'm inclined to agree."

After the evening meal, the father invited us to a village gathering and we were happy to agree. The villagers sang, played homemade musical instruments and young children danced. We talked and laughed with the people and Zaavi allowed them to persuade him to join in the dancing. It must have been well into the night before the people wandered home, when a man approached Zaavi and me with a small boy.

"We wish to offer you rest for the night my friends." We thanked him and accepted. Snuggled under animal hides, we were both asleep within minutes and with the warm fire nearby, I awoke knowing I had not slept so well in months. We were given a hearty breakfast by the man and his family, who all sported tattoos over their arms and backs. I asked about them and he told me they were the mark of his family's rank as tribal leaders. I noticed the youngest boy had no tattoos and the man nodded.

"Yes, he will soon be of an age when he can get his tattoos. Maybe you can help us with this problem." I groaned inwardly and glanced at Zaavi, who rolled his eyes in response. "There are only two men in our village who can do our tattoos," he said. "Come, I will introduce you to them." We got up and followed him out of the hut and through the village. Soon, we came to a small hut by a stream and we saw an old man covered in the most magnificent tattoos I had ever seen. The work was fine and the detail, incredible. His body was well kept, muscular and fit, while his hut was immaculate. I would not worry about catching an infection from him.

"This is Trajo." We smiled and he nodded. After exchanging a few pleasantries, the man walked on and we followed. Ten minutes later, we came upon a larger hut under a tree and the man shouted. A small wiry man emerged and I almost laughed aloud. I heard Zaavi gasp beside me and exchanged a shocked glance with him. The man was filthy and his tattoos were awful. A small blind child could have better executed them, I thought to myself. His hut was in disarray, with his few belongings scattered about and an all-pervading smell of body odour hung inside.

"This is Wenlas." We exchanged nods and smiles before the man led us back to his own hut and sat us down. "Which of them should tattoo my son? If you give me a good answer, and convince me why I should take my son to the one you choose, I will know you are indeed wise. I will leave you alone to think. There is food and drink whenever you need it, take your time."

"Well it's obviously the first guy, Trajo," Zaavi said.

"You'd think so. But since he's asked the question, it's obviously the other guy."

"You're probably right. It is a little too obvious I suppose."

I sat down, despondent. "Yeah, but why?"

We talked it over for hours, but neither of us could find a reason to pick the second man. I had sense enough to guess we were supposed to pick Wenlas, but coming up with a definite reason why, eluded us both. I lay back and closed my eyes as I massaged my temples. "That first guy, Trajo, his tattoos are fabulous though aren't they?"

"They are indeed. The highest quality workmanship I've ever seen, even more so than our own on Nahda 4 who do our women."

"So those designs on their heads are tattooed on?"

"Yes."

"I assumed they were painted on or something."

"The girls get their heads tattooed when they reach Chaneska, puberty. The designs are a mixture of family designs, mixed with symbolic representations of good virtues and those qualities the family hopes she will gain as she grows."

"Your girlfriend, Shyola, is beautiful."

"Thank you Sam. That is the best compliment to give a Nahdan man."

"Is it?"

"Yes. If you say his woman is beautiful, you are saying his choice is a good one, and Nahdan men believe that making the right choices in life is the mark of the best of men."

"What will happen to her if you get these superpowers you're hoping for?"

"She will rule the universe by my side of course."

"You still believe that the true power of the universe means you get to rule?"

"Of course. What else could the power of the universe be?"

I raised my eyebrows and shrugged. "I guess I don't know."

"Well you know," he began but stopped, his mouth falling open.

"What?"

145

"We take the boy to a different tattoo guy, a third one."

"But there's only two."

"No, wait Sam. We take him to whoever did the first guy's tattoo." Now it was time for my mouth to drop open. We stared at each other without speaking for several seconds before we both yelled together.

"They tattooed each other," we yelled in unison and fell down laughing.

I was so relieved and amazed we had not worked it out sooner. "Of course, that must be the answer."

Zaavi nodded. "They can't tattoo themselves can they? How does a man tattoo his own back?"

"He can't. He gets someone else to do it for him.

"So we take the boy to Wenlas, in the filthy hut."

I laughed. "Which is filthy because he's always busy with customers wanting his fabulous tattoos."

"Exactly."

We called the man over and told him to take his son to Wenlas for his tattoos, because he tattooed Trajo and his tattoos are so good. The man grinned and nodded, shook our hands and said he thought we were the wisest men he had ever met. He invited us to share lunch with them and we happily accepted.

With full bellies, we walked through the village towards whatever our next encounter was to be. I was getting very tired of all this quest stuff, magic and universal powers. All I wanted was a way out so I could restrain Zaavi, hand him over to the Law Enforcement Agency, and then concentrate on fighting my own corner and trying to save my liberty. Over the past few days, I had allowed thoughts of my impending imprisonment to languish at the back of my mind, but as we made our way through the village, they came back to haunt me. As a successful Freelance Law Enforcer with twenty years' experience, I have brought many people to justice, and I shuddered as I thought of the treatment I would get once word of my presence got around. I doubt I would survive more than six months, and I cannot imagine a pissed off Ambassador out for revenge would bother hiding my identity. Knowing Stell, he would no doubt make a point of spreading it around that Sam Sinclair was now in jail. My ass clenched involuntarily at the thought.

Over the years I have been doing this job, I have never had cause to doubt the Agency or question its standards. As we walked along through those primitive people who had accepted us so readily, I was not sure if the people I had given so many years of service to would have my back when I needed it. My heart sank even lower and I had to admit that for the first time, I doubted it. I had no faith whatsoever in Zaavi's promise to help me out once he got his powers, and I did not believe for a second there were any powers waiting for him anyway. As we found ourselves in the middle of the village, I felt more alone than at any other time in my entire life. I almost cried as the loneliness embraced me and thought back to when I was a kid and my parents had still been alive. They were nice people and treated me well, and I had never doubted their love. In those days, everything was simple. What I did not know or could not fix, my parents would sort out for me with a smile, and I wished very much that they were here to help me.

The sound of raised voices raised me from my self-pity. A crowd had gathered around two women who were arguing. We joined the throng and watched.

I leaned towards a man who stood next to me. "What's going on?"

"The woman with the red garment is demanding the other woman's child."

"Why?" Zaavi asked.

"Because her own child died, and she says her husband took this woman to his bed because she would not lie with him due to her grief. She thinks she is entitled to be the child's mother more than the other woman."

I could not believe what I was hearing. "But that's crazy."

"If they cannot come to a mutual agreement, the child will be cut in half and each woman will get one half."

"What?" Zaavi and I hissed in unison.

"It is the only way to give both women what they want."

I was horrified. "No. There has to be another way."

"If you know of another way, tell us so our women can be at peace again." He ran to the front and yelled for everyone's attention.

"Please everyone, listen to me. Our new friends from beyond our borders say there is another way to deal with this problem." Every face turned towards Zaavi and I, and my cheeks flushed. He nudged me.

"Okay Sam, time to exercise that wonderful diplomatic nature of yours."

I glared at him. "Hey this is your quest asshole, you sort it out."

"Come on, we're working together remember? You're the brains and I'm the muscle."

"Fuck you."

147

The Trials of Nahda

"Later," he replied and winked. I was shocked, but remembered what Cristik told me about Nahdan sexual attitudes. Oh hell, was I doomed to be the bitch of a seven-foot giant with a world domination issue? Anything but that. Forcing my mind away as my ass clenched in fright, I turned back to the crowd.

"My friends, we will think on this for a while. Please be patient."

Everyone nodded and the crowd dispersed until the village leader and the disputed child stood in front of us.

"You have proven to us that you are the wisest of men, and we will wait to hear what you say. The child will remain with you until then." He gave the kid a gentle nudge in the back and walked away. A pair of large brown eyes looked up at me, a single tear still tracing its way down one cheek. He was no more than five, and was scared stiff, so I picked him up and wiped his eyes.

"Hi there little fella. My name is Sam, what is yours?"

"Konyu."

"Hello Konyu, my name is Zaavi."

"Hello. Why was mother shouting? Was she angry at me?"

"No, she could never be angry with you," I said. "She was worried that's all, and mothers sometimes shout when they're worried. Mine used to sometimes."

"Mine still does," Zaavi said.

The kid brightened up and sniffed away his tears. "Will you play with me?"

"Well sure we will. We love to play don't we Sam?"

"We do indeed."

For the next three hours straight, Konyu had us chasing, catching balls, running and jumping, climbing trees, pretending to be all sorts of animals, and all manner of other games and by the time the village leader returned with the offer of food, both Zaavi and I were exhausted. In the village leader's hut, we ate and drank, Konyu sitting between us and quiet for the first time now he had food to distract him. After he had eaten his fill, Zaavi sat him on his lap and sang him to sleep, a beautiful melody whose words were foreign to me.

"That's beautiful, you have a wonderful voice."

"Thanks. My mother sang that song to me when I was his age. I haven't played silly games like that in ages. I enjoyed myself immensely, but I'm exhausted. I shall be more attentive when Shyola and I become parents."

"I used to play with my Boss's daughter when she was that age. She's fifteen now, but I remember like it was yesterday. They have so much energy don't they? How do mothers cope all alone when their men are out at work all day, and many of them with more than one child?"

"I have no idea, but I admire them for it."

"Hey that's it. There's our solution."

"What?"

"The woman could be a nanny for the whole village. People could take their kids to her for a little while so they can get some peace, have a sleep, tend to chores, or whatever. Once they've finished, they collect their kids again. The woman can play with them, even teach them stuff, and she would be real important in their lives."

Zaavi grinned. "What a fabulous idea. She could be the village child watcher."

"Yeah, and everyone could pay her by providing food for her. She won't have time to prepare food while caring for the village children, so the other people could pay her in food on those days."

"Yes. That way, she would feel as if she was mother to everyone's children. That would surely help to ease her grief."

I nodded. "I reckon so. Let's go and tell the people now."

We asked the village leader to call the whole village together, and he nodded. When the crowd was gathered, I stepped forward and regarded the two women. "There is no need to cut this child in half. Both of your needs and rights can be satisfied another way." Everyone mumbled and exchanged glances with each other. I looked at the child's mother. "You are this child's mother yes?" She nodded. "He came from your body and fed at your breast?" Another nod. "He shall remain your child." She cried out and sobbed with relief, while the other woman cried out in anger. I raised a hand to quieten her.

I turned to the grieving woman. "You will also be mother to the child, and every other child in this village." She frowned. "Children need to play, to learn, and they need to be cared for and watched constantly. All the other mothers are very busy. They have other children to care for, husbands to attend to, homes to keep, animals and crops. You can care for the children, play with them, feed them, and teach them, while their mothers are busy with their other tasks. The other mother's will repay your kindness by providing you with food as you will be too busy to provide it for yourself. You will be Village Child Watcher, a most important position. All the children will learn

149

from you, you will teach them to grow up to be strong and wise. You don't need to cut this child in half, when you can care for everyone's children."

The crowd nodded in approval and I was delighted. Konyu's mother came up, took her sleeping son from Zaavi, and thanked us. Everyone said it was a most beneficial thing to have someone to watch children and by the time the crowd dispersed, the grief stricken woman had three children for the afternoon.

The village leader came up to us and smiled, his already lined eyes crinkling at the corners. "Your wisdom, the choices you made, will now become part of our culture and will affect our lives, and the lives of our children, and their children. We are happy with the gift you bestowed upon us." He bowed his head and walked away.

I knew his parting words were significant, and hoped Zaavi knew too. "Do you realise what he was really saying?"

Zaavi frowned. "He said we did a good job."

"Yes, but I'm talking about what he meant, rather than what he actually said."

He shrugged. "Umm, you've lost me."

I tried not to groan aloud as I explained. "When he said our choices would become part of their lives and their kids' lives, he was talking about the effect we have on the lives we touch. Once you influence somebody or something, you can't take that influence back. For good or bad, once it's done there's no changing it. I guess he was really saying, take care that the influence you have on others is positive."

"Oh I see. Yeah, I understand. All one can do is hope that we affect others in a good way. We all want to impress others, don't we?"

"Yeah, but most of us could take a little more care than we do when affecting others. I know that I've affected people negatively, my job requires it, but for every one person whose liberty I take away, I make the lives of many others safer. For me, the good outweighs the bad."

"Whether I influence anyone for good or bad isn't something I've ever had to think about before."

"Then you'd better get into the habit of thinking about it now. The universe could very well depend upon it."

We made our way out of the village and the gloom of the cavern embraced us once again. At the far wall, we saw another set of steps cut into the rock wall. After a drink, we climbed up, and once again, I tried not to

The Trials of Nahda

notice the empty air to my side that tried to pull me from the steps. A door waited for us at the top of the steps and we entered, our legs tired from the climb. By now, my heart was no longer in the quest, if it ever had been, and I wanted to go to sleep and never wake up. Many emotions flooded through me. Anger at the situation was the strongest, followed by an overwhelming sense of impotence, with despair following along at the rear. A few days before, I had been ready to fight the false allegations but now, all I wanted was for everything to stop. The knowledge that the years of dedication and sacrifice had all been for nothing was too painful to bear at that point and I couldn't face it. I was too worn out. I did not know what had brought on this sudden depression, and I was too tired to fight it. Maybe it was being alone again after spending a couple of days amongst the villagers, who gave me a sense of belonging for a while. All I knew at that point was that I needed to sleep and was about to mention it when the door opened into yet another small square room. I almost burst into tears of anguish at the sight.

Vaylon was there waiting for us. "You have successfully completed the trial of wisdom Sword Bearer."

"Thank you," Zaavi said. "We are ready for the final trial."

"No. You go if you want but I've had it."

Zaavi gaped at me. "What? What's up Sam?"

"I'm sick of this, sick of everything. I'm not going on anymore. I just want to lie down and go to sleep and if I don't wake up, that'll be just fine by me. You go on, get your superpowers and rule the universe if you want to, but you're doing it without me."

"What's brought on this dark mood?"

"What kind of life do I have to look forward to huh? I'm a law enforcer who is probably going to jail for something I didn't do. I've been doing this job for twenty years and most of the prisons in the galaxy have inmates I put there. They are going to be mighty happy to have me as a cellmate. I'm not prepared to suffer that when I didn't do anything to deserve it. I never expect anyone else to go to jail when they're innocent, so why should I? All those wasted years I had no friends because of this job, all the times I was nearly killed and all the people who hate me, all because of this job. I lost the only woman I ever loved because of this damned job, and the only best friend I ever had, and I'm just as alone now after twenty years of service, as I was the day my parents died. Now they're just going to put me in jail for my trouble. I've had it Zaavi, I can't do this anymore."

151

"I've come to know you as a fighter Sam." He sat down beside me. Vaylon stood by, ignored by us both. "Why the change?"

"Because I'm scared that's why."

"And does being scared mean you can't fight?"

"I don't have the strength anymore."

"So what are you going to do? Lie here until you starve to death?"

"No need." I reached for my laser pistol.

Zaavi's eyes widened. "I thought you said you had no strength left." I frowned. "People think taking your life is a coward's way, something done by those without the backbone to face their life, but they're wrong, so wrong. You really believe it's so easy to pull the trigger that the greatest coward could do it? I don't. I reckon it's one of the bravest things anyone could do. It's easy to pull the trigger when someone else is doing the dying, but when it's you? Hell no Sam, that takes a whole lot of strength. Strength you just proclaimed you don't have. So that makes you a liar, and I thought a liar would be the last thing I could ever accuse you of being."

Zaavi had done it again; his logic had brought me and my runaway mind to a standstill and I burst into tears.

"Now that's more like it." He stood and looked at Vaylon. "Could we wait until tomorrow to continue?"

"Of course. I will return when you have awakened." With a wave of his hand, another magical meal appeared and he vanished.

The Trials of Nahda

CHAPTER TWELVE

I had not had a meltdown like that in a long time, not since my ex-partner Ren died and the feelings that came out scared me. With hindsight, I can see it was the culmination of many things that have happened to me, but which I had not dealt with in the right way. Given the stress of the situation we were in at that time, it was no wonder. Being trapped underground, having my beliefs and understanding of the very fabric of the universe questioned, and the call from Tinnias, everything festering inside boiled over. This was the first time I had ever contemplated ending it all, and with the benefit of hindsight, I find it difficult now to believe I felt that bad. I can remember feeling it, but the memory does not feel like it belongs to me. It was the lowest I have ever been in my life, and as I sat there on the floor of that small room, I was naked for the first time ever.

From that moment on, I had to try to rebuild myself in a form I would recognise and feel comfortable with, and the way to do that was to decide whether I was going to fight or lie down. Despite being a little fixed in certain areas of my personality, I am flexible about change and upheaval. There have been many times in both my personal life, and with my job, where things were going as I had predicted, and then something happened to turn everything upside down. Every single time that happened, I was able to adapt myself to the changes without too much trouble. Granted, those changes were mostly temporary, but change is change and I have shown I can adapt many times. There was no good reason why I should not be able to adapt this time.

By the time we settled down to sleep, I had reached a point where I understood that this turmoil might be a blessing in disguise. Although my life and my job are unusual in that no two days are ever the same, in another way, it is predictable, and I had settled into a narrow rut in some ways. The job may be eventful and different, but as a person, I was a little fixed. This job means I can't maintain a circle of friends; I'm away from home so much that I could never be the kind of friend they could rely on to be there, so I have always kept myself pretty much of a loner. Without the influence of other people I trust and respect, it is no wonder I became fixed and narrow in my outlook. There was no one else to conflict with, to debate ideas or argue with and have those debates alter my thought patterns.

The Trials of Nahda

I lay down, thought about my scepticism, and asked myself why I cannot accept the prospect of magic being real. When I thought about it in more depth, I had been experiencing it for several days now, and still I refused to accept it. As I lay down and tried to go to sleep I asked myself why, and the only answer that came was fear of what it would mean for my carefully ordered universe. Entertaining the thought that not everything in nature follows a predictable pattern, and that sometimes, a person can will something to be, was frightening for someone as fixed as I had become. I knew I had to unwind or I would run the risk of being someone I would not like to have around. It was time to grow and stretch my mental boundaries a little and by the time we awoke several hours later, the seeds of change had been tentatively sown.

"How are you feeling Sam?"

"I'm fine, thanks. I'm sorry for unravelling. I guess this whole business has affected me more than I would've anticipated."

"No need to apologise to me. You could say what I did was unravelling."

"Huh?"

"Stealing the sword and disappearing in the middle of the night? It's like something out of a bad movie. I was your average stuffy clever guy with a good job and the respect of my peers, and then I go and do something so out of character like that. I think that satisfies the criteria of unravelling don't you?"

I nodded. "Perhaps. I guess I've spent far too many years alone for my own good. My thinking is far more blinkered now than it ever was, but it's obvious that things need to change so I'm going to adapt. It can't be any worse than how I felt last night can it?"

"Exactly. And you never know, it might be the most exciting thing you ever experience. You might just look back on it as amazing and wonderful. Stranger things have happened."

"You never know. Okay, what's next?"

Vaylon appeared and looked at us. "You have one final trial to complete Sword Bearer. Succeed, and you will gain the true power of the universe."

"I will not fail," Zaavi announced. "What am I to do?" Vaylon did not reply, but pointed through a new doorway that he brought into being in the far wall. I took a deep breath and followed Zaavi through into darkness.

"So what is this trial again?"

"Self knowledge."

"I gained a lot of that last night."

"And what does your self knowledge tell you Sam?"

"That I'm a good person, despite what I do for a living. I care about people's wellbeing, even those crazies I have to restrain and take into custody. On the few occasions I've lost my temper with them, I always admit when I'm wrong. I know that I'm a likeable person, my ex-partner Ren would testify to that, and so would my Boss. Like everyone, I have flaws and limitations, but I know what they are and I do try to overcome them. It's not like I think I'm perfect or anything; I'm not in denial about anything. How about you?"

"I know I'm destined to gain the true power of the universe. The fact that my life has taken this dramatic path shows that and I trust destiny. I know I shall wield my powers effectively and do good with them. Everyone who knows me will tell you I'm hard working and dedicated, and I always keep my promises. I know I'm the right one for this job, I know that about myself more than anything else."

I groaned inwardly as I listened. Everything I had heard was about him and those powers he was expecting to receive. There was nothing about whether he was truthful, honest or compassionate with people. He said nothing about knowing his flaws and whether he feels he has the ability to overcome them or not, nor even whether he wants to overcome them. It was all about gaining those powers and what he would do with them. He was the most self-centred person I had ever met and not someone I could rely on unless it benefitted him first. Was the real reason he kept me around this long that he needed me to help him get those damned powers?

We found ourselves walking through another huge dark cavern, and as we picked our way along, I thought about how I would deal with things if I were in Zaavi's position. Superpowers have never entered my thought process except on the one or two occasions when I had to find and capture crazies with weird notions about ruling the universe. Suddenly finding yourself in the position of gaining weird abilities must be a temptation to give in to your most selfish desires, just because you can. To know that you can now do anything you want, no matter how crazy, would be like asking an alcoholic to work in a liquor store but not drink, and even if he did give in and drink, there would be no hangover or liver damage to worry about. Few people would be able to carry that and not lose touch with their real selves, I decided, and it gave me a new insight into Zaavi that told me to be careful. All I know is that if I were able to snap my fingers and have anything I want happen, I would find it very hard not to bring back a few people who died that I love and miss. The true power of the universe, whatever that means, also carries a huge responsibility. All the lives on all the worlds within the universe you have such power over would be very vulnerable to an emotional outburst or bad decision, which could have far reaching consequences. It was obvious to me that such power should not be accessible to any one man, at least no one I had ever known. I remembered someone I once met and smiled at the memory. There is only one man whom I would feel safe with having such power. He is a King I once met during a job and he is the only person I would say has the right mind set and level of compassion and understanding to carry such a burden. Then I thought of Zaavi. The gulf between him and that King was so wide it was too ridiculous to comprehend.

"What do you think will happen to us during this trial?" I asked, just to make conversation.

"I've been wondering about that myself. What can one do to demonstrate self knowledge?"

I thought about it for a moment. "Well umm. I suppose we could be faced with situations that necessitate us knowing whether we're able to get through or not."

"How do you mean?"

"For instance, back there in the first trial with the snake. I know I'm terrified of them, and I also know why. That means I should be able to use that knowledge when I'm faced with them. I know myself well enough to know that despite knowing why I'm scared of them, the fear is so all encompassing that I might fail to overcome it if I was given the chance."

"So you mean we could be faced with situations we're likely to fail in?"

I nodded. "It's a suggestion. Maybe we're meant to fail this trial to demonstrate our self knowledge."

"But as you just said. knowing why you're scared means you should be able to overcome the fear next time. Maybe we're supposed to face the self knowledge of our expected failings, but win through and learn new self knowledge."

The Trials of Nahda

"That's possible too."

Zaavi was about to reply when a sound to our left brought us both to a stop mid stride, instinct driving my hand to my laser pistol. The sound of someone stumbling over loose rocks caught our ears.

"Someone is here with us," Zaavi said.

"Someone or something. We're definitely not alone though. Please let it not be that snake."

For nearly an hour, we walked, and the sounds kept pace with us. We knew we were not alone in the cavern, but so far we had not been attacked or accosted, so I suggested early on that we remain alert but not aggressive, and so far it had paid off.

"At least until we know what we're dealing with. It could be something huge, or tiny and harmless, let's wait and see what happens."

"It might have hundreds of friends."

"More reason not to start something we can't finish." Zaavi snorted in reply but he kept walking and did not do anything provocative.

The cavern stretched on, the darkness all enveloping and my flashlight only served to highlight how dark it was. I found myself longing for eyes like Zaavi's that could see in the low light. When asked about the cavern, he described a huge rocky room that seemed to go on forever, with no distinguishing features at all. A small underground river ran along by the right hand wall and its rushing and tumbling kept us company as we trudged.

Another hour dragged by, and I was about to suggest we stop and rest when Zaavi stopped dead, staring straight ahead. "There's something ahead."

"What?"

He squinted into the darkness. "I'm not sure. It's sticking up out of the floor and reaches up a couple of hundred feet. There's also a sort of umm, structure high up there."

"What sort of structure?"

"Well it looks for all the world like that narrow bridge you crossed the other day, only right up in the air."

"Where does it go? Can you see?"

"No. It goes on too far. Shall we investigate?"

"I guess we're supposed to." I followed as he marched forwards.

We found the structure to be a stone column, into which steps had been cut. They spiralled upwards and Zaavi told me they led onto a platform high above. I swore aloud as I saw the steps had been made for people well over seven feet in height. With Zaavi leading, we climbed up and around the column, and I was glad that all around me was in darkness. Knowing that an aching chasm lay to my right was bad enough, but having to see it as well would have been too terrifying to contemplate. I am okay with heights, but these steps were no more than two feet wide, and there was no handrail from which to gain some sense of security. I clung to the column with both hands, which meant I had to put away my flashlight and do the climb by feel. My legs were killing me, but I did not dare stop to rest for fear of losing my nerve and freezing in terror.

By the time we reached the platform, I was exhausted and the muscles in my legs were twitching uncontrollably. I sat on the square platform to rest and regretted having made this climb. How the hell was I to get down again? When I had calmed down, I opened my eyes and noticed a narrow walkway leading from the platform and away into the darkness ahead. I asked Zaavi if he could see where it led.

"It leads to another platform just like this one."

"Is there anything to be gained from doing this?"

He shrugged. "I haven't the faintest idea, but it's here so I presume we're supposed to make use of it."

"Does it go anywhere we can't get from down on the ground?"

"Not as far as I can tell."

"Then I vote we go back down and walk in relative comfort. Why give ourselves more problems when there's no obvious need?"

"I umm, believe there is a need actually," he said as he peered over the side down into the gloom.

"What?"

"You know earlier you were saying about facing your fears and how you don't think you'd be able to overcome one particular fear?"

"Yeah. So what?"

"Well if we go back down to the ground, you'll have the perfect opportunity to find out if your words are true or not."

"Oh shit. Not that. Not again. What did I do to deserve this huh? I'm a nice guy just trying to do a good job. Who the fuck hates me so much?"

"Okay don't panic Sam. Let's talk about this. Which fear is the greater? The Snake or the walkway?"

"They're both bad."

The Trials of Nahda

"Well then, which carries the greater risk of death or injury, aside from the fear factor?"

"The bridge. I can shoot the snake, or you can slice its head off with that sword, but if I fall from up here, I'm dog meat."

"So you'd rather face the snake?"

"The trouble is I can't see the damned thing. I'm practically blind in here. It's all right for you with those eyes. All I have is a flashlight."

"So you'd rather do the walkway?"

"Oh fuck what a choice." I thought for a few seconds before deciding. "Well if I'm gonna die, I'd rather not do it by falling from a great height. That's a horrible way to go. I'm going down." I stood and walked back to the steps.

"Okay." Zaavi started down ahead of me whilst I sat down and shunted down each step on my ass, hugging the column with both hands like a groupie. Halfway down, something occurred to me that brought me to a stop.

"Hey Zaavi, do you reckon that snake caused those noises we heard earlier?"

"I'd say it's a distinct possibility."

I continued my inelegant shunting. "Hmm. Funny how knowing that it's a snake makes it more fearful. When I thought it was maybe a humanoid or some other creature, I was okay with it, but now I know what it is, it's taken on a whole new meaning for me."

"That's more self knowledge you're learning Sam, how appropriate."

"It's not me that needs it. It's you that needs to do whatever it is to display self knowledge."

"I'll get my chance, don't you worry. Destiny will require me to demonstrate the quality that is required for this trial, so an opportunity will no doubt present itself before too long." I continued down, and decided that would be an interesting experience to witness.

When we reached the bottom, I sat on the bottom step while I got my nerves calmed and my breath back. Zaavi scanned for the snake but could not see it anywhere. I could not decide what was worse, knowing it was there but not being able to see it, or having it trail us in full view. My next thought was to hope we got away from here before we needed to sleep. There was no way I would be able to sleep, knowing that thing was slithering around nearby, and I had mental images of us both fighting to stay awake while the snake stalked us, waiting for us to drop. The only comfort was the knowledge that at least I would be oblivious to my death.

We started out into the darkness, and it was not long before we heard the same sounds we had heard earlier. For an hour or more, Zaavi said there was no sign of the snake, and then he caught a glimpse of its tail going behind a rock to our left, right where the sound had come from.

Zaavi stopped walking and turned to me. "Listen Sam. Why don't we take a pro-active stance and go flush it out and kill it? That way you won't have to worry anymore, and I have to admit that it's beginning to bother me too. We're vulnerable out here, and it's big. All the time we're getting more and more uptight about it, we're losing our focus and that could cost us. We would've been safer up top." He indicated up to the platform. He was trying to make me feel guilty but I wasn't having any of it.

"If you remember, the last time we happened across a bridge that narrow, you said your height and weight would not be an advantage."

"Yeah, that's true but if we," he started but the loud screech cut him off. We both snapped our heads up and I saw his mouth drop open in obvious shock. His eyes widened in horror, and I knew I did the right thing getting away from up there.

"Oh shit," he whispered.

"What?"

"There are creatures up there."

"What sort of creatures?"

"Flying creatures."

I gaped at him in horror. "Oh fuck. Do they see us?"

"I don't know, but they've made their nest on that second platform."

"What? So if we'd gone across the walkway, we'd have walked right into them?"

"Yeah."

I glared at him. "Well that settles it. Next time you want to get funny with me about not wanting to do the walkway, remember this moment huh? How it could've gone but didn't."

He grinned. "Okay. Come on, let's keep going. The sooner we find a doorway or something, the better."

"And keep one eye on the sky and the other on the snake."

"My eyes may be different to yours Sam, but they don't move independently y'know."

161

The Trials of Nahda

"It's a figure of speech. Just keep watching okay? I wish I had some night sight goggles, or that low light enhancement the Drycenians have. I could sure use it now."

"What enhancement is that?"

"They do something to their eyes to give them natural low light ability like you have, but they can see in total darkness. It's really cool, and damned useful."

"How do you know? The Drycenians keep themselves very private, no one knows anything about them, apart from they're supposed to have amazing technology."

"They do. I met them once, during a job. They're wonderful people."

"Really?" He seemed genuinely impressed.

"Yeah."

"Wow, I envy you Sam. I've never met them, but I'd love to. Everyone would love to. Mind you, when I get the true power of the universe, I'll be able to do whatever I want, so I will get to meet them after all. I'll say hello to them for you shall I?"

"Yeah, you do that buddy." Was he losing his mind now the trials were almost finished? I hoped he was not going crazy on me before I managed to get out. Having a seven-foot high psycho on my hands while being trapped underground was not my idea of fun.

I was longing to stop and rest my legs, but the desire to get to safety, away from the snake and the flying things, was greater than my physical discomfort. I plodded on, and as we walked, I noticed Zaavi getting a bit ahead of me. If he ran off and left me alone now, I would not hesitate to shoot him for being asshole enough to do such a thing. At the same time, I felt annoyed with myself for being afraid of the snake, and for being so vulnerable down there in the dark.

"Hey," I called as loud as I dare. My voice echoed around the chamber and he turned. "Wait for me would ya?"

"You could try and hurry it up a bit."

I ran to catch him up. "Hey c'mon. Your strides are twice the length of mine, and you can see in the dark. Don't be an asshole."

"I'm not. It's just that we really need to get out of here as soon as we can, and you're slowing us down."

"Well I'm sorry I'm being such a damned burden to you. I'm sorry I saved your sorry ass by completing those puzzles for you, but I'm more sorry

162

that you were too stupid to do them yourself. Where would you be if I wasn't here huh? Back in the labyrinth with a broken ankle and sobbing for the superpowers you wouldn't be getting." Zaavi put his hands on his hips and closed his eyes, trying to calm his rising anger. At once, I was back in the cavern with the tribe of primitive people and remembered what happened the last time we fought.

"Look, Zaavi, I'm sorry okay? That was rude and I apologise. I'm well aware of the dangers down here, and of my vulnerability. I guess I'm a burden to you but I do have value, I've proved it so far. Maybe that makes up for my shortcomings huh?"

"You have helped me out Sam, and I'm grateful. I guess I owe you for it, but don't call me stupid, please."

"I won't. Let's get going shall we? What the fuck is that noise?" The moment I asked the question, we both knew what it was. The slithering was getting louder and I knew without a doubt that the snake was getting closer. The acoustics of the chamber made it almost impossible to tell from which direction the sound came, and it was too late that I realised the snake was right behind me. I whirled around on one heel and we locked eyes. As we gazed at each other, I went cold to the bone. Time stood still as the cavern doubled in size around me and I shrank to a couple of inches high. The snake was no more than six feet away, its front rearing up into the air. I met its mesmerising gaze, saw the similarity with Zaavi's eyes and presumed they shared a common ancestor. As my senses came back, I heard thudding footsteps that quickly faded into the distance. The asshole had run away and left me to fend for myself against a giant snake. Without me having to think about it, my mind switched from all-encompassing fear to naked survival instinct, and my shaking hand fumbled for my laser pistol. Panicking, I fought with the holster as the snake drew back its head, readying itself to strike. It was as I saw it thrust forward that I yelped in fear, dropped my pistol in sheer terror and fell to the ground, covering my head with my arms and hoping the end would be quick.

I heard the slithering coming towards me, then a crunch, followed by a screech of pain. I risked a peek through my arms. The snake was writhing around, curling itself around its prey and squeezing the life from it. The giant bird-like creature must have been flying silently down towards me from the darkness above, and I had not been aware of it. I saw clawed feet and part of a leathery wing sticking from between the coils and guessed the thing must be at least twice the size of me, if not Zaavi. At once, I was transported back to a hellish planet I remembered from a previous job, one where I was caught in a terrible nightmare with creatures very much like the one that was still dying within the snake's deadly embrace. All sorts of emotions ran through me at that moment. Horror at what had almost happened, relief at having not become something's dinner, disgust at the sight before me, and gratitude at the snake for saving me. In all my years of carrying this phobia, never once would anyone have been able to convince me that one day, I would be saying thank you to a gigantic snake for saving my sorry ass. At that moment I realised the true meaning of the phrase, the enemy of my enemy is my friend.

I sat down and watched the snake kill and eat its prey. I was far too puny to be of interest to it. There was nowhere near enough meat on my bones to fill his belly, and I reckoned he would leave me alone in favour of the bigger prey above. This was why he was following us. He knew the flying things would come after us, and was happy to use us as bait for his own prey. What did Zaavi call it? Simby-something? That is what we had, the snake and me. It seemed likely to me that he would choose to continue following me; I was useful as bait for his own prey so I figured that he would take the opportunity while it lasted. At least I hoped so.

After what seemed like a long time, the snake finished his meal and moved off, so I stood and followed him over to the left hand wall of the cavern. At least there was one direction from which I was safe from ambush. As I continued my course through the cavern, I heard the slithering not more than twenty feet away and laughed to myself when I realised it gave me some comfort. After a couple of hours, I was tired and took the risk of sitting down to rest. The slithering stopped. Taking off my boots, I massaged my toes and aired my feet as I stretched out my legs to let my muscles recover. Clambering over the rocky floor of the cavern was hard on the legs, and I was glad I worked out every day. What state I would be in if I didn't, was too terrifying to think about, so I pushed it from my mind as I took a drink and settled back against the rock wall.

I awoke some hours later and at first, could not work out where I was. I remembered sitting down to rest, but was not aware of having fallen asleep and silently cursed myself for it. As wakefulness took hold, I sensed a body to my right. Reaching out, I touched what I thought was yet another dark grey rock, to find my hand on the body of the snake which slept all around me, and I snapped my hand away in horror. As I slept, it had curled itself around my body in a protective circle and was itself now sleeping. I did not know whether it was protecting its precious living bait, or if it wanted to share my body warmth. Thoughts of the horrific experience when I was six and awoke to find a huge snake asleep on me flew back into my mind and I almost cried out. With the greatest effort of sheer willpower I have ever been able to muster, I fought through the fear and allowed that six-year-old boy to return to sleep. With trembling fingers, I reached out again and touched it, expecting it to be slimy, and was surprised to find it dry. It was cold but definitely dry; its scales making it so smooth it appeared wet and shiny, like something covered in slime.

"Thanks for saving my ass."

I am going to stop for a bit and get something to eat. I have some reports to write up and I need to Call Tinnias for an update on something. I will carry on in a few hours. This is Sinclair V-Log PA884/R, data log reference point 1956365/7989.

The Trials of Nahda

CHAPTER THIRTEEN

Okay I'm back, sorry to jump out like that. Now where were we? This is Sinclair V-Log PA884/R, data log reference point 1956365/7990, continuing report.

When the snake showed signs of waking up, helped along by my uncomfortable shuffling due to a full bladder, I took a pee and headed off. Within a few minutes, I heard the slithering, though this time it seemed slow and laboured. It took me a while to remember that this was a cold-blooded creature, so I slowed my pace a little. How could a cold-blooded creature live down here with no sun? I was again reminded of Vaylon's remark about truth and untruth. We took that to mean that much of what we might experience may not be real. I guessed the snake was another of Vaylon's tricks, which further helped allay my phobia.

As I walked and the snake, whom I soon christened Squeezer, slithered along twenty feet to my left, I told him about myself, my life, and my job. I guess it was a kind of therapy for me and I supposed that he did not mind. He was a good listener and it helped keep the creeping loneliness away from the front of my mind. Ours was indeed a working relationship. The flying things did not dare get too near for fear of their greatest predator, but Squeezer kept far enough away to lure them into a false sense of security and it was not long before he was enjoying another meal.

By the end of the second day, I was wracked with hunger but did not know if Vaylon would bother giving me another magical meal. I was not the Sword Bearer, so I figured I was not worth saving now Zaavi had gone on without me. Squeezer was a good listener, but offered no solution to my problems as I voiced my concerns. As I found a place to settle, I wished there was wood for a fire, and tried to prepare my mind for another cold night on the rocky floor of the cavern. After a few minutes trying to find a comfortable position to lie down in, Vaylon appeared, and with a wave of his hand, a dish of meat and vegetables appeared, along with a jug of hot liquid and a thick blanket.

"No one is ever unworthy of saving".

"Thank you." I could not decide whether to grab the food first or the blanket.

"You have done well to survive this long, and I am confident you will get through and see the sun again."

"Before I get sent to prison or after?"

"Your life, your future, depends upon you Samelan Sinclair. It will be what you make it, and you can make it anything you wish it to be. All it takes is the will and determination. Do you have those things?"

"I do, but others have them too. They have more power than me and lower moral standards than mine. I fear their power to change my future will be stronger than my own."

"But despite that, you will still try, because that is who you are."

I nodded. "Yeah. I always have been a bit stubborn where my personal freedom is concerned."

"Eat well, sleep and then continue. You are close to completing the quest."

"Thank you for the food and the blanket. I really need them both right now."

Vaylon said nothing. He bowed his head, and vanished.

With a full belly and a wonderfully warm blanket, I was asleep within a few minutes and awoke to find Squeezer snuggled up close around me, my body warmth filtering out to him and keeping him alive. I allowed myself a few minutes to lie there in the warmth and found considerable comfort knowing Squeezer was there keeping me safe. When my bladder became uncomfortable, I stretched, yawned and got up. Squeezer's coils were all around me and my movement had not woken him. I was bursting to pee, and had to resort to physically climbing over him. All the time I expected him to wake and kill me, but apart from regarding me with one sleepy eye, he ignored me and went back to sleep. After clambering back inside the safety of his coils, the cold got the better of me and I snuggled back under the blanket to wait for him to wake up and signal the time to get going.

Small stones skittered down and hit me on the head, raising me from my slumbers. Squeezer was awake and slithering around, so I got up, folded the blanket and slung it around my shoulders.

"Okay, let's get going huh?" I looked at my new companion and set off, flashlight leading the way.

Several hours later, and another meal for Squeezer, the end wall of the cavern loomed into view in the gloom. I prayed there would be a door, a set of stairs or something that would mean I was not a prisoner here and quickened my pace a little. Perhaps I would find Zaavi, frantic as he searched for a way out, or perhaps even dead on the floor. In my anger at being abandoned, I hoped to find his dead body half-eaten by the flying things, but remembered his size and strength were useful, so I checked myself.

A walk along the bottom of the far wall revealed two options. The river that ran along the right hand wall disappeared through a large hole, and off to hell knows where. If I took this option, it would mean two things. I would have to swim, which is not a problem for me, but it would also mean I would get soaking wet and freezing cold, which was a problem. With no wood to light a fire, drying my clothes would be impossible and I would likely die of exposure before getting out. The second option was a set of steps leading up and into the darkness above. This option had its own problems. First, it would take me well within the territory of the flying things. Second, I cannot see them in the dark, and as they fly in complete silence, my chances of avoiding them would be very low. I had no idea whether Squeezer would follow me up there, but with no other obvious options, I had little choice. After a deep breath, I started up the stairs, pressing myself against the rock wall to my left to try to avoid the aching chasm to my right. To my relief, Squeezer did indeed follow me up and I was so thankful I told him so aloud. The steps ended in a large ledge overlooking the cavern, the end of the high walkway adjoining the far end telling me that this was the obvious option, especially as the high walkway would have brought me here too.

The opening to a tunnel invited me in, and with a deep breath, I gripped my flashlight and entered. I found a short tunnel, which opened out into another ledge within a much smaller cavern, and my joy at having left those flying things behind vanished. Another huge chasm fell away into darkness ahead, and this time not even a narrow bridge waited for me. Walking up and down the ledge, I scanned the rock walls for steps but saw none. I heard the river rushing below, and thought that perhaps I should have taken that swim after all.

"Shit and fuck." I tore my hands through my hair in frustration. The chasm ahead was around thirty feet across, another ledge on the other side and another dark tunnel entrance laughed at my predicament. Squeezer crossed the open space with ease; slithering down the sheer rock face into darkness, then appeared moments later coming up the other side. For a moment, I had a fleeting image of myself astride his body as we both sailed across to the other

169

side. For several minutes, I did consider it. Would he allow me to ride him? I doubted it; real or imaginary he was a wild animal and although we enjoyed a mutually beneficial working relationship, I did not believe that would extend to giving me rides. Even if he would allow it, his body was so smooth and shiny that I feared falling off. With nothing to hold on to, I would be reliant upon nothing but balance. No, I concluded that it was out of the question. There was nothing for it, I would have to find a way to climb across on the side walls, or go back and swim for it.

After careful examination of both side walls of the small cavern, with Squeezer going back and forth over the chasm impatiently, I picked the right. It was more uneven than the left, with more possibilities for hand and foot holds. After a few minutes during which I tried to get my courage up, I reached for the nearest hand hold and started making my way across. Everything was going pretty well until I got three quarters of the way over. Although it was damned hard work and I was exhausted, I thought I would make it without killing myself. One wrong foot hold was all it took, one moment of carelessness, one moment of sheer bad luck and I felt myself falling. I cried out in shock as empty air embraced me, and as I waited for the inevitable crunch, I squeezed my eyes shut despite the darkness. After what felt like several long minutes, but which was probably no more than a couple of seconds, I entered the river below. The icy water took my breath and froze my bones and it took me a moment or two for my chilled brain to understand that I had fallen into the river and not onto the rock floor. Naked survival instinct kicked in and with a monumental effort, I fought for the surface and gasped in air as I scrabbled for the rocky shoreline nearby. I was thankful the river was no more than ten feet wide, my body was seizing up with the cold and I knew I would not last much longer.

I lay on the rock floor of the cavern, my body shaking so hard I thought I might fall apart at my frozen joints. I saw Squeezer slithering down the valley towards me, the uneven nooks and minute ledges giving him enough purchase to make the journey safely. Although still a little scared of his sheer size, I found myself hoping he would wrap himself around me and warm me up. Being a cold-blooded creature of course meant he would not enjoy cuddling up to me at that moment, so I guessed I was on my own. What he did do, stunned me, and still does now. He kept slithering behind me, between myself and the river. Using his muscular body, he inched me away from the edge by undulating his body and pushing me little by little. I thought he was trying to encourage me to get up and walk, but I was so cold I could not imagine I would be able to make my legs work. I lifted my head and caught sight of the blanket that had fallen from my shoulders, landing a few feet from the water. It was dry and a dry blanket meant a chance at warmth.

I stuttered through my chattering teeth. "Thanks Squeezer. I get the point." The sight of the blanket and the knowledge that with it, I had a chance at not freezing to death, gave me renewed hope, and this gave me the strength to drag myself towards it. With numb fingers, I struggled to remove my clothes, but I did not want to get the blanket wet and ruin my chances of being warm. Eventually I shivered naked on the rocks and wrapped the blanket around myself and within minutes, I felt sensation returning to my extremities. As the blood flowed again, I cried with relief. The shock of the fall, the struggle through the water and the adrenaline rush that accompanied it all, sent me into a fitful sleep within minutes and I awoke some time later, warm and with Squeezer once again wrapped around me. I heard the squeals of the flying things and guessed they knew how to negotiate the tunnel I had walked through. I stood and looked over the top of Squeezer's body and my mouth dropped in shock. There on a rock were my now dry clothes in a neat pile, alongside my backpack, a bowl of food that steamed in the cold, and a jug of hot liquid. Clambering carefully over Squeezer's sleeping body, I made my way over to the food, wincing as small stones stabbed the soles of my bare feet.

Once dressed and re-wrapped in the blanket, I ate the hot food; meat and vegetables in a rich gravy with a hunk of bread on the side that warmed me inside. I drank the hot liquid, which was a little sweet for my usual taste, but I guessed it would give me energy. After a few minutes, I felt the need to lie down again, so I clambered back into the relative safety of Squeezer's coils and was asleep within minutes.

I was woken by Squeezer moving around, so after a drink and a pee, I took some time to assess the situation and try to figure a way out. We were at the bottom of the chasm I had been trying to cross earlier, the two steep walls loomed up on either side, and equally steep ones loomed at each end, which continued up and met overhead in the domed roof of the small cavern. I knew which wall I had to climb to reach the new ledge and doorway, but I could not fathom how it was to be done. I went over to the river. It disappeared through a hole in the wall and out of sight. I did not fancy getting wet again, so I turned away and resumed my examination of the rock wall. Squeezer could make it up the almost sheer rock face in seconds, the tiny undulations and inequalities in the rock giving him enough purchase to slither up without a problem. How the hell could he make it without legs or arms, and yet I was incapable? The irony was not lost on me.

The only possible solution was a narrow crack in the wall, just wide enough for me to stand in. I knew what I had to do, but I had never done it before and I doubted I had enough strength to make it all the way up. With no other solution, I had no choice, so after putting my backpack on back to front and fixing the blanket to its straps, I stood sideways in the crack. With my back against one side of the crack, I shunted upwards slowly and painfully. Using each leg in turn, and pressing my ass into the wall behind me for extra purchase, I made slow progress up the wall. Every few minutes I had to push my back hard against the wall so I could stretch both legs out in front to rest my knees. I have no idea how long it took me, but I was almost at the point of giving up and sliding down, when I felt something bump against the top of my head.

Craning my head around, I found that the crack stopped in a blind end and I yelled out in frustration and despair. I craned my head as far to my left as I dared, and peered up. The ledge was above me and I cried out in relief. Reaching an arm up, I grabbed hold of the edge and tested it for strength. It held. I knew this was going to be hard, but I had to try, so after unhooking my backpack and the blanket, I threw them up and over the edge. After taking a minute to rest my knees, I shunted up as far as I could, before reaching out and up with my hands. I had to risk leaning out a little to make room to shunt my legs a little further up, and the empty space behind me throbbed against my back. I felt horribly vulnerable in that position, my whole body shook with adrenaline and I do not remember breathing for fear of losing my focus. If I fell again, I would not survive. With a determined effort, I leaned out and took most of the weight of my upper body on my hands. My fingers found small ridges and inequalities in the rock floor of the ledge, which I used to brace my hands and help stop them from slipping off. Squeezer slithered around above me and I wished he could send a coil down and lift me up.

Bracing my legs against the back wall of the crack, whilst holding my upper body with my hands, I walked my legs up as far as I could. Another deep breath and I pushed off with my legs, whilst pulling with my arms and I got my head and chest above the ledge. My legs were now swinging in empty air and for an agonising second or two, they flailed as I scrabbled for purchase.

The Trials of Nahda

Once I found the wall of the cavern with my feet, I was able to pull myself up with my arms and with a loud grunting effort, I flopped over the ledge and rolled onto my back. Every muscle and bone in my body hurt, the blood in my temples throbbed and my throat was raw but I had made it. After allowing myself a minute to get my strength back, I had a long drink, picked up the blanket and backpack, and stood. I felt pleased with myself at having made the climb, and yelled in triumph, my voice echoing around and flying back at me.

"Hah, can't keep this little guy down for long motherfucker!"

The ledge was identical to the one across the gap from which I had come, and as Squeezer was already making his way into the darkness of the tunnel, I shrugged and followed.

The tunnel wound its way along and down, in a gradual sloping curve around to the right and in places, I found myself having to stoop. At the bottom, it opened out into a small cave into which the river ran, creating a pool that led away through a small hole in the far wall. Squeezer suddenly took off like a rocket and by the time I entered the small cave, his prey was taking its dying breath in his embrace. I heard its bones breaking and winced at the sound.

"Squeezer, you're awesome but could you do that a little quieter?"

I sat on a rock while he ate his meal and took the time to fill my water bottle from the pool. It was cold down there, so I wrapped the blanket around myself while I waited for Squeezer to finish. I thought about this peculiar relationship we had, and it both amazed and scared me. On a previous job, the one during which my ex-partner Ren died, circumstances were such that I ended up with a pet, a huge scary looking thing who I named Essy, after my ship. She lived with me for around eight months or so before she was killed taking a bullet for me, and I was very attached to her. I recognised the feelings as I thought of Squeezer and laughed at the thought of hauling a thirty-foot snake around on jobs. It was not going to work, so I mentally detached myself a little and settled for respecting him for the role he was playing in my survival. Common sense told me he was not real, and was another product of Vaylon's magical doodlings, but I was glad that I was playing an equally important role in his survival, and was glad that I now felt more at ease with him. Maybe this would end my snake phobia.

Once Squeezer was satisfied, we continued and found another tunnel entrance to the left of the hole through which the river plunged. The ceiling in here was lower than the last tunnel, in places I was almost doubled over and I hoped that I was not going to end up crawling on my belly. Squeezer was good at it but I doubted my own ability to move in such a manner. The tunnel wound around and began to climb uphill, which was a relief to me. Although I knew I was underground, the knowledge that I was going uphill gave me hope. Funny how your mind works sometimes.

Round another left-handed bend, and we exited the tunnel to find ourselves on yet another ledge. Another yawning chasm lay in front of us, its far side lost in the gloom. A bridge ran across the void, and I was thankful to notice this one was wide enough for two men to walk abreast. Squeezer was already slithering across it, so I guessed it must be safe and followed. As we walked, I noticed that this bridge had a handrail at some time in the past, for I spotted post holes at regular intervals, and broken ends of now rusting metal stuck up from some of them. At one point, we came to a much wider section; a large circular space into which the narrow bridge entered and exited out the other side. I assumed it was some kind of viewing platform and imagined people strolling along, gathering together and admiring the underground view. This must have been inhabited at some time in the past, maybe even an underground city of some kind. The memory of Zaavi telling me that this was once a Temple came back to me. The Temple of Power he had called it, and I remembered how appropriate it was that a fusion reactor now lay on the site. Maybe there was once a city tending to the temple and its needs.

It took twenty minutes to reach the other end of the bridge, and by the time we got there, we had passed another three of the circular viewing platforms as I now assumed them to be. How in the hell men had built this structure was beyond me, and I was seriously impressed. Maybe they did it with magic, I thought to myself and laughed at having even considered the option. When I reached the end of the bridge, I saw a wide ledge and a double doorway. This ledge had been made by the hand of man; that much was obvious right away. The edges were straight and smooth, the angles precise and a stone balustrade still stood around the entire circumference. The doorway was, as everything else connected with Nahda and its people, too big for me, but that was not what caught my eye and made me gasp. The whole of the double door and its surround was carved from the same grey stone as the natural bedrock and must have weighed hundreds of tons. The rock at each side of the two doors had been carved so that a series of stone loops stuck out down each outer edge of each door, forming hinges. These loops encircled pillars of the same stone, and when I examined them up close, I saw each loop hinge was lined with some kind of metal. The doors themselves were carved with swirls and loops, stylised leaves and vines and some kind of continuous looping knot. I looked at the looping knot and smiled. It reminded me of a maze or labyrinth.

"That's a labyrinth," I said to Squeezer, who was slithering around the edge of the ledge, winding his body in and out of the balustrade. He did not seem that interested, so I turned my attention back to the doors and the problem of how to open them. Their sheer size told me that I would never have the strength alone to push them open, and I saw nothing like a switch or even a counterweight system. Each of the two doors had a raised bar about five feet from the ground that spanned the whole width of the door, and it occurred to me that they were at the right height for a Nahdan who might wish to lean against them to push the doors open. Images of banks of slaves in loincloths came to my mind, all sweating and leaning on the bars to open and close them.

"I watch too many bad movies." I put my hands around the bar and pushed to test the resistance.

The door slid open and I gaped in shock. Stepping through, I found myself in a tiny market square. Assuming the door led into a building, I was surprised to find myself in a courtyard surrounded by smaller buildings. A fountain, long since run dry and covered with moss and other minute plant life lay in the centre, stone seating arranged around its circumference. Everything was carved out of the same grey stone as the surrounding bedrock, but mouldering fragments of cloth still hung limp from the seating. In my mind's eye, I saw bright cushions and fabrics adorning this dark architecture; it must have been amazing.

Turning, I saw Squeezer coiled in the doorway, his eyes fixed upon me. The only time he ever looked at me that way, was the first time I saw him, when he caught the flying creature that had been flying down to catch me.

"Hey buddy, come on in. This is the only option we have so I guess we go this way." He lifted the front six feet of his body off the ground and met me eye to eye. We gazed at each other for long moments and I knew without being told that this was the end of the line for us. He had brought me as far as he was able and knowing I was now to be alone saddened me.

"You're not coming are you? Thank you, for everything." Another couple of seconds passed before, with a flick of his tongue, he slithered out of my life. I did not know why he chose then to leave me, and for a moment, I contemplated running after him and remaining with him. Real or not, he afforded me safety, and most important for me, companionship. It was as he left me that the importance of his role in my life hit me. A silly thought struck me and I laughed. If I did get out of here alive, no matter what happened to me afterwards, I would get a snake tattooed on my body somewhere. It would be my homage to Squeezer.

Forcing myself not to dwell on my sudden loneliness, I turned back and examined my surroundings. The obvious thing to do was investigate the buildings, so I worked my way around from left to right and found them all empty of life. Furniture remained, rotten and decayed, and here and there I saw garments, kitchen utensils and even a weaving loom stood in one building, a few threads still hanging rotten from the frame. Seven small buildings stood in my immediate vicinity, and once I had investigated them all, I followed the path between buildings five and six, to find myself in a tiny street. On each side, I found more small buildings that revealed nothing of interest within their walls except for one, which may once have been a bar, inn or some other gathering place where drink was brewed and served. In another, I found an oil lamp and a large vat of oil, which lit after a bit of fumbling on my part. It gave a comforting glow to the room and I decided to stop and ask for a meal, which once again appeared out of thin air the moment I asked. I was getting used to accepting the idea of magic. I now did not hesitate to call for a meal and felt confident it would appear. My whole way of thinking about the nature of the universe was changing, and while I found the changes unsettling and wished everything could stay the way I had always believed, I knew I had no choice but to evolve as my environment demanded.

Once my hunger was satisfied, I set out. I considered taking the oil lamp with me but found one of my flashlights still had a full energy cell and even though the one I had been using was almost dead, I had several spare cells in my backpack. I could do without more stuff to carry anyway, so I reluctantly left it behind. The street turned through ninety degrees and I found myself in another tunnel, this one big enough for me to walk upright. After walking for a half hour, I noticed the tunnel was getting damp, and drips from the ceiling found their way down the back of my neck, no matter what I did to avoid it. Puddles littered the tunnel floor and as I rounded another bend, I noticed a pile of rubble up ahead. Part of the rock wall had collapsed and the rubble lay around my feet. I picked my way carefully over the pile, which was loose and moved under my weight with each step. It was at that moment my foot settled upon what looked like a large rock that felt firm underfoot, so I moved my weight forward to take another step. As I did so, the rock moved, my foot slipped and I went over. I heard the crack and felt the pain of something breaking inside my ankle and I screamed in pain as I sprawled headlong. The pain was more intense than anything in my experience, and I lay there screaming in agony for many minutes until my throat was sore. Trembling in agony, and sweating with adrenaline, I tried to get into a more comfortable position but it was too painful to move, so I lay there in agony until the shock sent me to sleep.

CHAPTER FOURTEEN

The pain woke me, both from my ankle and my back from the position I lay in. Instinct took over and I tried to move into a more comfortable position as I awoke, which sent red-hot pain stabbing up from my ankle, through my thigh, and into my lower abdomen. Immediately awake, I yelled in agony as I remembered my predicament, and forced myself to keep still, my eyes rolling back into my head with the pain. Biting my tongue in an effort to gain more control, I waited until the pain subsided to a more manageable level. I knew I had to move, so I took a few deep breaths, then moving my whole body as one, I rolled onto my side, the broken ankle now resting on top of my good leg. Pain seared through me, taking my breath away for long moments, so I lay there and prayed for it to subside. With great difficulty, I managed to wriggle out of my backpack, and rummaged for a sedative dart. I keep these as part of my restraining kit, for those prisoners who choose not to submit to restraint willingly and they are very effective, rendering a person unconscious within twenty seconds. Another rummage and I found my auto injector. I didn't want to be unconscious, so I bled two thirds of the sedative out of the dart, before loading the remainder into the injector and jabbing myself in the thigh. It was not a painkiller, but it rendered me dozy enough not to care quite so much.

Feeling drunk, I got the backpack on and dragged myself along the tunnel, pulling with my arms and using my good leg to push from behind. I was soon soaked through from the wet tunnel, and the numbing cold dulled the searing agony a little, so I tried not to complain. It took me four hours to drag myself along the tunnel and find the bottom of another flight of far too steep stairs, which I knew right away I was not going to be able to climb in my condition. I slumped against the first step and cried with despair, the sedative making it difficult for me to retain emotional control. I was in agony, exhausted, cold and thirsty but did not have the strength or the will to rummage in my backpack for my water bottle, so I allowed myself to fall asleep.

A searing pain dragged me from the depths of my sleep and I awoke feeling as if my ankle had been torn clean off. I screamed in agony, and heard my own screams echoing around me within the cavern. Another stab of red-hot pain took over my consciousness and I begged for death amidst my screams. Anything please, just take me and stop the pain. A thousand other screams came at me from all directions within the cavern, but I was so consumed with pain that I barely felt my leg being restrained and something tied tightly around it. The pain gripped my entire being and all I could do was scream and beg for oblivion. A prick of pain in my thigh caught my attention, but I was in too much pain to care. Long minutes went by, during which I cried aloud in pain, but it eventually diminished enough for me to notice that it was getting less, and after several minutes, I was able to wake fully and notice Zaavi crouching over me.

"Zaavi? You fucking shit. You left me you asshole."

"I know, and I'm sorry Sam. I thought you were dead when that snake appeared behind you. There was no way I could take that thing on and save you in time, so I ran for my life."

"So why come back now?"

"I heard you screaming. This whole place echoed with it and I was amazed to know you survived, so I ran back and found you at the bottom of those steps with a broken ankle. How did it happen?"

I was so relieved not to be alone that I could not maintain my anger any longer. "I slipped on some wet rocks back in that last tunnel. I guess I'm glad to see you. What have you done to me?"

"I'm chief first aider at the museum, and I always carry a basic med kit with me whenever I leave home. I had to realign your ankle before splinting it, and I've given you a shot of painkiller. How in all the world did you escape the snake?"

I grinned. "Squeezer? He was a good friend to me."

"Huh? Are you delirious?"

"What did you call it? Simby something or other?"

"Symbiosis."

"That's it. That's what me and my friend Squeezer had. He wasn't after us. He wanted those flying things. They wanted us, and he allowed us to be bait for them, and hung around close enough to grab 'em when they came for me."

"Wow."

"I fell from the wall in that other cavern; you know the one right after the big cavern with the flying things? I didn't make it all the way across, and I fell into the river below. I struggled to get out of the water; it's colder than anything I've ever experienced by the way. Anyway, he helped me out of the water, pushed me with his body."

"You are delirious after all."

"Nope. When I slept, he curled his body around me like a protective wall so the flying things didn't get me while we both slept. He was too big for them to take on, so I was safe with him. He kept me alive because I attracted his prey, and he afforded me safety from them. It was a working relationship."

"That's incredible. I've never heard of anything like that before."

"He is quite a guy." Now that the pain was wearing off, I felt much better. "Where are we?"

"Oh, I carried you up the steps and into here where there's more room to sort you out. We've not come far."

"Thanks I guess, for coming back for me." I chose not to say so, but I doubted his story about presuming my death and hearing me screaming. Everything in my mind told me he was here because he needed me for something, but seeing the circumstances I was in, I had to admit I was glad he felt I still had a use.

"I'm sorry for leaving you Sam. It was an honest mistake, and not surprising given the circumstances. That snake is huge."

"How far ahead did you get?" I noticed him hesitate a moment too long before replying, which confirmed he was lying.

"Not that far actually. That door over there leads into another long tunnel, which ends in another small square room, but there's no door out of it."

"Were you bothered by the flying things?"

"One caught me in the cave with the pool." He showed me his chest. Several long scratches stretched from his right shoulder down to his navel and I winced as I imagined how he got them. "I managed to injure it with the sword and run away through the next tunnel and thankfully it chose not to follow me in there."

I grinned, remembering how Squeezer shot past me in the tunnel and how I'd found him chowing down on something. "Squeezer says thanks for the easy meal."

Zaavi laughed. "He ate it? That's great. Where did you get the blanket?"

"Vaylon. When I was cold, I wished for warmth and immediately, he appeared with a hot meal and this blanket. Later, when I fell into the river, I took my wet clothes off and wrapped myself in this, and when I woke up, my clothes were dry and folded, waiting for me. He's been providing me with a hot meal each day, a hot drink too and I'm mighty grateful for them I can tell you."

"That's great." I noticed a quick flash of darkness cross his face, which told me he did not think it great at all. I was tempted to question him, but thought better of it and kept my mouth shut.

"We might as well get going then. We can rest and have a meal perhaps."

"Okay, come on, let me help you up. Here, use this as a walking stick." He handed me a stout piece of wood.

"Where did you get this?"

"From one of the buildings back along that tunnel. I needed something to splint your ankle with, and I found some wood that wasn't too rotten."

Zaavi and I made our way along the next long tunnel, me hobbling along behind in much less pain now, but he soon got ahead of me. Should I call out for him to wait? I decided against it. I had come this far without him, and although he had helped me, I did not want to rely on him anymore. Besides, if what he said was true, and a blind-ended room was waiting for us, where could he disappear to? I saw him disappear round a corner up ahead, and to my surprise, saw him come back and look for me.

"Sorry. I'm a bit slower than my normal slow."

"No problem Sam. Take your time. You want me to carry you?"

"No I'm okay thanks; this stick is helping just fine. Is it far?"

"Just another couple of hundred yards or so."

Sure enough, a small square room waited for us and no doorway was evident anywhere.

I thought this odd; surely Zaavi should have been offered the chance to continue? "I wonder why Vaylon didn't appear and offer you the chance to continue?"

He shrugged but did not look at me or reply, so I guessed there was something he did not want to tell me. Not wanting to push the matter yet, I kept my mouth shut and sat down in a corner. "Are you hungry Sam? I'm starving."

"A meal is always welcome."

The Trials of Nahda

"Welcome Sword Bearer." Vaylon appeared before us in a flash of bright light. "You have triumphed in the four trials of Nahda. Never before has anyone made it far enough to claim the true power of the universe."

"Thank you," Zaavi replied. "Can we eat and drink before continuing?"

Vaylon bowed his head, waved a hand, and a big meal appeared before us. Meat, vegetables, fruit, some kind of sweet cake and jugs of the same hot sweet liquid he had given me over the past days. It was a magnificent sight, and it smelled wonderful.

"Take your time, refresh yourself, sleep perhaps. When you are ready to continue, it will be my honour to endow you with the true power of the universe, as is your right as Sword Bearer." Before either of us could reply, he vanished. Zaavi fell upon the food like a mad thing and it looked to me as if he had not eaten in days. Maybe he was getting his appetite back now his crazy quest was almost over, I thought as I tucked in. He did not seem to want to talk much, and no amount of questions or conversation from me encouraged him to open up. He was a different person than the one I spent the past few days with, and as I pride myself on my people reading skills, I knew he was hiding something. My dilemma was whether to confront him about it or not. On the one hand, if he got annoyed, I would be in serious trouble. With a broken ankle, I would be unable to defend myself against someone his size. On the other hand, it annoyed me that he was holding out on me and after everything I had been through because of him, I reckoned I deserved some kind of explanation. I turned the choices over in my mind until my mouth made the choice for me.

"What's up?" I heard myself asking the question before I had consciously decided to do so.

"Huh? Nothing, why?"

"Come on, don't insult my powers of observation please. I've been doing this job for a long time, and I'm something of an expert at reading people. You've changed. You're holding out on me. So what is it?"

"I umm, just feel guilty that's all." Again, he hesitated a moment too long, which told me he was still lying. "I feel bad for leaving you behind, and you got injured."

I decided not to push it further. "Well you came back. That's the main thing. Let's get some sleep huh?"

He nodded and we settled down to sleep. I was warm and comfortable under the blanket, which I had managed to hold on to throughout all the drama of the day before, and I did not feel like sharing it, not after he left me and lied to me about why or what happened since. I knew, as I tried to doze off, that he had not come back for me out of compassion, and I knew that the real reason would no doubt make itself apparent soon enough. My heart sinking at the fresh drama I knew awaited me, I closed my eyes.

Zaavi shook me awake a few hours later and gave me another pain killing shot. He told me I had been keeping him awake moaning in pain, and before I could prevent it, I heard myself apologising to him. A few days ago, he would not have said that without expressing concern for me, but that night he seemed annoyed with me for being a nuisance. As I tried to go back to sleep, I worried for my safety at the hands of this crazed giant, and I experienced one of those rare moments when I seriously doubted that I would survive another day. I have had moments like that in my twenty years as a law enforcer, but they are thankfully rare. Each time it happens though, it is new, fresh and terrifying, leaving me feeling anxious and impotent to do anything to save myself. Most days I feel happy that the life I have lived has made me a good person, and I do not have a family or close friends to leave behind to mourn. Most of the time, I feel that if I were to die today, I would be untroubled by who I am and how I have lived, but when these moments happen, I always find myself scared. It is only when a situation gives you zero control over whether you live or die, that you find out how much you want to live. When it is another person who has that control, it is much scarier, and it took me a while to get back to sleep.

Throbbing from my ankle woke me, and I winced in pain as I turned over and tried to get comfortable. It had been difficult to get into a comfortable position, and once I did find one, I had not dared to move for fear of bringing the pain back, so I awoke stiff from head to toe.

"Morning Sam."

I rolled over onto my left side and saw him putting on his boots. "Morning." I yawned and winced as I sat up and tried to stretch.

"You need another pain killer?"

"Not at the moment. I could only find one fairly comfortable position to sleep in, so I didn't dare move and now I'm as stiff as a board."

"Let me help you up." He came over and lifted me to my feet. "Here's your stick."

"Thanks. I'll just have a pee and then we can be off. You must be eager to get done here."

"Yeah. Eager is right."

After struggling into my backpack and securing the blanket, which I still refused to be parted from, Vaylon appeared.

"Are you refreshed and ready to proceed Sword Bearer?"

"I am indeed," Zaavi replied. "Isn't that right Sam? We're eager to be done here."

I nodded weakly. "Yep." I knew there was going to be some drama today that would show me his true motive in coming back for me, and I knew it would put my safety in danger. Although I was eager to get away from this place, I was not eager to meet whatever fate he had in store for me. I then reminded myself that my career was over, and that I would be spending at least some time in jail while Ambassador Stell had his revenge. Maybe I should not be so keen to get out of here after all. For a moment, I had a crazy idea of running back into the tunnels and staying down there for good, working with Squeezer for both of our mutual benefit, and a snicker of fear ran up my spine as I contemplated whether to run, or to stay. Vaylon decided for me however, by indicating a door that appeared in the wall as he waved his hand.

"Then it is time to come and claim the true power of the universe." He stood aside and smiled. Zaavi took a deep breath, puffed out his chest, and strode through. I hobbled after him, wincing as my ankle twinged.

The sight that greeted us made us both stop and gasp. We had spent the last few days in dark dank tunnels and caverns, almost been eaten by creatures and I had nearly died in agony several times in a system of huge underground caves that had once been occupied. The room we stood in however was modern and clean. Although carved out of the bedrock like the previous caverns, these stone walls and the floor were smooth and shiny, light illuminated the large room and it was warm. We walked between two rows of statues towards a large circular area ahead. The statues were all clearly Nahdans; some held large spheres, the shapes of landmasses on them telling me these represented planets. Others carried what appeared to me to be scientific instruments, and one carried what I now recognised as the Singing Sword. We climbed steps up to the main circular area, and I noticed a jet-black square column directly ahead of me, in the centre. Vaylon appeared out of thin air, and stood beside it.

"It is time for the very last task Sword Bearer. Within this column, is the Thillial." He waved his hand and the central portion of the column rose another foot. In the front of this central portion, I noticed a niche, and in this niche was a carved stone tablet, about six inches long. Regularly spaced notches decorated its outer edges, the top portion, rounded and much larger than the bottom, which tapered to a point. Carved symbols covered its entire surface. As I stood and wondered what it was for, I noticed Vaylon wipe his hand in front of the niche, and heard a low hum as some kind of force field appeared over the front, almost obscuring the tablet within.

"The Thillial is the key to the final gift we have for you. Remove it from its niche and you may place the sword within the Silembar, the stone within which it will sing."

"Seems simple enough," Zaavi said.

My heart sank as I looked at that force field. "Okay. Go get it, you worked for it."

Zaavi rolled his neck around, took a deep breath and walked towards the column. With a little hesitation, he reached towards the force field. I was not surprised when I heard a loud hiss that sent him leaping back, yelling in surprise and clutching at his hand in pain. What did surprise me was that he lacked the insight to foresee it. It was too easy to assume he wanted to help me, there had to be a catch, and a creeping feeling of dread told me what that was.

He shook his hand and gasped in pain. "You have a go Sam."

"Hell no. You're the destined Sword Bearer; this is your job buddy. I'm just here to watch."

"Oh come on." His smile did not touch those strange orange eyes, their vertical pupils now angry slits. He opened his arms to the sides in frustration at my refusal. "I've already promised to make everything all right for you afterwards."

"Then you do it and make it better for yourself afterwards."

He rolled his eyes up to the ceiling. "I thought you were going to be less trouble than this. You've slowed me down and held me up all the way through here and now you decide to be awkward. I've saved your life, put up with your emotional outbursts, listened to your inane conversation and tolerated your ridiculous moral standards without complaint, and this is how you repay me?"

"Excuse me? Put up with me? How about when I saved your sorry ass huh? How about when I used my brain to solve your stupid riddles so you could get some ancient superpowers? Where would you be without me? Still stuck in that labyrinth, that's where. How about a little clarity for once?"

The Trials of Nahda

"And you'd be still lying in that tunnel in agony if I hadn't come back for your sorry ass. How about a little gratitude?"

"And why did you come back? It sure as hell wasn't out of concern for my welfare. You've been distant and uncommunicative ever since you came back for me, and I think I know why. You knew you needed me for this didn't you? You came all this way yesterday and didn't have the nerve to put your own hand in there, so you came back and decided to use me instead. Even the thought of superpowers isn't enough to give you the balls to stick your own hand in there. I had to listen to you drivelling on about being destined for the true power of the universe, and all the time you're no more than a petty thief who doesn't like being told what to do."

Zaavi grimaced in anger and walked towards me. I knew I was in no physical shape to take him on, so I reached for my laser pistol. My hand grabbed empty air, and my heart sank. Either I had lost it, or he had stolen it. He grinned when he saw my shock.

"Sorry Sam. You lost it back there in the tunnel. At least once I'd disposed of it you did. Can't have you shooting me now, can I?"

He stalked towards me and kicked my stick away, catching me before I could rummage in my backpack for my other sidearm. I struggled as he whipped me around, grabbed me around the chest with one arm, and the waist with the other. My legs swung in empty air as he hoisted me off the ground and marched towards the column, the hum of the force field getting louder as we approached. He was too big and too strong for me in my disabled state, and he had no problem grabbing my right arm and shoving it in through the force field.

My whole body exploded with pain from the inside out, and I was unable to cry out or struggle. I went rigid and Zaavi leapt away as energy coursed through me, burning its way up my arm from the inside out. My eyes rolled into the back of my head as my whole body shook. It was like being struck by lightning whilst sticking my finger into an electric socket and being shot by a laser rifle, all rolled into one. My eyes bulged from my head with the pain, my tongue curled to the back of my throat and my feet twitched. More by accident than design, the shaking and trembling of my body as the burning energy coursed through it, made my fingers catch the edge of the Thillial. The sound of it clinking onto the stone floor vaguely registered as fluid jetted from my throat and soaked my front. All at once, the force field disappeared and I dropped to the floor, the wetness in my crotch making itself apparent as I lay there still twitching from the after effects. Although the immediate pain from whatever energy source powered the force field was gone, the effect it had upon my body caused me much agony. I lay, twitching and vomiting, my blood vessels now turned to fire within.

I rolled onto my side as a fresh jet of fluid rose up from my stomach, and I saw another column rise from the shiny stone floor. As black as the first, this one had a slot in the top, which Zaavi was now approaching with the sword. Still not able to move from the after effects of the force field, I watched as he brought the tip of the sword towards the slot in the column. With a forceful thrust, he shoved the sword into the slot, and the column lit from within. The energy bolt shot up through the blade, which Zaavi still held onto with both hands, and coursed through his body, sending him flying twenty feet through the air, still clutching the sword in his hands. He coughed twice and died, the sword falling to the floor beside him. It was as quick as that, no last profound words nor even an angry curse, two coughs and he was gone.

Now that Zaavi was dead, I could concentrate on my own state of health and looked down at myself. My right arm was withered from the force field, where once was a hand and fingers was now a rounded stump, and the smell of scorched blood reached my nostrils. With a broken ankle and a withered arm, I knew my career was over even if I could fight the Ambassador and his lies. All the stress of the past few days boiled over, and I cried as I lay there on the floor, disabled, covered in sick and having pissed my pants with the pain. I was so tired that I did not care if I lived or died at that moment. What I did not want, was to linger for days, trapped down there and in agony.

A new noise made me calm my cries, and I opened my eyes. I saw nothing new from which the noise emanated, and wondered where it came from. In less than a minute, the whole room was vibrating with it, and as the stone floor on which I still lay, vibrated beneath me, something happened within my body. A feeling like electricity coursed through me, but this time it was not painful. The energy flowed down my arms and legs, and as it did so, I felt cells come to life and divide, bones knit together, flesh reattach, veins flow and nerves fire. It was the strangest experience of my entire life so far, feeling my body repairing itself from the inside out in less than a minute. Within two minutes, I had the splint off my leg, my arm was as good as new and I felt better than ever. I stood, frowning with disbelief at what I had experienced. Not daring to believe I was mended and expecting to fall down in pain again at any moment, I examined my arm and was amazed to find that even the small scar on the inside of my elbow where I scratched myself on a Mosnar bush was gone.

There was no way I could hope to understand that last couple of minutes, so being a practical sort of person, I decided to do something I knew was familiar, something I knew was right. I walked over to Zaavi and confirmed he was dead, took a DNA sample and retinal scan for my record, before noting the date and time of his death. My next problem was getting him out of there. He was far too big and heavy for me to carry far, even if there was a way out. If I hauled him over my shoulder and came to a set of Nahdan stairs, I would be screwed. There was a high probability that I would end up having to leave him here if I did find a way out.

I picked up the sword and had my first good look at it. Zaavi had always been very touchy about showing it to me, so I gave up asking after the first time he brushed me off. It was five feet high and even with both my hands, I could not wield it without struggling. At least it was not too heavy for me to drag along behind me, so I wrapped it in my blanket to keep it from getting further damage. After having a drink of water, I set about trying to find a way out, and walked the perimeter of the room, scanning the walls for steps, ledges or doorways. I was concentrating so hard that when the voice spoke, it almost made me jump out of my skin.

I spun around and saw Vaylon smiling at me. Unlike all our previous meetings, this time he was not alone. Eight similar holograms stood beside him, all mature men and all smiling at me. The third from the left turned and spoke to his neighbour, his Nahdan language meaning nothing to me. His companion nodded and replied, before turning to his other neighbour and saying something. Soon, all eight were deep in conversation, and it was obvious that I was the topic of discussion. I hoped they were discussing how much they liked me, what a nice person I was and how good it would be to set me free at last. Surely no good could come from killing me or keeping me imprisoned down here? Eventually they stopped their chatter and Vaylon stepped forwards.

"You have successfully completed the Trials of Nahda Sword Bearer, and the true power of the universe is yours."

The Trials of Nahda

CHAPTER FIFTEEN

I stood for several seconds, staring at Vaylon without replying. How to reply was beyond me, so I stood, open mouthed as I tried to take in what he said. My jaw flapped a couple of times as I tried in vain to articulate something, but in the end, I had to resort to running a hand through my hair and sighing.

"What?"

"The true power of the universe Sword Bearer is yours. You completed the trials and displayed all the required character traits. You are truly deserving of your prize."

"But," I began and my mouth flapped again. "Zaavi is, was, the Sword Bearer, not me. I'm just the law enforcer sent to arrest him for theft who got stuck down here with him."

"You went through the trials of your own free will?"

I reluctantly nodded. "Yeah. I had little choice. There was no way out so it was either stay there and starve to death or go with him and see if I could find another way out."

"When you were offered an immediate evacuation, by myself, you refused it of your own free will?"

"Yeah. I did, didn't I? But it wasn't because I wanted to win superpowers or anything. It was because I can't run for the rest of my life. I'm not cut out to be a fugitive. My job is over and my life is in ruins, but I can't run."

"Since you entered the trials of your own free will, and having refused to leave when offered the chance, the fact that you completed the trials successfully makes you the Sword Bearer and the recipient of the true power of the universe. We have done all we can as Temple Keepers to ensure that only the man with the right character completes the trials. Now it is up to you how you use that power. Come, sit with me."

We sat on the stairs and he explained everything to me. What he told me was so out there, that at first I could not take it in. He was patient with me though, and eventually I understood.

"Samelan Sinclair. How much these past days have troubled you."

"You got that right."

190

The Trials of Nahda

"Before I explain everything, tell me what this experience has taught you. What do you feel you have got from it, whether good or bad?"

I frowned. "Well. I've learned that everything I ever believed about life is not true."

"Explain, please."

"I've always been a straight down the line sort of guy. I know what the rules are and I follow them ninety-nine percent of the time. I know what the boundaries are and I try not to go over them. But I also like to think of myself as flexible, spontaneous, creative even. Doing the job I do, I mean did, means I have to think on my feet, sometimes with just a moment's notice. You can't plan in this job, and sometimes I have to be creative. Being the person I am and living the life I've led has made me the kind of person who likes boundaries. They're necessary to keep order and although everyone, including me, gets annoyed with them at times, I know the universe needs them. I'm no scientist, but I've always known that there's no such thing as magic. Mystical stuff, fairies and all that, it's from storybooks. I like it in storybooks, that's where it feels right. Now I've had to force myself to accept that my view of the universe and my place in it was all wrong. There are no boundaries now. With a wave of a hand, someone can make a monster appear, give you a meal, destroy a world. That makes me feel very insecure."

Vaylon listened intently, nodding from time to time. "What else has this experience taught you?"

"I learned that my life has fallen to pieces through no fault of my own."

"How so?"

"My boss managed to get a call through to me a few days ago. I guess the rocks must've been different and let the signal through or something, I don't know, but he managed to tell me that I'm probably going to jail. To cut a long story short, my last job was on Abastra 7. I had to find and restrain the leader of a group of political insurrectionists who had killed several politicians. I had managed to infiltrate the group, posing as a recruit, but somehow, the Abastran authorities decided to storm the place before I told them to. There was a firefight and several people died, including a female member of the group, who was the daughter of a high ranking Abastran Ambassador. He refused to accept that his daughter was a member of the group, and tried to accuse me of using her as a shield. I thought we had got it all sorted out, but my boss told me when he called that the Ambassador definitely doesn't feel he's had satisfaction, and he's pulled a few strings to get a warrant issued for my arrest. He knows I was sent here, and probably has a whole crew waiting up top to arrest me when, and if, I ever get out."

"That upsets you?"

"Well yeah, of course it upsets me. I've been doing this job for over twenty years. I'm good at it and don't want to do anything else. I've put away many crazy assholes over the years, and there's hardly a prison in the galaxy that doesn't contain someone who knows me for all the wrong reasons. I'm not going to enjoy prison at all, and knowing I'm innocent just makes it worse."

"But you refused to run when I offered you the chance. Why?"

"Well. First because it's wrong. I've been on the right side of the law for a long time and I like being honest and truthful. I like being able to hold my head up in public and know what I do is for the greater good. I do this job because I don't want crazies and psychos out there roaming free and hurting people. To run would make me feel like one of them, and everyone who knows me would think of me in a way I really would not like. Second, I'm not built to be on the run. Being a fugitive would get seriously old very quickly, and besides, I'm innocent so I should fight for acknowledgement of that. The right thing to do is fight. That's what an innocent person should do, not run. Even if I lose, which I probably will, at least I'll know I did the right thing as much as I was able to. I'm a law enforcer, I have a code y'know."

"What have you learned about yourself Samelan Sinclair?"

"I learned that I'm strong. Over the past days, I learned that I'm strong enough to face my fears. I've learned that I do have a brain, that my job hasn't destroyed my ability to work stuff out. I've also learned that my people reading skills are as sharp as ever. I knew as soon as Zaavi came back for me that something was up. Even though he denied it, I knew, and I was right. Now that this experience is in the past, I can understand it objectively. I guess the best thing I learned was that despite everything that happened, despite losing my job and my reputation, no matter what Zaavi did, I was still able to be a good person and do the right thing. As he got crazier and crazier, I realised just how strong my morals are. I'm glad about that, real glad."

Vaylon nodded. "Are you hungry?"

"Yeah, I guess so." He waved a hand and another meal appeared from nowhere.

"Eat, and enjoy. I will explain everything." I ate, and listened.

The Trials of Nahda

"My name is Vaylon Rabramas, and I am indeed, Temple Keeper number 43852382693. This is truly the third month of my watch. I am not a hologram though; I am as much of a man as you are. What you see before you is a highly advanced communication portal, via which I have been monitoring you."

"So you're a laser holographic comms signal?"

"Sort of. The unit is more highly advanced than anything you will have come across before. Essentially, it allows us to appear solid at the required location and interact naturally with people. I appear almost solid to you, as do you to me."

"Wow, that's umm, amazing. So where are you? Physically I mean."

"We are three hundred feet below where we now sit. The other Temple Keepers and I remained here when our people left the planet several thousand years ago, to wait for the Sword Bearer to arrive and take him through the trials. Now you are here and when we are finished, we shall leave and return to our own planet."

"But you're Nahdan. Even though you're not as tall as those on Nahda 4. Surely your home planet is now over there?"

"We are the race who originally colonised this world. A comet destroyed our first home world, and we had to leave. We were lucky enough to have many years notice of this impending doom, so we built a fleet of ships and left. We roamed the galaxy for several generations before we found a planet with no indigenous humanoids on which we could settle. By that time, our numbers had dwindled to a few thousand, and we were not sure we could survive. Our technology enabled us to ensure our race made it through and became fruitful. Over the next few generations however, those bred and born here on Nahda 3, were different from the rest of us. The oxygen here was much richer than that on our original home, so those born here were bigger, and continued to grow until they reached their present size. Not only did they grow bigger, but they did not have the capacity to accept the old beliefs, the spirituality we had enjoyed for millennia. They were politically motivated, power hungry, greedy consumers and we of the original Nahdan race, eventually kept to ourselves. Things came to a head when the government at the time tried to force us to reveal the location of the sword and give them the secret of the true power of the universe. We refused. Over the course of a few years, as things were getting difficult for us, we built and extended the Temple below us and hid there. We used our technology to make them think we had all died in a massive rock collapse, so they would leave us alone. When the modern Nahdans had to emigrate to the neighbouring planet, we seized the chance and sent all but the Temple Keepers away in one of our ships. They found a new planet, far away from anyone and with the help of some dear friends, the Drycenians, they shrouded our new home so that it is invisible to anyone who happens to stray into the area."

"You know the Drycenians? I've met them. They're nice people."

"They helped us find a new home where no one would find us, and when you have claimed your rightful prize, the Temple Keepers and I will leave to join them."

"Can I come with you?" The question leapt from my heart before I could stop it. "My life here is over. I could be useful."

Vaylon laughed aloud. "Your life is far from over Samelan Sinclair."

"Call me Sam."

"Sam, your life is not over. Not by a long way. How easily you allowed yourself to believe when what was happening was bad. Why could you not believe so easily when what was happening was good? That is very strange to me."

"Huh?"

"You struggled to allow yourself to believe the meals, the magically appearing doorways, and the blanket that came out of thin air. All those things that were to help and assist you met with scepticism. Yet, the moment you get a Unicom transmission while deep underground, that you'd never been able to receive before because of the depth and the rock, you believe the terrible news it brings without hesitation. Explain this to me Sam." He frowned.

I stared at him for long moments while allowing his words to sink in and form a recognisable thread inside my confused mind. As the realisation took hold, I was both relieved and angry. "You mean that wasn't true?"

"It was all magic Sam." He waved his hand across his body in a dramatic gesture. I almost slapped it away.

"You mean you let me believe my life was over? You chose to watch me cope with that and not tell me? Even later on, you still didn't feel it prudent to tell me? You fucking asshole."

He held up his hands in a placating gesture. "Now Sam. Just moments ago, you told me of all that experience taught you, and remember, those experiences were trials. Despite believing your whole life was now in tatters around your feet, you chose not to run because it's the right thing to do."

The Trials of Nahda

"So I haven't lost my job?"

Vaylon shook his head. "That Unicom transmission was a complete fabrication, designed to test your character under the most extreme emotional turmoil."

I cried with relief and apologised to him for swearing earlier. "I'm sorry for swearing at you. I thought everything was gone y'know? I thought my whole life was gone. Why did you do that?"

"To test you. It wouldn't be a trial without problems to overcome now would it? It gave you the chance to show that even when you thought everything you believed in was gone, you would do the right thing, and you did. I gave you the chance to run and you chose to stay and fight later. You learned about yourself in the process. It enabled you to grow, and to demonstrate that growth."

"Zaavi said that to complete the trials, he had to show courage, resilience, wisdom and self knowledge. I admit I probably scored on the courage and resilience, maybe even the wisdom a little bit, but the self knowledge? I didn't do anything to actively demonstrate that, so how come you say I won?"

"Ahh. Well, first, the trials were indeed designed to allow you to demonstrate courage, resilience and wisdom, but self knowledge was never a requirement, although it is always desirable don't you think?"

"But Zaavi said," I began but he cut me off.

"He got the translation wrong Sam. The fourth trial wasn't self knowledge, it was selflessness. Zaavi never showed compassion that didn't have an ulterior motive attached somewhere."

I nodded as these words sank in. "But he saved my life a couple of times. I can't take that away from him."

"Only because he knew that he needed you to help complete the trials."

"How do you know that?"

"Because he told me when he came here to try to claim the true power of the universe. You were still in the tunnel suffering your injury, and only when he realised he needed someone to get hurt retrieving the Thillial, did he go back for you. I asked him why he had left you in the tunnel, when he had previously saved you, and he said it was because you were useful. He was worried that he might not survive the trials, and wanted you around to help him if he got into difficulty."

"He got all the way here before he came back for me?"

195

"Yes. Once he found out that he was not the Sword Bearer, he decided to use you to gain the true power for himself."

"I knew something was up when he came back." I ran a hand through my hair in frustration. "By the way, talking about my injury, how did I get healed so quickly? Magic again I guess huh?"

"No, not magic Sam. Just technology. You must've already experienced sound healing, yes?" I nodded. I have had sound healing a few times. "Well we have taken the technology much further. That sound you heard, the vibration you felt, it was our Frequency Modulation Healing Unit in action. Using our unique carrier wave, the sound waves are able to penetrate the body to a much deeper degree than ever before, and have a far greater effect upon the body's cells than before. Your injuries occurred very recently, and your body had not yet adjusted to them and consolidated them into its energy frequency. That means it is very simple to readjust everything back to the way your body knows it should be."

"Okay, thanks. So Zaavi's lack of compassion ensured he failed?"

"Not only that, but yes. He was never destined to be the Sword Bearer. You see Sam, although there were four trials, you demonstrated all four of the required character traits, all of the time. At no time was there ever a rule that said only courage was needed in the first trial or only wisdom in the third. Zaavi chose to think of it that way, and that further shows his lack of insight. At all times, you were courageous, resilient, wise and compassionate. That is what makes a Sword Bearer."

I shrugged. "I was just me." I was finding it almost impossible to take all this information in.

Vaylon pointed at me. "And that's the key Sam. That is what makes you stand out. You weren't trying to make yourself appear courageous, resilient or anything else, you were just you as you are all the time. You are always courageous, resilient, wise and compassionate. It's not an act for you. When you cried for the child who died in the stampede, you felt genuine pain at the loss, and at having caused it. You learned from it, and acted differently because of it. That is not something that can be learned or put on for a show." My gaze fell to the floor at that memory and I nodded.

"I think that was when I finally had to admit that the thought of Zaavi having so much power really scared me. It was so easy for us to cause something like that, in the blink of an eye a kid died and I can never change that. Just think of the damage he could've done if he'd lost his temper when he had the powers he spoke of."

Vaylon nodded. "Indeed. The true power of the universe would not be put to good use in his hands."

"Y'know. Thinking back now, I did wonder why the trials sometimes seemed a little devoid of action. I would've expected to be fighting monsters and running from all sorts of horrors all the time, but most of the time we just spent walking and finding our way around."

"And why do you think that should be?"

"Well. Knowing now that it was me being tested, I understand why I was the one affected the most. The things we had to do were more trouble for me than Zaavi, I was the one who got hurt and upset, it was me who got scared and had to overcome it. Most of the time, the battles were going on inside my head. We never had to fight anything physically. Sure, we had to cross chasms and climb walls, but I guess that helped to provide an opportunity for me to demonstrate endurance, and whether I was able to do the right thing, even when scared for my life. I couldn't see in the dark, I felt trapped and vulnerable knowing there was a sheer drop all around me. Like when we climbed those columns for instance. I'm okay with heights but knowing nothing but empty air was all around me was hell. I guess there are more ways to demonstrate the qualities you wanted, than by fighting monsters or answering riddles."

Vaylon nodded. "Indeed. You went to a place inside yourself that you have never been to before. A place where you had to face things you've never faced before. You had to pull yourself apart, come to terms with everything you were experiencing and try to make sense of it and forge a brand new future for yourself. You never lost sight of yourself Sam. Not once did you lose sight of who you are."

"Well I did have a bit of a meltdown." I blushed, embarrassed at the memory. "I didn't want to continue, and I contemplated ending it all."

"You did, but you did it because you knew who you were at that moment. At that moment, you knew that what you had experienced was beyond your capacity at that time. It was then that you had to pull yourself apart and rebuild, or wither under the stress. You did not wither, and that moment was not one of weakness, but a moment of growth."

"Yeah." I understood his words but did not know how to reply without sounding boastful. "Can I ask your advice about something?"

197

"Of course."

"How the hell am I supposed to come to terms with the fact that magic really does exist? I don't know why I have such a problem with it, but I like the fact that everything in life, everything in the universe, follows some kind of predictable pattern or rule. Some of the patterns are weird and some of the rules are difficult to understand, but they're there. Now everything is turned upside down. Someone can change everything by waving a hand, and that makes me feel really insecure. How can I feel okay about that?"

"Ahh, that." His cheeks reddened a little. "Well, you see Sam, you don't have to come to terms with it, for magic doesn't exist. At least not the magic you're speaking of." I frowned and shook my head. I assumed he got the wrong end of the stick.

"No, I meant like the meals, the blanket, the disappearing paradise cave, and the doors. When you did stuff by waving your hand."

"As I said, that kind of magic doesn't exist. Unless of course, you wish to think of technology as magical."

My eyebrows shot to the top of my head and my jaw dropped. "Just what are you telling me here?"

"The people in that village where the child died in the stampede, the paradise cave, they were all seven dimensional holograms, projected by our ship's holographic multi-phase projector."

"Seven dimensional holograms?"

"Yes. Solid enough to touch and interact with, but projections nonetheless."

"But we spoke with those people in the village."

"That was Temple Keeper 43852382692 using the voice modulation generator that is part of the holographic projector."

I sat there staring at him, wide eyed and open mouthed. Annoyed but relieved. "You stiffed me?"

"If you want to put it like that, yes."

"And the meals, doors, and the blanket? What about those?"

"Now they were real, not holograms. We cannot yet produce holographic food that actually nourishes the body. No, they were real. The doors are self moulding adaptations that we put in thousands of years ago, when we first inhabited the place on a permanent basis. They mould right into the fabric of the surrounding surface so no cracks can be seen. Press a button and the process reverses, revealing the door. Very simple technology and aesthetically very pleasing. As for the meals and the blanket, well they are a slightly different story."

"Which is?"

"We recently invented a single phase transporter device. The meals you enjoyed were prepared by our own chefs and sent to you via this device."

I laughed aloud. "A transporter? That's crazy. No one has ever invented a transporter. Not even the Drycenians have one of those."

"Actually it was a collaboration between them and ourselves that helped to make it as successful as it currently is."

"You're shitting me. They have one of those?"

Vaylon nodded. "Yes. At the moment, we can only send non-living tissue. That's why you got your meals and your blanket so easily. We do not yet feel able to risk it on living tissue, as the tests do not yet give us the results we want, to enable us to be sure it is safe to try it on a person."

"So how do you explain the animals I caught and ate? When Zaavi and I spent that time in the paradise cave, I caught our food, we fished in the stream, ate fruit from those trees."

"As I said before, the seven dimensional holograms are so lifelike that you can interact with them naturally and not know they're not real. We can make the animals behave naturally, so you will see them die on the end of your fishing line, or the point of a spear. Turn your eyes away for a second however, to put away your spear or watch where you step, and we switch the hologram for a previously killed specimen that you are able to eat and enjoy."

"And what about the books?"

Vaylon frowned. "What about them?"

"You said that whoever read them would find them written in his own mother tongue. I read a book Zaavi had read and it was written in Sigman. When he read it, it was in Nahdan."

"Ahh yes. That was easy. The books are made to look like real old fashioned ones, but their outer covers are a technologically advanced bio-racial recognition system."

Now I frowned. "Bio what?"

"Bio-racial recognition. When you touch the outer covers, the oils in your skin, which contain minute quantities of your DNA, are analysed by the technology built into them. Within seconds, the books know which race you are, and the words inside change to that of your own mother tongue. Simple technology really."

The Trials of Nahda

"If I didn't feel so relieved, I would be angry that you've been dicking me around these past few days."

"But you understand why, don't you Sam?"

"Yeah."

"We had to be sure only the right person made it this far."

"Before you continue." I put a hand up to silence him. "I don't want this power you speak of. I don't want superpowers; I don't want to rule over anyone. Nobody can wield such power in the right way, humanoid nature won't allow anyone to be sufficiently just, wise or compassionate. People are selfish, greedy and aggressive, believe me I know. Please don't be offended, but I don't want the power, and I hope you never offer it to anyone else, ever."

"You already have the true power of the universe Sam. There are no superpowers. No one but the creator can rule over the universe. No, the true power of the universe is that which you already have, and have shown during these trials. The courage to endure hardship with fortitude and grace, the resilience to overcome the worst of your fears, the wisdom to know your place in the universe, and the selflessness to show compassion to all others, no matter their station in life nor their purpose for good or evil. You have those qualities, you have always had them. The difference now, is that you know you have them, and you know how they've made you who you are."

"But lots of people have those same qualities. Why me in particular?"

"First because you are here and have done the trials, but mostly because you knew from the start what the goal was, and despite knowing what was on offer to the Sword Bearer, you didn't lose any of those qualities. You didn't let your ego get in the way and influence you. That is the difference Sam. That is what makes you different. You already are the true power of the universe my friend, and that is why we are happy for you to be Sword Bearer of the Singing Sword.

By this time, I had tears in my eyes as I listened to his wisdom. Call me an old softie if you want, but his soft voice and his ability to help me understand affected me. It all made perfect sense to me now, and I was so relieved I cannot put it into words.

"It really does sing?"

"It does indeed. This Sword represents everything we stand for, and have ever stood for. The greedy, power hungry, politically biased people who killed this planet are not us Sam. They are what they made themselves when they turned their backs on our ways, the old ways. The sword is our belief system, our values and our hopes for the future, personified. Only he who is of the right character can bear this symbol of universal truth."

"So I was right. It is a symbolic thing, not a conduit of power in itself."

"You were right."

"You know I have to return it to the museum. I can't keep it."

"We know. You do not have to carry it with you. It doesn't matter if you never set eyes on it again. The important thing is that you are here, now, and we hold you as Sword Bearer. Nothing can change that, and no other man will ever be here in the future to claim the title from you."

"How do you know that no one will try this stunt again some time?"

"Because we will be gone from here." I gaped at him in surprise and he nodded. "We chose to remain only until the Sword Bearer had been found. As I have already told you, I am Temple Keeper 43852382693. Out of that large number, there are just nine of us left waiting for you. The years we spent in cryo sleep, each of us taking a two-year watch at a time, took their toll upon our numbers, and we were becoming afraid you would never arrive before we all died out. Now that you are here, we can go and join our friends on our new home planet. We have been here for many thousands of years waiting for you, and our own families are long since dead, but being here to witness the sword meeting its true bearer makes the sacrifice worth it. It was said that when the Singing Sword was forged, many thousands of years ago, it would seek out the one with the right character to wield it. The legend was that the one who forged it was a man with two sons. The two men were always disagreeing and fighting with each other. Their father tried everything to bring the two together, but they would never embrace each other's differences without aggression. As a blacksmith, he decided to forge a mighty sword that would be a weapon against tyranny and aggression, but a weapon that would never need to be used in a physical way. His emotions and belief were so strong as he forged it, that they became part of the very fabric of the blade itself, and caused it to seek out the right man. When this man was found, the two sons would finally be able to recognise each other with compassion."

"That's a nice legend. But those two sons will be long dead by now."

"Indeed they will. But somewhere, there are descendants of those two men, and who knows, maybe they will all find themselves more compassionate with each other now."

"How can I make that happen just by being here and doing those trials?"

The Trials of Nahda

"Maybe it'll happen by magic." At first, I bristled from his sarcasm, but my relief took over, and I laughed with him. When we finished laughing, I thought of Squeezer and felt the need to express my feelings about him. It was weird for me. I had been terrified of snakes since I was a kid, but during these trials, I was forced to face that fear and overcome it. I had formed a real attachment to him and I knew I would miss him.

"What about Squeezer? Was he real or just a hologram too?"

"Well he was," Vaylon began but I cut him off.

I threw my hands up. "No, don't. Please don't say anything. I don't want you to answer that question after all."

"Why not?"

"Because I don't think I want to know that he wasn't real. I would feel happier if I remembered him as a buddy I made during a strange experience, and that we helped each other out to our mutual benefit. How did you know I was scared of snakes anyway?"

"As soon as you entered the Temple complex, we looked into your background and found references to your phobia. We couldn't resist using this knowledge in the trials."

"Of course, you spied on me. I should've guessed."

Vaylon smiled. "Judging by your feelings towards the animal now, you are surely glad we did."

I blushed. "Well yeah, I guess I am. I'm sorry, I didn't mean to be offensive."

"I understand perfectly. Now, it is time for you to hear the song of the sword. Come."

The Trials of Nahda

CHAPTER SIXTEEN

My mind was reeling as I thought about everything Vaylon told me. I found it almost impossible to believe that I was anything special. It was almost embarrassing listening to him talking about me in such glowing terms as I have never tried to be anything other than a normal person. The one thing that did please me though, was that there were no superpowers waiting for me. No humanoid I have ever met could have superpowers and use them properly. Greed and ego would always get in the way. Ego has never been something I have thought about much. It has never driven me like many of the people I am employed to apprehend, and I guess being around such people so much might be the reason that ego is not a part of my own life. Watching how it twists people has put me right off it and I tend to avoid it in myself wherever possible.

Knowing that my job was still intact and that I would not be going to prison after all, was such a relief to me that it gave me a whole new perspective on my job and my life in general. Whenever I get complacent about things, bored with a job or annoyed at having to do something I do not enjoy, I make myself remember when I believed with all my heart that it had all been taken away. It is powerful motivation to see things in a different light and I know it changed me permanently. The sad thing is that it usually takes something like this to make that change in people.

Vaylon led me back up the steps to the large circular area, and I saw the pillar into which Zaavi forced my arm to retrieve the Thillial. Memory of the pain floated to the front of my mind and I clutched my arm to my body, instinct driving me into a defensive posture. The other pillar, into which Zaavi tried to thrust the sword, stood a little to the left, and Zaavi's body sprawled twenty feet away. Vaylon called to me.

"Come Sword Bearer. Take up the sword."

I hesitated, remembering the dramatic way Zaavi had died and having such recent memories of the most horrendous pain inflicted by the pillar on the right. I was not keen to experience that again, so I was reluctant to move.

"Do not be afraid Sword Bearer. Take up the sword and approach the Silembar."

"The what?"

204

Vaylon pointed towards the pillar with the slot. "The Silembar. Take the sword and thrust it into the Silembar and it will sing for you."

With a deep breath, I hauled the sword from the floor and dragged it across to the black pillar, its slot open like a mouth, inviting me inside before biting my head off. I blinked hard and tried to calm myself, before lifting the blade and resting the tip at the entrance to the slot. With a moment's hesitation and Vaylon nodding his encouragement, I shoved with all my weight and the sword entered the pillar, right up to the hilt.

"Keep hold of the sword Sam. Don't let go or it won't sing."

Grabbing hold of the hilt with both hands, I waited for something to happen. After a few seconds, a beam of light streamed out of the slot and shot to the ceiling like a searchlight. As the light hit the ceiling, waves of it oozed over the surface of the rock, like syrup running down your hand after eating Malcot Berries. Another beam of light streamed from the Silembar, entwined with the first, and I heard the sound. It was like a million voices all raised in exaltation, the whole cavern rang with it, the rock floor on which Vaylon and I stood, vibrated with it. As I watched the light oozing its way around and over the entire rock surface of the cavern, I felt the vibrations come up through my feet and course through my body, but this time it felt awesome. A mixture of emotions and feelings streamed through my mind. The sheer power of the experience was intoxicating, but at the same time, humbling. I felt big and proud, but tiny and insignificant too. What I had experienced these past few days, the troubles I'd gone through came back to me but this time the memories were balanced by the knowledge of what I had achieved, the self knowledge I had gained and the growth that happened within me. I felt all at once, both important and humble.

As the light oozed its way across the shiny floor on which Vaylon and I stood and reached the base of the Silembar, I heard a soft bang from within the pillar and sparks erupted from around the blade as it sat in the slot. I leapt away and watched as a fountain of sparks flew from the top of the Silembar. Suddenly, flames licked from around the blade, more bangs from within the pillar and finally, one loud bang that cracked the Silembar from top to bottom. The light stopped oozing and the cavern returned to its normal grey self. The voices stopped singing and all was quiet, apart from the crash as the Silembar fell in half, sending the sword sliding ten feet across the shiny floor.

The Trials of Nahda

After the noise, the sudden quiet was spooky, and I crept over to the sword, its intricate symbols and sigils now gone, an ugly black scorch in their place. Vaylon nodded as understanding crept over me.

"That is why I am confident no other will ever try to find their way here again. The trials of Nahda can only be done once, there has only ever been one Sword Bearer and the sword will only ever sing once."

I nodded in understanding. Without the inscription on the blade, nobody would know of the legend of the true power of the universe, the temple, or its likely location. "That was amazing. Did it really happen or was that a hologram too?"

"Oh it happened. Everything you saw and heard was real. We've always believed the sword to be the final part in an extremely advanced circuit, and only with the sword in place, can the whole thing do what it was designed to do."

"But you people designed it, don't you know?"

"The story of the blacksmith who forged it many thousands of years ago is just that, a story. The truth is, we don't know who forged it or built the Silembar. Even with our current technology, we couldn't produce such an artefact. Many believe it was someone from a very ancient race who may have visited the Ancient Nahdans as they first evolved. He may have been a space explorer who crash landed on Nahda and couldn't repair his ship, he may have been the only survivor of his race, we don't know. We believe he may have bred with the primitive ancient Nahdans and produced a line of descendants who possessed great knowledge and had skills that enabled us to evolve as we have done. It's all speculation. The important thing is that it has now been done, we can go home and you can return to your life."

"So what is the point of having gone through this experience? Just to teach one man how to be compassionate and humble?"

"We cannot know what the point is, nor even if there was one. One thing I'm sure of though is that if there is a point, it will be a very important one, and it won't matter if anyone knows what it is. Whether you choose to believe in any kind of point is up to you. Me? Well after the other Temple Keepers and I have spent thousands of years waiting here for you, we choose to believe there is a point, and that one day, when humanoids have evolved in the right way, that point will become clear."

I nodded. "Yeah, so do I."

The Trials of Nahda

"You may now return the sword without worry that someone else will take up where Zaavi left off."

I will admit that knowing I would not have to return at some point in the future and go through all the things I had endured during the past few days, all over again, was a great comfort. Nodding, I ran a hand through my hair as I bent to pick up the sword. Underneath, I saw the Thillial, the key Zaavi had forced me to retrieve for him, and I hesitated before picking it up. A frisson of fear pricked inside, and for a moment, I was scared that touching it would bring back the pain. Having a withered arm would make it almost impossible for me to do my job, and I doubted the existence of a sound healing device as powerful as the one Vaylon and his people possessed. Remembering his assurance that the process happened only once, I shook away the fear and picked it up.

"What's this for? It never did get used. I thought it opened the Silembar or something."

Vaylon shook his head. "No Sam, the Thillial is not for the Silembar. It is for the vault. Retrieving it from the niche which hurt you so, was necessary to make the Silembar work, but the lock it fits is elsewhere."

"So what do I do with it? Do I give it to you?" I held it out to him.

"It belongs at my feet."

I frowned at his cryptic reply and looked at his feet. On the ground where he stood was a slot in the shiny floor and I nodded. "Oh, I see." I walked towards him. "Is this gonna hurt?"

He laughed aloud. "No Sam, it won't hurt a bit. Go on, insert the Thillial into the keyhole and enter the vault."

"The Vault? What's in there? A monster perhaps. Not another trial. Please tell me it's not another trial."

"It's not another trial. It's your prize for having endured. Only the Sword Bearer can use what's in this vault in the right way."

I crouched at Vaylon's feet and hesitated, my hand holding the Thillial an inch above the keyhole. What was in there, I did not know, and I was a bit apprehensive after everything I had been through. I silently counted to three and dropped it into the slot before leaping back and waiting for something awful to happen. Nothing awful happened, but the sound of stone grinding on stone reached my ears. A portion of the shiny stone floor, three feet wide by at least eight long, sunk into the surrounding floor and slid sideways and out of sight. Behind me, a portion of the cavern wall, of similar dimensions, swung on some invisible hinge, revealing a door.

"Below here is the vault Sam. Enter and claim your prize. That door behind you will take you back up to the surface of the planet. There are steps beyond that door, a short tunnel and another door. Upon that second door, you will find nine square carved tiles, much like the ones on the first door you entered. There are three rows of three tiles, numbered from the left, one to three on the top row, four to six on the middle row, and seven to nine on the bottom row. To open the door, press three, seven, one, six, and two, in that order."

"Three, seven, one, six, two." I repeated it over and over to myself as I approached the hole in the floor. Before me were a set of steps leading down, a dull yellow glow lighting the darkness. With great caution, I descended the steps and almost fainted in shock when I reached the room below. The room must have been twenty feet wide by at least twice as much long, and was filled with crates, sacks and chests of precious metals, jewels and priceless artefacts that glittered in the dull yellow glow.

"Holy shit. How many banks did you rob to get all this?"

"This is the Treasury Vault of the Ancient Nahdans. This is what remains of our original nation. We brought it with us when we left our original home world, and hoped to use it for our benefit as we colonised a new world, this one, Nahda 3. Over time, it became obvious to us that subsequent generations viewed it very differently from the way we had. Eventually, we moved what was left out of sight of the general population, who were going through some turmoil at the time due to the interest caused by the high quantity of Esplonite TX5 found here. We built the Vault down here, and created the Thillial to open it. Our engineers were able to link it with the Silembar, so that only by retrieving the Thillial would the Silembar appear. We hoped that by hiding this wealth, they might avoid descending into materialistic chaos. Alas, they still destroyed this planet, but have since sown the first seeds of reform, which we hope will bring our people back to the way we were on our first home world. As Sword Bearer, it is now yours."

"Mine? You can't be serious. What the hell would I do with all this?"

"It is yours to do with as you see fit. As Sword Bearer, we know you have the right mind to use it wisely, and we will trust your judgement. You can either keep it for yourself, give it away or let the modern Nahdans have it and see how they cope with it. Whatever you decree shall be done Sword Bearer."

The Trials of Nahda

The sheer amount of wealth in that room is impossible to describe. There was tons of it. Jewellery, pots, jugs and ornaments, bags of coins, and all manner of other things, made of precious metals of several colours. Precious stones of every colour imaginable, some as big as my fist, glinted in the dull light and sent rainbow sparkles dancing around the walls as I picked up handfuls and let them rain down to the floor. There was no way I could deal with all this, and the thought of explaining its presence to Tinnias, made me laugh. My next thought was to give it back to the Nahdans and I thought this was the most sensible thing to do. After all, it was theirs to begin with.

I picked up a bracelet of some silver coloured metal and admired it. It was chunky, and carved with animal designs, each animal chasing the one in front. I thought of Tinnias' daughter Ambella and smiled, the comforting familiarity of our pseudo sibling relationship making me feel loved no matter where I was in the cosmos. She is like a little sister to me, and I always get her a gift whenever I go off world. I thought this bracelet would be perfect for her. The next thing that caught my eye was a gold coloured bracelet, the size and style of it telling me it was obviously made for a man to wear. It was quite plain in style, and had been twisted around on itself many times over, forming a thick stiff rope design. I slipped it on and smiled as I felt the weight of it gripping my wrist. As I wandered among the piles of riches, I wondered how the Nahdans would react to this. All their carefully constructed rules and regulations regarding the pursuit of wealth and power would take a serious blow if this haul arrived on their doorstep. I imagined the people rioting over who got a share and who did not, and saw the swift downfall of the Nahdan way of life.

My thoughts drifted to my flight from Nahda 4, how I gazed down at the planet and understood what the government was trying to do and why. I did not want to do anything to ruin that; with no other place to run, the people need to get things right this time. As an ego driven race, they need strict controls and I foresaw this burden causing nothing but chaos. I turned to Vaylon, my mind made up.

I held out the two bracelets. "I would like to keep these two if I may."

"You need not ask me Sword Bearer. It belongs to you now."

"Yeah, I know. It just takes some getting used to. I'm used to working for my money and having all this wealth dumped on me feels wrong somehow, dishonest y'know? I also believe that this would do more harm than good to the Nahdans. They have no other place to run to if they get it wrong again, and I couldn't live with myself if I hastened their downfall. None of the humanoids I've met could be sensible about dealing with this, and I've seen people's lives ruined by sudden wealth more times than I've seen it help them. I want you and the other Temple Keepers to take it back with you when you leave. It is yours and should remain so. You had the strength to hide it away, which tells me you have the strength to use it wisely. Take it home, and if you feel it right, give it back to your people so that it can do good for you."

Vaylon did not reply for several seconds. Then he smiled and nodded. "You are truly the Sword Bearer. Come, I have something more that will help you on your journey out of here."

We made our way back up the steps to the cavern and I removed the Thillial from the slot in the floor. The sound of grinding stone filled the room as the slab slid back across and slotted back into place, the self moulding technology ensuring that no visible trace remained. I took a last look at the Thillial and smiled, before placing it on the floor at Vaylon's feet. I nodded in satisfaction. Vaylon indicated to the other Temple Keepers who still stood in a line where they had first appeared and had remained silent until now. The one on the right of the line stepped forward.

"It has been a most interesting experience watching you Sword Bearer. I am content that the sword has chosen wisely."

"Thank you."

He stepped back and the second stepped forward. "You have taught us much Sword Bearer, and we are all the richer for it."

The third smiled as he stepped forward. "Remember this experience for the growth it has inspired within you. Use the memories of it to promote further growth."

"I'll try."

"Your life will never be the same from this moment on," the fourth declared. "Ours is changed too. We can now go home and join our kin, and your courage, resilience, wisdom and compassion has made this possible."

"Have a safe journey."

"You are indeed the Sword Bearer," the fifth said. "I knew it from the moment we first saw you enter the Temple."

"Thank you for having faith in me. In many ways I'm glad I didn't know until now."

"Those qualities that brought you to this point," the sixth said, "are the very qualities that make you the unique person that you are. Use them as you've always done. Be the person you've always been. Don't assume that this experience means more is, or ever will be, expected of you. Continue to be as you are and always have been."

"Thanks. I'm glad to hear that. It does feel like a bit of a responsibility and I'm just me. That's all I'm capable of being. I hope it's enough."

"It's enough Sword Bearer," the seventh replied. "It has always been enough and always will be. This is our last gift to you, to help you make your way out of here." He pointed to the floor at his feet, and I saw six small metallic cubes, and what looked like an advanced digital control mechanism.

"This is a personal hover device," the last explained. "Attach the components to whatever you need to move with these straps. This controller will allow you to move bodies or other large heavy objects without having to struggle with their weight. You can use it where the size and bulk of a normal hover cart would be unsuitable or unavailable, and you can use it on anything that needs to be moved. Arrange the six power packs evenly over the lower surface of whatever needs moving and you will never have to struggle."

"Wow, thank you. This is a very welcome gift."

"This is very advanced technology Sword Bearer. If it should be stolen or lost, it is designed so that each of the components will explode if anyone attempts to take them apart or interfere with them. I tell you this so that you don't try to find out how they work and get injured or killed. If they should fail to work at any time, discard them without trying to fix them. We give these to you to show you our trust, and because we sincerely wish to make a positive impact on your future. This is a small way for us to do that."

"Oh this will be a very positive impact. I can't count the times I've needed something like this."

"Now you are free to leave and return to your life," Vaylon said. "You can return the body of Zaavi and tell them he died from falling into an underground cave. His body will display all the injuries one would expect from a fall, so don't worry about how to explain the Silembar and its function."

I nodded. "Okay. How do I explain the sword though?" I indicated the black scorch mark that now marred the blade where the inscription and symbols used to be.

"Tell them Zaavi poured some Galminastrel Runoff over it in a deliberate attempt to prevent anyone else from deciphering the inscription."

"Galminastrel Runoff?" What's that?"

The Trials of Nahda

"It's a liquid residue from the Esplonite TX5 fusion reactor. Tell them he found some drums of this liquid near the reactor and decided to try to remove the inscription."

"What if they decide to go look for the stuff?" How would I explain further if they could not find any?

"They won't be able to. Remember, the Nahdan's don't live on this planet anymore. The atmosphere is poisoned and they don't have the resources to clean up their mess. Even if they did, by the time they can mobilise safety technicians to get here, the underground volcano that lies several miles beneath us will be erupting. It will not be safe for anyone to be here for a very long time. This whole system of caverns in which you've spent these past days, everything will be consumed, leaving no trace."

"A volcano? I'm glad. I would hate for someone to stumble upon the place and be stuck down here, especially as you'll not be here. My ship's scanner didn't indicate a volcano though."

"It has been dormant for many thousands of years, but a carefully placed charge will begin the process of waking it up again. When everyone has left, we will leave invisibly and detonate the charge. The caverns in which you spent these past few days were once chambers filled with molten lava during its last active phase. It seemed a natural place for us to build the Temple and install the Silembar, and it gave us enough room to live comfortably when the modern Nahdans moved away from our ways and made life difficult for us as we waited for you."

I nodded. I was glad to be getting out, and even more glad that my life was still intact. It would be good to get back to a more normal existence again. "Thank you Vaylon. For taking care of me down there." He said nothing, just smiled and nodded. I walked over to Zaavi's body and attached the hover power packs to him. Vaylon showed me how to operate it, and I was amazed to see Zaavi lift into the air and float around without any obvious means of support. This gizmo was going to earn its keep many times over.

"Remember Sword Bearer. You will need your breather on the surface."

I am glad he reminded me, as I had forgotten. I rummaged in my backpack and put the breather around my neck, before picking up the sword and with a last look around the enormous cavern, walked towards the door in the far wall. I glanced back and saw Vaylon and his companions smiling. I nodded at them, turned away and climbed the steep steps, Zaavi's body floating effortlessly ahead of me. As I climbed, I recited the combination to the tile lock in my mind. Three, seven, one, six, two. The last thing I needed was to forget and be stuck down there after everything else that happened. At the top of the steps, I pressed the tiles in the combination Vaylon gave me. The sound of stone grinding against stone was music to my ears and I was relieved as the door slid open, allowing the poisoned air inside.

I walked out into the grey I had almost forgotten during the last few days, and despite the poisoned atmosphere and the grey dust that blanketed everything, I was glad to be out. The experience had been traumatic and life changing, and I was glad to move away from it and get on with the job. Now I was back doing what I knew how to do, what I am comfortable doing and I was so relieved I cannot explain it adequately. I set out on the walk back to my ship, Zaavi floating ahead of me, and before I had walked a hundred metres, my Unicom beeped.

"Sam?" Tinnias' voice asked.

"Hi Boss."

"Oh jeez, I'm so relieved to hear you. Are you okay?"

"I'm fine thanks."

"I've been calling and calling for days but there was never a signal. I've been worried sick."

"Sorry. Things happened quickly and I didn't have time to call you. I got stuck in some underground cave system chasing Zaavi and there was no signal. I tried to call you too, several times."

"I sent a team to find you. They should be arriving in around a day or so. Do you need them or shall I call them off?"

"You can call them off. Everything is fine and I have Zaavi, although he's dead I'm afraid."

"No problem Sam. Okay I'll call them off. Jeez, I'm so glad you're all right. Are you able to give me a report now?"

"Can you give me a couple of hours? I've only just got out of there and I'm hauling Zaavi's ass back to the ship as we speak. Once I get him settled, I'll call you and tell you everything."

"Okay, no problem. Call me in two hours."

I guess that is where the story of the Trials of Nahda ends. I got Zaavi secured in my ship and called Tinnias back with my report. I did not tell him about the trials, the Temple Keepers and especially the Treasury. I said it was an underground cave system below the fusion reactor. My official report said how Zaavi fell whilst trying to evade capture, and how he tried to destroy the sword by pouring Galminastrel Runoff over it to remove the inscription. I returned Zaavi's body to Nahda 4, along with the sword and everyone was upset that he had destroyed the inscription. I visited Zaavi's mother and girlfriend to express my condolences and both were distraught but thankful to me for returning him. Shyola Mastak, Zaavi's girlfriend invited me for a meal and I was more than happy to accept. As I left the next morning after a night of amazing sex, having indulged her passion for off worlders in every conceivable way, I visited Cristik Noya and went for a drink with him to say goodbye. While we were drinking, we heard talk from some people about a volcano on Nahda 3 that had woken up after thousands of years being dormant. I knew then that the Temple Keepers had left and were making their own long journey home. I was relieved to know that the Treasury would never be seen again. There was no way anyone I've met would be able to use that much wealth without bringing about their own destruction, and it was far better staying with its original owners. The Temple Keepers had sacrificed thousands of years of family life to wait for me, and they deserved any good the wealth could bring. It would bring nothing but trouble to anyone else.

I was happy to leave the Nahdan system and still to this day, I cannot get my head around what happened to me down there. I struggled with it for a while, until I remembered one of the Temple Keepers telling me to carry on being me and living my life as I always have. That helped me a lot, and I was able to let it go and not try to understand it. I kept my word and got a tattoo of a snake on my shoulder. Its tail is on my shoulder blade, and it snakes up and round my shoulder to its head in the centre of my chest. I am pleased with it and those who have seen it say it is cool. I call it Squeezer.

Now I had better close up here. A new job has come in and I have to go and find a soldier who went AWOL from the military after blowing up his whole company. This sounds like it is going to be a long job.

This is Sinclair V-Log PA884/R, data log reference point 1956365/7991, Sam Sinclair signing off.

THE END

COMING SOON

Psychomanteum

A story of one man's obsession.

It starts out innocently enough, but soon becomes the conduit through which a monstrous horror gains entry to our world.

Harlon Drake wanted to know about his famous ancestor, but finds her difficult to track down. When he gets the chance to buy one of her paintings, his trip to the auction room turns out to be the catalyst for a horror that threatens not only his own soul, but that of every other person alive.

Two New York cops and one reclusive psychic find themselves thrust together in a perilous battle to save humanity from annihilation.

www.ingramcontent.com/pod-product-compliance
Lightning Source LLC
Chambersburg PA
CBHW072052170626
46813CB00004B/1313